Praise for the Val Cameron Mystery Series

PRACTICAL SINS FOR COLD CLIMATES (#1)

"A strong plot and engaging characters make for a well-crafted mystery, and Val's humorous attempts to cope with the wilderness do much to lighten the tension. The core of the story is Val's discovery of her own self-worth."

– *Publishers Weekly*

"Costa hits all the right notes—vulnerable but likable characters, a compelling plot, a clearly drawn setting, and a tangled web of past and present events."

– Sheila Connolly,
New York Times Bestselling Author of *A Gala Event*

"Taut, well written and suspenseful, *Practical Sins for Cold Climates* draws readers into a community where the past haunts the present and residents' motives are buried deep...just like the truth."

– Kylie Logan,
Author of *And Then There Were Nuns*

"An engaging, deftly-plotted mystery with a smart, tough-minded heroine. Shelley Costa delivers a terrific series debut."

– Daniel Stashower,
Author of *The Hour of Peril*

"If you want to read a beautifully written story with a twisting and turning plot, this book is for you. Five stars out of five."

– *Examiner.com*

"A brooding, atmospheric story, you can almost feel the weight of a blizzard bearing down. Highly recommended."

– *For the Love of Books*

A KILLER'S GUIDE *to* GOOD WORKS

**The Val Cameron Mystery Series
by Shelley Costa**

PRACTICAL SINS FOR COLD CLIMATES (#1)
A KILLER'S GUIDE TO GOOD WORKS (#2)

A KILLER'S GUIDE *to* GOOD WORKS

A Val Cameron Mystery

SHELLEY COSTA

HENERY PRESS

A KILLER'S GUIDE TO GOOD WORKS
A Val Cameron Mystery
Part of the Henery Press Mystery Collection

First Edition | September 2016

Henery Press, LLC
www.henerypress.com

Trade Paperback ISBN-13: 978-1-63511-061-6
Digital epub ISBN-13: 978-1-63511-062-3
Kindle ISBN-13: 978-1-63511-063-0
Hardcover Paperback ISBN-13: 978-1-63511-064-7

Printed in the United States of America

For you, Joyce
...my dear friend from that day in 1975
when you turned from the blackboard in the Writing Lab
and said hello

ACKNOWLEDGMENTS

This is a story about how far people will go to possess what more properly belongs to all. When that happens, there is a whiff of brimstone, and for me, as a writer, a story worth telling. Thanks to editors Rachel Jackson and Erin George for holding the line; thanks to Casey Daniels, Emilie Richards, and Serena Miller for helping me figure out what, in the early stages, was possible; thanks to my daughter Jessica Bloomfield for, once again, being a fine beta reader; thanks to Paul Gaston for being my go-to on craft beer; and thanks to Sisters in Crime for—back in January 2014—providing time, space, three squares, and great company.

*Men never do evil so completely and cheerfully
as when they do it from religious conviction.*
— Blaise Pascal

Prologue

Veracruz, 1595

The Franciscan friar lifted his eyes to the open window in the room he had rented by the harbor. Veracruz was a coastal town, more liberal in its ways, and only an outpost of the Inquisition. So it suited his purposes. After working in secret for the last two days, he set down the goose quill and stared impassively at the final page of his work, a satire about the Inquisition he titled "The Entertainment of Spain." Then he carefully set the pages inside the acacia wood box that used to hold family papers.

Even after all this time, his fingers trembled as he pressed the finely carved rosette in the lower right-hand corner of the box, which released the hidden spring. Out slid the small, shallow shelf, and with it the heart of his family's inheritance throughout the ages, from their Judean beginnings as Essenes. Ink on thin leather with ragged edges, the writing in a hurried Hebrew. That scribe, who was his family's earliest ancestor, recorded the mystical statement of the master that night in Gethsemane...*the Son of God in this night among the olive trees of Gat Smanim. For he says what binds his feet, what pierces his flesh, what crowns his head are the way to life everlasting among the world of living men.*

Tonight the weary friar would write a letter in the guise of an unimportant priest, attach it to the satire, and set the lid in place. In the morning, dressed humbly in a stolen cassock, he would deliver the box to the administrators at this outpost of the Inquisition. And he knew them all well enough, without ever having met them, that they would record the receipt of this heretical work.

Ah, so much easier than cataloguing the official trials of the accused. This, this was just some, well, literature of dubious harm. Then they would put it in the archives where they would all quickly forget about it. And as the disguised friar would turn away, with their bored thanks, he would smile, knowing he had placed the ancient document that could topple cathedrals in both the Old and New Worlds, in the hands of the Inquisition, its enemy.

But it was a way of buying time and safety for the words of the master. Over centuries, possibly, the box and its contents would gather dust in a vault. He had to believe that somewhere away from this benighted place and time in human history, a new place across vast waters, where concertinas still made evenings sweet, someone would touch the little rosette, even accidentally, and the shallow drawer would appear. And with it the inscribed words. And perhaps by then they were no longer dangerous. Or perhaps—here, surprised, the friar's breath caught in his throat—they were no longer in the very least...important.

1

New York City, present day

Val Cameron was taking a break.

She had been at her desk since 8:43 a.m., slogging away at the line edits on *Plumb Lines*, an exposé by a hotshot neo-journalist named James Killian who posed as a plumber for three years in Beverly Hills to get into celebrity homes and get the dirt—or as he put it, "the real sewage"—on them. This nasty trash had been acquired by her former boss during his period of extreme bad taste, which immediately preceded his present period of extended time in a Canadian prison. With the kind of alacrity no publisher ever shows in terms of actual book production, Schlesinger Publishing undertook a massive "redeployment of human resources" (read: head rollings) and renovation of the offices.

It was a purge, a slate wiping, a dry wall response to murder.

But the bad taste remained, as bad taste often does. Val had inherited his line, been promoted to vice president of something, and dealt with the remodeling of the space. When an interior designer breezed through, Val fought for a corner—double the windows, wall-to-wall carpeting with enough pile to feel like something other than Astroturf, taupe on the walls, and a desk made out of anything other than pressed wood. She got it all. Including, on the debit side of the ledger, Ivy League Ivy, her with the doomsday personality.

Miraculously, the girl who had been hired by their former boss had been promoted to assistant editor and was now actually included in editorial meetings, where she bored the whiskey-soaked stuffing out of the other editors with her talk of where things fit in the grand literary tradition.

Within three months of the arrest of their former boss, his beloved Fir Na Tine—Welsh for *Men on Fire*—had been renamed because corporate felt it to be "too gender provocative." So some branding whiz on the ninth floor got it changed to Words on Fire, forget the Welsh. Ah, words on fire! To no one in the company other than Val Cameron, apparently, it evoked a whole grim history of book burnings—although there were a certain amount of titters on Twitter...and smirks over parmesan-encrusted chèvre salads wherever the publishing pantheon lunched. One blogger referred to all the changes at Val's imprint as Pants on Fire. In the end, she had come cheap. She had saved the imprint from a certain amount of disgrace. Surely more windows was the least her employers could do for her.

Val set her slippered feet against the edge of her new desk—the Belmont Writing Desk with Bluestone Top in Natural, from Arhaus—and pushed back. The slippers had been a present from Wade Decker, the single best thing to come out of her time in Canada all those months ago. The affair lasted several months, despite the fact that she inspired faux-leopard, bow-tied leather footwear in the man. But finally they ran up against the unsolvable problem of where a smitten fish and bird could live. When it became clear Decker wasn't about to permanently relocate from Toronto, and Val wasn't about to head back to the land of more long-suffering jolliness than she could stand, he took a job flying small planes for a Canadian international aid agency.

When her cell phone buzzed on her desk, Val half hoped it was James Killian calling to cancel their meeting that afternoon. No such luck. She sat up and grabbed the phone. *Adrian Bale.* "Hi, Ade." Her college roommate. Her partner in boozy line dances and ill-advised open mike poetry slams, now a curator at a private antiquities museum on the Upper West Side. "Howdy, Valjean."

She sounded good. Whenever Adrian felt good she took a shot at sounding like her idea of a cowboy—which was about as far from the brilliant, prim, beneath-it-all salty Adrian Bale as anything in nature could get. "Where in the world are you?" Val asked her.

Adrian's warm laugh came right against Val's ear. "I'm at Heathrow, dear heart."

"Doing what?" Val's eyes scanned the glossy white ceiling while she waited for one of Adrian's tales of swirling dunes and storybook lovers.

"Coming back from a visit to my brother."

Ah, the pious Antony, a Carmelite monk. "Is he sick? Besides all that piety, I mean."

"No," she said archly. "That's not Antony at all, Val. If you weren't such a pill about meeting him—" Still, she said it affectionately, like it was just some lovable quirk of Val's. They had made it through seventeen years of friendship without Val's having to tangle with the one she always thought of as Monk Man. Although she never talked about it, Val had a secret fear of clergy, who she suspected always wanted to cure her of sarcasm and save her soul, in that order.

During their long friendship, anytime Adrian suggested a trip to the coast of England to see the sainted Antony, Val always had an excuse. Finally she got it down to a speedy "no," followed by an eye-rolling sigh from Adrian. Val never knew which idea was more repellent, trailing unsaved behind the pious Antony in a drafty cathedral, or getting stuck in a game of beach volleyball with the pasty Monk Man. There was no place she could picture pulling off a meeting with Adrian's silent, gliding brother. So it was just more fish and birds. All of life was just fish and birds.

"I'm calling to nail down dinner later this week," said Adrian.

"Absolutely," Val smiled. "I can hear all about the trip then."

"Oh." Adrian sighed in that big, airy way Val had always liked. "The abbey's donating a funerary urn to the Coleman-Witt Museum. I bubble wrapped the hell out of it last night, since I'm carrying it on the plane—"

Val glanced at the ceiling. "Are you sure there aren't any ashes in it?"

"You forget the Catholics bury the body."

"Ah."

"No," she went on, "it's one of those funky Victorian black and white Jasperware things. Not terribly valuable, but it's bigger than they usually come, and in good condition." Val heard a voice crackling behind Adrian's, who overrode it. "Maybe we'll plant some nasturtiums in it and—" A pause. "Oh, listen, Val, they're boarding my flight."

"Take good care of the prize." At a knock on the door, Val barked, "Come in!" Stepping onto the threshold was Ivy League Ivy. The associate editor widened her limpid eyes, tapped her watch, and turned on her heel. Ivy's way of reminding her of the weekly editorial meeting...

"Not such a prize, really. I'm only accepting it—" Adrian's voice dropped "—because the Prior insisted. He's this sweet old magnanimous thing. Believe me, Val—" said Adrian, who sounded at that moment like she was lugging a Victorian funerary urn and heading for the gate at Heathrow, "there's nothing about this poor little urn that anyone could possibly want."

2

Stepping inside Kyoto, the Asian fusion restaurant where she was meeting James Killian, Val shook off the rain and squinted around the small room. Never having met the man, she was relying on his promise to wave at her like a fool. She had only found one fuzzy online image of Killian, on location on Kauai where he was guest blogging about GMOs. It was the kind of terrible shot you get of shy guys who seem happier on the margins everywhere. At that moment, a man at the back of Kyoto raised an arm at her, shooting her a quick smile. More like minor royalty signaling for the limo to pull 'round than anyone she'd describe as "waving like a fool." Was it the right guy?

As Val neared the small corner booth, the man slid from the seat. "Val?" James Killian was reasonably tall, reasonably slim, and more than reasonably good-looking. Older than she expected, maybe forty, with a shock of well-cut dirty blond hair prematurely heading toward white. The lightweight lamb's wool sweater was camel colored, the leather bomber was the color of old saddles, and the eyes were dark gray. She gave him a speedy scan for some demerits—no matter how unfair—she could fixate on quickly to keep herself from slipping off to unprofessional places. Ah, there it was. One crooked front tooth.

She thrust out a hand. "I'm Val Cameron," she said with a thin smile. "Nice to meet you finally." The red-wrapped hostess slid two menus into place with an even thinner smile, then glided away. As Killian, pretend plumber to the stars, murmured something about a real pleasure, she noticed he was scanning her right back. Not in a sexy, heavy-lidded way, but as if he was cataloguing her somehow. In case he had to pick her out of a crowd of other wavy-haired brunettes with excellent taste in footwear standing on a badly lighted subway platform.

She shot him a frank look. "I'm 5'7" and 142 pounds."

As they sat, he shrugged, waving it away. "I like to know who's sitting across from me."

"I'm pretty harmless." As soon as she said it, she regretted it. Mainly because it was true.

"You can work on that," said Killian helpfully. Then he frowned at the bright green bamboo in a small square vase, and moved it six inches to the left.

When their waiter, a lad with a high forehead and unworkable poodle curls, hovered, unable to tear his eyes from Val's dinner date, Killian ordered a double Oban, neat, and Val a Bombay gin and tonic. They sat in silence for a moment, evaluating each other's choices.

Val went first. "You like the idea of a peculiar Scotch more than the actual taste of it."

His expression stayed neutral. "You hesitated before you ordered, which makes me think the gin and tonic is a throwback, something you haven't had for a long time." Killian narrowed his eyes. "I'm guessing you recently got out of a relationship."

She gave him a flat look. "What about the Scotch?"

"Actually," he told her, "I like both—the idea and the taste." He smiled, and for a moment she thought he was talking about sex. Crooked front tooth. Crooked front tooth. "Otherwise," he went on reasonably, "what's the point? Why choose," here he opened his hands wide in an innocent way that was about as far from innocent as she could stand, "when you can have it all?"

She was holding her breath. "Are you talking about the Oban?"

"And one or two other things besides." Then he grinned in a speculative way.

Was the man actually flirting with her? Do people still flirt?

She looked him straight in the eye, which felt more disturbing than a Words on Fire business dinner at a friendly little Asian fusion place should be. This was Midtown. There were rules. She was pretty sure.

At that moment, the smitten waiter showed up and set down the double Oban in front of Killian. Then he turned an inattentive face to Val. "Sorry, but we're out of Bombay."

"Then make it Tanqueray, please." She flashed Killian a sickly smile. "I just got out of a relationship."

He nodded, resting loose fists on the table, and waited.

Val studied him. "Where do you live?" she asked after a moment.

"Wherever I'm working," said Killian, sipping. "I'm not one for a permanent address."

"Well, where did you grow up?"

His face clouded. "On the Ohio River, actually. Which is surprisingly fast-moving," he added. "Unless you're a human."

"So you got out."

"There was nothing stopping me."

She shifted in her seat. "How long have you been writing?" The quality of her conversation was definitely slipping.

"A few years. It's my day job." Suddenly, Killian seemed delighted. "Are you interviewing me?"

"Just trying to get the picture," she told him. That writing was his "day job" wouldn't play well on the back cover of *Plumb Lines*. Words on Fire was certainly paying this man pretty well to do something that floated him until he sold his screenplay or scored a dance audition. "What would you rather be doing?"

"I have other interests." He pushed himself back from the table. "Don't you?"

Val fixed him with a blank look. She could tell him her work was her life, but it only that minute occurred to her, and she wasn't sure she wanted to lay bare any single other thing about herself. She changed the subject. "I'd like to get down to business now."

He smiled at her, then struck a match and held it to the votive candle the management had forgotten to light. "I'm sure you would."

"Thank you." A slow tilt of her head. Why was he so maddening?

Her drink arrived, and Killian raised his double. "Here's to the woman sitting across from me. She is loyal, hard-working, trustworthy, thrifty, humble—"

Never had a list of virtues seemed quite this disheartening. With a long sip of the gin and tonic, she sat back slightly. Fizzy juniper berries, that was a gin and tonic, her college drink—and Adrian's. She had to admit, she liked the idea of it. And the taste. Reaching for her tote, she pulled out the manuscript of *Plumb Lines* and pushed it across the table.

As Killian pulled out a pair of drugstore reading glasses and paged expressionlessly through her marginal comments, Val folded her hands and stared at nothing. All she had to do was make it through another hour or so, interrupted by some seared ahi tuna served over soba noodles with black sesame seeds and shredded kale, followed by a quick handshake and a half-shouted goodbye. The rest she and Killian could do through email.

She would have to stay very far away from this handsome and unsettling man.

3

A man called Alaric stood safely away from the entrance to Olde Bandylegs Pub, where he couldn't be overheard, then looked at his phone. Eight p.m. here meant it was the middle of the afternoon in New York.

The man he was calling was no doubt at his three o'clock private prayers in that inexpressibly sweet church on Gramercy Park West. The man known as Animus, the soul of their secret organization, called it the Chapel of Robus Christi. The Might of Christ.

"Yes?"

That one word, Alaric knew, spoke so much. "I have news," he said evenly.

"Go on."

"It's disappeared." There was no way around it.

"Disappeared?" the other man repeated. "What do you mean, disappeared?"

"The boy lost it."

"Lost it!"

Alaric went on to explain what had happened. According to the boy monk, Fintan, the theft itself went off smoothly, but when he was coming to meet Alaric, out on the ridge trail, he was very nearly caught out by his mates. At that moment he secreted the holy relic in an empty urn, then led the others away, knowing he could retrieve it later. Only when he returned, the urn was gone, and with it, of course, the relic. He searched everywhere.

"Has he been discreet?"

The first, and in some ways the only question. "Not perfectly discreet, Animus."

The other man groaned. "What has he said?"

"He asked the abbey maintenance crew. He asked the monks who tend the gardens, thinking maybe the urn was a planter. He even asked his mates."

"Has he put an ad in the London *Times*?" he cried.

"Not yet," said Alaric humorously.

Through gritted teeth, he whispered, "The relic has to be there."

After a moment, Alaric murmured. "Unless—"

"Unless what?"

"Unless we have...a rival."

That possibility had actually never occurred to him. A rival. A competitor for the holy relic. A crusade that needs no knights and no equipment—no clanging public journey awash in the blood of reluctant converts. Oh, no. In this twenty-first century of sleek subterfuge, a lone operative could most certainly do the job. Hadn't Alaric?

In all the grand planning, all the years and crimes dedicated to the founding of Robus Christi, the elite organization with a holy prophecy at its core, had their leader been every bit as careless as that hapless boy? Was there a breach in the heart of the organization? A mole? All this operative would have to do is follow the boy in his holy mission, wait for an opportunity alone with the stolen object, and complete the task. A rival. A faceless and nameless rival with unknown motives.

They both fell silent.

Finally: "Alaric," the man in Gramercy Park said softly into the phone.

"What do you want me to do?"

"Get as much information as the boy can give you."

"I understand."

"After all," he went on, "he may get a lead in the—disappearance."

"I agree." Alaric waited.

"When you're sure he has no more information..." said the other man slowly.

"Yes?"

"Confess him." The voice gained strength. "Be careful not to alarm him. Robus Christi does not deal in terror." It seemed an important point.

Alaric stood very still. "I see."

"Then kill him."

With that, Animus ended the call.

After staring for a moment at his phone, Alaric took off down the road from the pub at a good pace. *Kill him, but don't alarm him.* What counted as alarm? Anything from struggling to a quick flash of understanding in those young eyes now destined never to achieve cataracts?

For all the planning ahead, murder, he had come to appreciate, had a large element of improvisation to it—which, of course, was where mere talent parts ways with brilliance. An unexpected witness, a weapon malfunction, even the vagaries of weather.

If murder was the object, stay open to mischance. That much he knew.

Alaric. A corruption of "wings," because as Animus explained to him at his first meeting of the inner circle, the position required soaring above everything terrestrial—law, convention, memory, and personal history. Whatever it required. And he was suited to the work. With the piety he kept to himself, his great social ease—and no attachments. In another generation, he would have been a spy worth the hanging.

For all of his life he had found no meaning in anything other than the Church, with its irreducible mysteries and its soaring hymns. The Church was the one thing he had never been able to get to the bottom of—and so he became Alaric, the winged spy, the agent, the effective killer.

He sighed with the half-smoked American Spirit cigarette cupped in his steady hand. Nothing quite as good as a cigarette in the night air of Norfolk, perched on its cliff. Something barked twice in the woods. Nothing approached. And the slight breeze was warm on his cheeks. It was a perfect life, even with the instructions he had just heard from the soul of the organization, safely stowed in his personal chapel there in Gramercy Park.

How easy murder must seem when you're three thousand miles away in a fine Manhattan afternoon still lighted by the April sun. How many codicils you can apply when there's an entire ocean between the desire and the act. Confess him, kill him, don't scare him, use a three-inch knife, hum a few bars of something Gregorian, thank him for his efforts, be sure you're wearing your scapular, stand on one goddamned foot.

Robus Christi does not deal in terror.

Maybe not. But terror, Alaric took a long final drag on his cigarette and tossed it over the cliff, the glowing tip disappearing in a sudden arc—terror was at the heart of everything we think we know for sure. Even Animus at his mid-afternoon prayers was terrified. Terrified he might fail in the mission, and terrified too that the mission may not be worth a good goddamn when it came right down to it. And all Alaric, the wings of the organization, could do was to keep those two points of terror as far away as possible from each other. Because if they ever touched each other, everything would fly violently apart.

They had invested too much to have that happen.

It was a matter of action—which, when it came right down to it, most things were. Here he was, about to confess, kill, and somehow not alarm an indiscreet boy who only ever wanted to earn a place in an organization very ill-suited to the ordinary man. In these final days before the theft, the boy had whispered to Alaric that by stealing the holy relic he would be living the body of Christ, touching what he had touched, becoming indistinguishable from history—and there was no one, not anywhere, he could tell. All the glory had to stay bottled up.

There in the dark, Alaric could tell it felt painful to his young heart, and the boy had stammered he could only hope that over time it would enlarge him. His bones would reach up and out, his flesh would thicken, his blood would course that much harder. "Glory," he'd said to Alaric, "will shine from my pores." If it was what the boy Fintan needed to believe to perform his part, Alaric saw no lasting harm in it.

And as they shared a smoke in the April midnight, Alaric thought he had made it very clear to the boy that their holy organization depended on absolute discretion. "From every single one of us," added Alaric, his voice low. "Glory is not a public thing." He thought the boy had understood.

But now it was fatally clear.

They never should have recruited him.

New York

"Look at this." Greta Bistritz swiveled her red Macbook Air around to face Val where she sat on a high padded stool at Greta's breakfast bar. Once every two weeks Val walked the fourteen blocks to her aunt's apartment on E. 65th off Lexington for homemade chocolate croissants and designer espresso before they both headed off for work. Today her mother's younger sister was wearing a ruffled white blouse and camel slacks, pulled together with a wide, soft leather brown belt with a gold clasp. Greta Bistritz had put on a few pounds in recent years, but not so many that she went in mortal fear of belts. She had artful blond hair that came in soft waves to her chin, a fine, long nose, a wide mouth that looked especially good when it was wry, and green eyes. Helplessly vain about her hands, Greta Bistritz sported about half a dozen rings on various fingers.

Val peered at the screen. It was a bibliographic entry for

holdings at the Morgan Library, thirty blocks south of where they sat next to each other peeling off the perfect layers of their pastries. Playing low in the background was Placido Domingo's "Nessun Dorma," one of Val's favorite arias, piercing the simple air it touched and making all things everywhere suddenly and achingly important. Val read the heading on the screen and turned to her aunt. "A catalog of Inquisition materials?"

Greta nodded. "Morgan has one of the finest collections of holdings from the Spanish Inquisition, which means," she lifted her coffee cup, "everything in it is almost five hundred years old, which was when the Holy Office opened for business." Greta Bistritz was the specialist—head of the office, in government-speak—at the Artifact Authentication Agency, an obscure branch of the U.S. Department of Commerce housed in a nondescript building on Seventh Avenue. The Agency was the gatekeeper for questionable pieces imported by reputable museums, galleries, auction houses, collectors, and other commercial interests.

Greta leaned closer to Val. "Get anything from it?"

Val scratched her cheek and read the page carefully. "This is a transcription from the original documents."

"Correct. A Morgan Library employee transcribed—and microfilmed—the original records of the documentary holdings."

"Where are the originals?"

Greta laughed. "Not in the stacks."

Val studied the screen, scrolling down. Columns and rows, entry after entry, mostly a record of names of the accused, charges against them, date and place of trial by The Holy Office, disposition of the case, and any other descriptive notes. All the entries had been translated into English. Val pointed to one: a trial against Fr. José DeMarzo, S.J., 6 June 1594, for soliciting sex in the Confessional. "So they prosecuted their own."

"As well as Protestants, Jews, witches, bigamists, you name it. Yes."

"Very busy."

"Zealotry is what they had instead of Red Bull."

Val slid her a look. "Or, I'm pretty sure, Viagra."

Greta pushed the bright blue IKEA plate to Val. "Have another," she said, waving first at the croissants, and then at the screen. "Read on."

From what Val could tell, this scrupulous recording of the official business of the Inquisition spanned hundreds of years. Mostly they were the *procesos*, the trial proceedings, but there were some entries that simply acknowledged receipt of royal decrees, Inquisitorial edicts, and the daily dealings of the Holy Office that had nothing to do with torture or execution. In terms of location, Sevilla, Spain saw the most action. And in terms of the *procesos* themselves, that terrifying business of the Inquisition, the formal accusations against the citizens unlucky enough to come to their attention were varied. Succinct. Even bizarre. A single row would contain the date, the place, the number of pages related to the matter, the name of the accused, and the accusation. Blasphemy, bigamy, polygamy, superstition, apostasy, heresy, practicing Judaism, witchcraft, misconduct with women, denying the sinfulness of paid fornication, being a priestess, an accomplice, a visionary, or an impostor.

You could certainly get into a lot of trouble in medieval Spain.

Down, down, down she scrolled, through the painstaking recorded rows, then back to the first page where Greta had begun. One entry caught her eye. A line item tucked in between an entry in 1594 for the *proceso* against Diego Mendez, tried for practicing Judaism, which Val knew probably ended in a trip to the stake— and an entry also in 1594 that was a receipt of two copies of an edict issued by the Inquisition listing "various forms" of sacrilege and heresy. Between the stake and the disobedience that could lead up to the stake was one little item. "Ah," Val murmured, "interesting..."

1595 Veracruz

# of Leaves/Pages: 16

Accusation/Subject: Satire

Val turned to her aunt, who sat back, and sipped her coffee, eyeing her. "A satire?" When Greta nodded, Val held her mug between both hands and thought about it. "It's the first work of—"

Greta interrupted. "The only."

Val whistled softly. "The only work of actual literature that's recorded," she said, tapping the screen with the backs of her fingers. "I'm wondering—"

"How bad can it be?"

"How bad can it be."

"Apparently this work was turned in to the Holy Office as a suspected piece of seditious material, otherwise how did it come into their hands?"

Greta's point made sense to Val. "And then the Inquisition simply—" She rotated her hand, searching for the idea.

"Filed it." Raising an elegant eyebrow at her, Greta logged out.

"That's absolutely what they did. Did they even read it?"

"We'll never know." Greta closed the lid of the laptop and set it at the end of her breakfast bar. "But the real question—" she said slowly, pulling her long, ringed fingers through her blond waves "—is why they kept it at all, wouldn't you say?" She lifted her arm to check her watch, those beautiful fingers dangling. "Why didn't they destroy it?"

Val grabbed the plates and walked them into the kitchen. An interesting question. "Dangerous to keep it, dangerous to destroy it."

"Why do you say that?" Greta clipped her U.S. Department of Commerce laminated ID badge to her belt.

"Because even if they didn't know what to make of the satire— or what they called a satire because they didn't know what to call it—it's better to know what's out there." Val lifted her shoulders. "What if there were copies?" Distracted, Greta murmured, pulling on a belted white jacket. Val went on, "It's better to keep the original out of reach. Filed away."

"They had enough else to keep them busy."

"Lucky for somebody they only had the satire," said Val, slipping into her street-length black fleece. "And not the satirist."

"True." For a moment, while Greta pointed the remote at her

sound system and Placido Domingo disappeared into silence, they didn't speak.

Finally, Val slung her red tote over her shoulder, and it was then she was struck. "What's all this have to do with you, Auntie?"

Greta Bistritz closed her wooden shutters, angling what little seeping daylight was left to thin streaks on the ceiling. "I got a call at work yesterday from someone," said Val's aunt, turning slowly with her arms crossed. In the soft light of Greta's stylish apartment, where the likes of Placido Domingo flavor the air and Kandinsky prints give the walls a small place in the world, Val watched as her aunt looked past her as she spoke. "He's in the Romance Languages department at Hunter College. Says he's writing a book on prose style during the Mexican Inquisition. I asked him how the Artifact Authentication Agency could help him." Greta frowned at her shoes for a second, then went on. "He told me this is a book he's been writing for about two years, and naturally he's done a lot of his research at the Morgan Library because of the wealth of their holdings. Imagine his excitement, he told me, when he found the record of the satire from 1595. From what he could tell—"

"What's his name?"

Greta lifted her head. "Saul Bensoussan."

"Go on." What a coup. Bensoussan may have unearthed a forgotten manuscript. Untranslated, most likely. Unstudied, for sure.

"He's made several trips to the Morgan over the last two years, working on an English translation of the original. Everything was going fine," Greta went on, "until last week, when the librarian brought him the satire in its very old wooden box and set it down. Imagine his chagrin."

"Why chagrin?"

Greta gave her a long look. "Because he's pretty sure," she said as they headed for the door, "it's a fake."

4

Norfolk

It was the small one, the young monk with the restless eyes, called Eli, who had come to Antony Bale to report his friend missing. First the one named Fintan had missed Lauds that morning, the boy standing before him ticked off on his fingers, and then he failed to show up in Housekeeping for the chores. Tick two. The boy stared frowning at his fingers, clearly wishing the evidence of something off, something amiss, had been more.

"Is that unusual?" Bale asked, where he sat at his small desk in the Warming Room. It was a cool April noon, and the guttering fire felt especially good while he went over the abbey books.

"Very," said the boy, one hand absently patting down a cowlick that made him look twelve. "Fintan is very devout." And when he seemed dissatisfied by that account of his friend, he added, "Which is not to say he can't let loose."

Bale smiled. "When the occasion calls for it."

Eli nodded once.

"No harm in that," Bale reassured him, although this was a boy who didn't appear to need much of that.

Suddenly the boy blurted, "There was that whole thing about the urn."

"With—Fintan?" He wished he could remember the boy who hadn't shown up for Lauds or chores...

The boy chewed a fingernail with a kind of intensity, while Bale simply waited. Then the one called Eli told him how it was the urn they had passed outside one of the outbuildings two nights ago, when the four of them—Fintan, Eli and their mates—snuck out after Compline to get up to some fun in the woods. Bale had a flicker of admiration for the boy who could easily recount a tale that included about three or four broken rules. By the next morning, Fintan was asking around about it. Had we seen it? Did we move it anywhere? Did we see anybody mucking around with it?

Colum told Eli that Fintan had questioned the maintenance crew. And Miles overheard him asking Brother Martin and two of the other—here the boy stumbled over his words—garden monks. But what really disturbed Eli was when, about an hour after lights out in the dorter, they were all supposed to be asleep, and he heard a small sound and opened his eyes just enough to see Fintan pulling aside the clothes and books and personal stuff in Miles's locker. Eli stayed still, not asking his mate what the hell he was up to. One by one Fintan went methodically through his mates' lockers—looking with a penlight for the damn urn, Eli had to think, when they had already all told him they hadn't touched it.

"What happened then?" Bale asked him.

Through narrow eyes, Eli watched his mate sink onto the foot of his bed, and—here the boy looked away—let out what sounded like a sob. In the morning, Eli had dawdled until the others had gone down for the Daily Service, and he checked each of the lockers. Nothing looked at all disturbed. Fintan was careful to set everything back the way he had found it. It was strange, Eli thought, and sneaky. And Fintan was gone. Even after Eli and the others had told him they hadn't touched "your bloody urn," Fintan didn't believe them. But he had wanted them to think he had. And now he was gone. Bale watched the boy take a mighty breath. Two more things, the young monk said then, ticking off another two fingers.

"Yes?"

Eli with the restless eyes said he was embarrassed to tell it, but Fintan had peed in that very urn as the other three joined him that night, although when Eli got closer it didn't smell like piss, so he had good reason to doubt Fintan's explanation for what he had been doing. Finally, the boy said with tight little shakes of his head, he felt terribly sorry for Fintan, since he must have been so disturbed about the missing urn that he wasn't thinking straight, mucking about in his mates' things despite what they had told him. From what Eli had seen, there was no way in heaven that urn could have fit in any of the lockers, even if they had been completely empty.

"Why have you come to me?" said Bale softly, interested.

"It was Prior Berthold," the boy explained with a quick little shrug. "He said it was your sister's urn. He had given that urn to your sister."

"Ah." Mystery solved. Adrian had it. "Did he say why?"

"For her museum. Which was what he told Fintan yesterday. Plus the name of the museum." A church warder who lived in town had offered Adrian a ride to the train to London, which was why none of the monks Fintan had asked could account for the urn. Antony stared at the fire which still crackled even though it was nearly down to embers. "Sir," said Eli, his left leg jiggling, "I'm thinking it's a good guess your sister has the urn Fintan's been looking for." Then he made a grand two-handed gesture, like he was turning over an important piece of information on a platter, and now it was the responsibility of the old-timers.

"Yes, Eli, I'd say we've found the urn." He'd give Adrian a call to verify. Although locating the urn didn't explain why it was desperately important to the missing young monk. "And now," said Bale, pushing himself decisively out of the old, high-backed chair that in better days had adorned the nave, "I think we had better find Fintan."

New York

As she and Aunt Greta pushed their way onto the 4 train at the 68th Street station, Val did her daily two-handed clutch of her red leather work tote against her chest. No seats, not at that hour. As the doors slid shut, Val managed to find a bare-handed pole position and pulled in her aunt, who was wearing blue kidskin gloves. Greta wore gloves, Val wore germs. When the train started with a lurch, Val staggered backwards, mashing the instep of a guy about her age with a fleshy neck, earbuds insulating him from subway boredom and panhandlers, and a black topcoat that had the look of those somber men who direct cars out of the parking lot at funeral homes. He actually gnashed his teeth, then recovered quickly when she muttered an apology. She guessed he had a long ride ahead of him down to Wall Street and hers was just the first of the day's foot mashings.

"What are you going to do?" she asked Greta, who gave her that long, thin-lipped smile Val remembered from her childhood. It was a smart, worldly look, suggesting great things to come, mostly in secret.

"About the satire?" When Val nodded, she narrowed her green eyes and seemed to study the MTA map mounted behind plastic next to the doors. "I'll send a field op from the office first," she answered, swaying into Val as the train picked up speed. "See if we can get the good professor to meet with us. Beyond the fact of the fake, he wasn't particularly forthcoming." Greta's simple shrug didn't have much room in the tight crush of riders.

"And if he's right?"

"Then it depends. Our next move is to figure out how long it's been a fake. A year? Five? Two hundred? Forever? If we believe it's recent," she fixed Val with a lively look, "we have one or two crimes we can pursue," Greta moved closer to the pole, "with a certain amount of delight." A short, very pregnant woman pushed by to claim a seat a crazy-haired student with a violin case awkwardly stood to give her.

At 59th Street, the train disgorged a few commuters, exposing more pole positions. With an exhale a little more audible than she would've liked, Val slung an arm around the pole, tucking herself in tight. She still clutched her red work tote against her chest with two bare hands like it held all her money in the world plus a one-of-a-kind satire on parchment from the sixteenth century. If the Hunter professor was correct, and the holding at the Morgan Library was a fake...who could possibly want to steal such a document? Legitimate scholars and researchers would content themselves to see it, read it, and study it there at the library—even springing for a hard copy or the microfilm. It seemed to Val that the ones who came to study it for its possible literary value were precisely the ones most likely to respect it.

If Greta's professor the whistleblower was correct that it was a fake, someone had gone to a lot of trouble to steal the original, substitute a good forgery to avert suspicion, and—what? What on earth was Greta dealing with? What could a little satire—if that's what it truly was, not simply described incorrectly by the Inquisition's scribe who quite possibly didn't know what he was looking at—what could a little satire matter to someone desperate enough to remove it? Was the work itself dangerous somehow? Or something the thief did not want available to all those other scholars? Was professional jealousy at the bottom of it?

The easiest explanation was that the professor was wrong.

Val watched a few commuters cluster around the closed doors as the train pulled into Grand Central. She and Greta should be able to get seats for the rest of the ride. Val would push her way out at 23rd and walk to the block to the Flatiron Building and the renovated offices of Words on Fire, leaving Greta to press on alone down to 330 Seventh Avenue. She leaned into her aunt and said in a low voice, "Can you really imagine anyone being able to pull off that kind of theft at the Morgan Library? It's like a fortress."

Greta Bistritz gave her niece a quick, fond look. "Oh, nothing is impenetrable, darling," she said with a smile. "Not even you."

5

By the middle of the afternoon, when Bale had interrupted his investigation into Fintan's disappearance and prayed None with the others in the sanctuary, the lines of Psalm 118 felt troubling. *I shall not fear when foes abound. My God, my Savior is near.* Sometimes, he had to admit, he didn't know which line felt truer to him—that foes were afoot or that the divine was there to help. The psalmist believed that both were true. Which felt like a bit more faith than Antony Bale himself could bring to bear on the problems of modern life.

Where could the boy be?

Bale had at least determined a few things. By the time Eli had come to the Warming Room to report his friend's disappearance, Fintan had been missing—or, at any rate, had not been seen—for more than half a day. From the time Eli had caught him going through their lockers in the dark, about eleven p.m., they figured, until now. A discreet search of all the buildings yielded nothing. Bale hadn't wanted to send out a general alarm, not yet, so he had enlisted Eli in the hunt.

The clever boy knew Fintan's favorite indoor spots—the choir loft, the back of the monks' frater after the meal had been cleared away, and the window seat in Misericorde, when no one was excused from fasting—and was thorough in poking around everywhere else. Bale had talked to the maintenance crew—no luck—and had put out a few feelers among the shops in town. Getting there would have been a hike, and none of the bikes were missing, but Fintan could conceivably have done it given enough motivation. Whatever that might be. And from there he could have caught the train anywhere. Calls to his cell phone went unanswered.

Bale himself checked the boy's locker, while Eli stood nearby, looking distracted. When Bale called him closer, to see whether everything appeared to be present, the answer was yes. Fintan's set of "off-world" clothes—what he had come to Burnham Norton wearing—and a Manchester United hoodie Eli swore Fintan would never leave behind. None of the others were allowed to touch it, especially the sleeve clapped by the hand of Beckham himself when Fintan had gotten his autograph after a match. Very fussy about that hoodie, he was. A jumbled stack of books, a worn Dopp kit holding toiletries. On the single shelf, a tin holding trinkets. For Bale, while Fintan was simply missing for not even a day, it was enough to have Eli verify that the locker's contents looked normal—as far as he knew.

Bale turned slowly to Eli, who was clearly waiting for one of the two of them to blurt something brilliant that would lead them straight—and quickly—to his missing mate. "Had he been himself lately?" asked Bale.

"Yes."

A little too fast. "Sure?"

"Well, himself but more, oh, keyed up."

Bale looked closely at the boy. "Worried?"

Eli snorted softly. "Not hardly. More like—" He narrowed his eyes. "More like he had been paid a visit by the Blessed Mother herself and was just enjoying it privately for a bit." The boy shot him a look a little too wry for someone committed to the religious life. "If you know what I mean," he added.

Bale did. "He was keeping something to himself."

"Oh, yeah." It was as if it was the first it had occurred to Eli, and now that it had—Fintan was keeping something to himself—it fit.

Was Fintan planning to run off from Burnham Norton? Not

without that Manchester United hoodie, that's for sure. Bale made a few discreet calls to key shopkeepers in nearby Mundesley, but no luck. And the station master didn't recall anyone by that description boarding any train in the last half day. Bale heaved a sigh, there was no way around it now. If Fintan hadn't escaped to town, or bolted on the train for parts unknown, or was hiding in some favorite spot inside the monastery, then it was looking more and more likely to Antony Bale that the boy was taken against his will. Or worse. Either way, it was about time to call the police. And announce the disappearance of Fintan to the community as a whole.

But there was one more place to search. The woods Fintan and his mates headed for when they wanted a smoke. Beyond that, the ridge walk. And this was part of the search for the missing boy—here he glanced smoothly at the clever Eli—that he wanted to do alone. So he sent the boy to interview what he had referred to as the garden monks, and Bale slipped out the side door of the East Range.

The afternoon was overcast and cool, weather Bale enjoyed. He cut across the paved paths and the north lawn, the breeze pushing his white robe against his legs as he strode. Four days ago, he had hiked the ridge walk with Adrian, toward Cromer, where the cliffs rose lower against the sea. Not like here at Sidestrand, the highest point along the Norfolk coast. The walk with Adrian hadn't been one of their old slogs from when they were in their twenties, when they could head to the Catskills and hike the Hunter Mountain trail in half a day and still be game to get back to the city for a night at Swing 46. All the while testing each other's resolve to defer future fun for what might be all time to pursue the monastic life or a doctorate in art history.

Over the years, the hikes became more urban—from the studio walk-up where Adrian was living at the time in the East Village to the Metropolitan Museum—and they still went swing dancing together, but had given up the sidecar step. Other pleasures continued. For both of them, despite vows and scholarship.

The woods between the abbey grounds were small and really rather thin. No more than a quarter mile across, by the looks of it. There were thickets of gorse and second growth pine trees, and a few docile beeches, but light had no problem penetrating these woods. In the bright overcast, Bale could just about see through to the ridge walk. Heading in, he slowed, keeping to the closest thing to a path he could find. What if the boy was lying hurt? "Fintan," he called, scanning left and right. Nothing moved, not even Bale, as he stood still and listened for something human. Bale cupped his hands at his mouth. "Fintan!"

A dreary inevitability settled over him. Mostly, in this life, boys get in over their heads with secrets. Either because they can't keep them, or they keep the wrong ones—or the secrets sadly have something to do with adults. Mere boys are no match. If the young monk Fintan wasn't artful enough to search his mates' lockers without being seen, no matter how quiet he thought he was being, no matter how skillfully he had kept from disturbing the contents, Bale doubted he was artful enough to keep clear of the secrets of dangerous adults.

Bale strode out to the ridge walk that lined this point on the Norfolk coast that was barren and rocky in both directions. Overhead a bittern wheeled and shrieked, white against the thin overcast. Bale crossed the trail that wound bleak and beautiful as far as the eye could see, empty of human habitation or industry of any sort, and stepped to the cliff's edge. At the foot of the cliff hundreds of feet below was a plume of white. For a second he narrowed his eyes against the thudding of his heart as he imagined what he saw was some bright outcropping of chalk. Or a lost sail that had found its mysterious way over the gray blue water.

With fingers suddenly cold, Bale stripped off his robe and started to find easy footholds sideways down the cliff toward the plume of white he knew was the missing boy. A boy who had kept his very last secret, only not very well.

*   *   *

New York

When Val emerged from the subway at 23rd Street, and stepped out of the way of glazed pedestrians jockeying for sidewalk position on the way to their offices, she checked her phone. There was a voicemail from Adrian. *Val, I don't care what you think your lunch plans are for today—*her voice was excited—*I want you to change them. No, make that your breakfast plans. Come to the museum if you want a once in a lifetime chance to see—*here Adrian took in a mighty breath—*the finest example of* Euphorbia milii *in the known world. I can't hang on to it very long.*

The street was clogged with cabs and delivery trucks, maybe half an hour before rush hour reached the hysterical honking stage. A New York tradition. The only outlet for expressing a shared outrage over a situation that, clearly, insistent honking wasn't going to help. She checked the time on her phone—7:43 a.m.—and debated taking a run up to see whatever it was Adrian was so excited about. *Euphorbia milii.*

A quick Google search sent her to Wikipedia, where she gleaned about as much information as she could handle at 7:43 in the morning before she got her hands on a second cup of dark roast coffee: *Euphorbia milii (crown of thorns, Christ plant, Christ thorn), is a species of flowering plant...introduced to the Middle East in ancient times, and legend associates it with the crown of thorns worn by Christ.*

Val clicked on her calendar. Nothing in the office until a ten a.m. meeting with the Digital Design geeks, who wanted to discuss branding the exciting new Words on Fire, such a stellar improvement over poor old decrepit Fir Na Tine. "I mean," the head of the department rhapsodized, "how do you brand a foreign language like Welsh, like we're not Bob effing Dylan, please." At which Val gave the two ambassadors sent to her to "sched" the meeting a wide, bright smile, spending only a slip of a second feeling bad for both Dylans who had suddenly become interchangeable commodities, apparently.

But she went right ahead and scheduled the meeting with the Digital Design geeks because she liked their repressed energy. They were the closest the company could come in age and look to a college chess club. Up to the Coleman-Witt and back in an hour, factoring in rush hour and time to slip into her ghastly moccasins—she walked the long block to Fifth Avenue, stepped off the curb, and raised an arm in the general direction of anything yellow that was moving and empty.

A yellow cab finally slid to a stop in front of her, and Val flung herself inside, giving the driver—an inscrutable woman who wore a gray burka—the address of the Coleman-Witt. The wordless driver imperturbably swung their way through what to Val appeared to be total gridlock. When they got to W. 73rd, up ahead Val saw a red and white FDNY ambulance with its rear lights strobing, blocked in against the curb by three patrol cars. Plus a late model black Chevy sedan disgorging two police detectives.

Muttering thanks, Val thrust a twenty-dollar bill at the driver and slid out of the cab without waiting for change. She loped her way up the sidewalk, shouldering past the dog walkers and joggers who were clutched together, arms crossed, waiting for something to happen. A forty-something woman with light brown hair rubber banded into a ponytail, wearing pale blue nylon shorts, started shaking her head. "That's the murder squad," she said to no one in particular, although everyone around her turned and gasped. "Well," she added defensively, "it is."

As Val turned onto the walk that led to the back entrance of the office wing, she was cut off by a cop who looked like he had given up a lucrative career as a digital designer in favor of a better wardrobe. "Ma'am, you can't go in," he told her, barring her with an arm.

Val looked wistfully at the door, where another uniformed cop stood in the entrance. She was no more than fifty feet away from Adrian who had a fine example of a flowering plant to show her.

Val's legs started to shake. "I have an appointment," she said finally, her voice sounding strange to herself. "With Adrian Bale." *Why is this dread the only thing we ever know with certainty?* Not love or beauty or how hummingbirds make it all the way to Central America for the winter. And when the cop pressed his lips tight and shook his head, Val knew the truth.

Later she would remember how she had to step wide to stay steady on her feet, and even then the cop had to grab her arm. Later still she would remember the Mexican jumping beans Adrian had sent away for sophomore year as a silly gift for Val who was having fits over studying for the History of Western Civilization final exam. The beans popped and flopped in her sweaty palm as she sat in the lecture hall with a blue exam book open in front of her. And her poor heart had felt like nothing more than beans as it trembled inside her—even all these years later, all these years later, when she didn't know what happened to the silly beans and she didn't know why the Coleman-Witt Museum was dissolving into vapor before her very eyes...and she didn't know what in the name of everything sweet she would ever do without Adrian Bale.

In the end, Val waited until they brought out the body. Someone had told her to go home. Someone else told her to go to work. Yet someone else advised a good stiff drink, and she lifted her chin, mildly interested. "Maybe the Beacon Bar on Broadway is open?" added the guy who had advised a drink. He had a flat, kind face, his hands stuffed into his Yankees jacket. She felt her eyes slide away from him as the Eyewitness News Channel 5 van pulled up and sleekly double-parked. Out rolled the A team, taking charge of the bloody event in a way that was making the crime scene techs bristle.

"No good could come of sticking around here," said one of the cops to Val after they got her contact information. She sat hunched on the edge of a low stone wall around the museum, her legs splayed like a bag lady, and she didn't give any kind of a damn. On the sidewalk the crowd got bigger, although some of the early dog walkers dipped their heads—sad to watch, sad to go—and went on their way. Dogs trotted, unfazed. Murder was a good time to be a Dachshund, thought Val, when no one could hold you responsible.

"I'll wait," said Val, although she wasn't sure anyone was listening, her ribs collapsing in on each other when she watched the agitated guards pull at their hair, saying Adrian Bale was a goddamn mess, that was for shit sure. Such a nice gal, always brought them fudge at Christmas. The kind with walnuts pressed into the top. The two of them had come running when the number five security camera was shot out. One added something low and quaking that might have been *head blown clear to New Jersey*, but the only way Val could swallow a scream was to think he said *get to go cheer for New Jersey*. Yes, that had to be it. Nets, Giants, some team always playing.

Inside her tote was an apple that she should have eaten days ago, that much she knew, and she'd have to be sure to tell the landlord about the silverfish in her bathroom. Maybe she should take a closer look at James Killian's manuscript. You can never be too sure about shocking tales of plumbing. And just that morning she had used up the very last of the hotel shampoo sample she had tossed into her suitcase at the end of her trip to Havana last September with Adrian. The last of the shampoo. The last trip together. The last of Adrian.

Head blown clear to New Jersey.

Val would have to face it.

Have to face it.

Only how?

The crowd got noisier as the cops pushed back to let the wheeled stretcher come through. At that moment, the director of the Coleman-Witt showed up, looking dazed. Adrian had introduced Val to Eva Toscano at the opening a month ago for the illuminated manuscripts exhibit. Now the sharp-beaked redhead was shoving her way through the television crew and gawkers. "Terrell!" she called out to one of the guards. Even what Adrian had told her was the mighty Eva was sounding shaken. "Tell me what the hell happened—" she demanded, as though she was trying to figure out what she was accusing him of. But Terrell didn't get a chance, because the coroner's van attendants rolled the body noiselessly along the walkway. Val pushed herself off the wall. Under the taut sheet smeared with blood was what was left of her best friend.

She pressed the heels of her hands into her eyes. There was something comforting in how some tech had wrapped Adrian tight, a child tucked in at last for a long and final night. As the van doors closed behind the stretcher, Val made a weak swipe at the handles of her tote, and she realized the strange keening as she shambled down 73rd Street in the direction of life, or just elsewhere, was her own. *Come see the finest example of a Euphorbia milii,* Adrian had tempted her early that morning. Everything left her, every gnawing truth about her work life, every twinge in a joint, every dark worry about how to skirt the strangers she didn't trust, a list that could now populate Tokyo. Even dread rolled clear off her. Because Adrian was dead.

As Val made her way over to Broadway on legs she couldn't feel, it occurred to her that for the first time since high school, she was fearless. Her jaw tightened up, but it was good. At that moment in time, Valjean Cameron was dangerously at home in the world. She would go and do whatever she had to. But first, on this day she would never quite be able to put behind her—and why should she?—she had to think. At the light, she ran across the street toward the entrance to the subway. Was the crown of thorns plant left trampled in the wreckage of Adrian's office? Not everything gets wrapped kindly and wheeled away. *Are we all just lost and beautiful things?* Who had her friend surprised that morning at the museum? In the act of...what, exactly?

6

The NYPD homicide detective at the 20th precinct who explained she "caught" the Bale murder was Lieutenant Shay Cleary, and Val had agreed to stop by the precinct house over her lunch hour. For Val, no contest: no food. The idea of eating with a homicide detective while the medical examiner was off somewhere disassembling Adrian felt entirely too casual. But after a morning spent staring at a red push pin on her bulletin board behind the closed door of her office, Val took a cab up to the address on W. 82nd Street that the detective had given her.

Cleary's handshake was surprisingly strong considering she had hands the size of a twelve-year-old. As they both sat, Cleary tugged at the creases in her belted khaki pants. She had a small-breasted, broad-shouldered, narrow-hipped kind of body that looked good in nearly anything, especially beachwear, but her face was plain. Cleary dyed her straight hair a tarry black, parted it with a laser, and pulled it back severely behind her ears with what was actually a pink rubber band at the back. Her eyes were narrow and dark, and freckles scattered over a short nose.

Sitting in front of her on her old wood desk that had been tortured decades ago with cigarettes was a meatball sub. While the homicide detective smoothed out the creases in the wrapper with her small, precise fingers, she said, "We've been in touch with the victim's next of kin, who lives out of the country." She lifted the sub. "He'll be making final arrangements once the ME releases the body.

Antony.

Val exhaled hard. Poor Antony. She had forgotten about him. Maybe not forgotten, exactly. He was such an abstraction for her, like quadratic equations or a book by Tolstoy. But she realized Antony Bale was even a greater stakeholder in the death of Adrian. By law he was contacted to handle the "arrangements," and by custom he might even be conducting the services. He'd be the one going through Adrian's closets. Closing out her bank accounts. Notifying all her friends. At least, thought Val, he wouldn't have to notify her.

Suddenly it felt powerfully sad to her that she had been such a bitch about meeting her best friend's brother the monk. How bad could it have been? Why was she such a bigot when it came to clergy?

For Adrian she should have done it, should have met the damn brother, no matter how blind Adrian had to be about him. And as she sat in a hard plastic chair there in Precinct 20 of the NYPD, Val realized that for a long time to come she'd deal with a lot of regret.

"That's right," she told Cleary, after the detective took notes on Val's home and work addresses, any phone that could possibly reach her, and the nature of her relationship with the victim. *Best friends, seventeen years.* Then: "Adrian called me at 7:08 this morning. It went to voicemail." She sat up straight in the creaky chair just to help keep her thoughts together. She wanted to be useful to Adrian. She wanted to get it right.

Cleary eyed her, then dug into the sub. "That typical?" she spoke out of the side of her mouth.

Val shrugged. "Yes and no," she answered. "We were used to talking to each other at odd hours." Trashing bad boyfriends or processing a screwy dream. Old college habits hadn't changed even as they moved along in their careers—and aged.

"Today—?" Cleary dabbed a napkin at her lips.

Val pulled out her phone, clicked through to the voicemail from Adrian, and put it on speaker. As her friend's voice sailed out into the air between Val and the detective, Cleary set down her lunch. *Val,* said Adrian, maybe less than an hour from her murder,

I don't care what you think your lunch plans are for today, I want you to change them. No, make that your breakfast plans. Come to the museum if you want a once in a lifetime chance to see—a brief silence—*the finest example of* Euphorbia milii *in the known world. I can't hang on to it very long.* When Val set down her phone, she looked at Cleary, who was frowning.

"I'll need that voicemail," she said, tipping her head toward Val's phone.

So will I, thought Val. The last of Adrian's voice. On her phone she pressed through to all of her voicemail messages, waited 'til the 7:08 a.m. message from Adrian ended, followed the prompts and tapped in Lieutenant Cleary's cell phone number.

They gave each other a tight-lipped nod, as though something great had been accomplished, then Val dropped her phone back into her purse. Adrian was increasingly becoming the property of the NYPD. A matter of reports. Evidence bags. Theories.

Cleary leaned closer to Val. "What did she want you to see?"

"I had to look it up," said Val. "A crown of thorns plant."

Cleary wrinkled her short nose. "Crown of thorns?" she said skeptically. "Like Jesus or whatever?"

"From what I read."

"So it's a plant—" said Shay Cleary, pointing her lunch at Val "—named because it resembles—"

"The Crown of Thorns, apparently." Why was this such new information for Homicide? Then it struck her. "Didn't you find it near—Adrian?" She couldn't bring herself to say *the body.*

But Cleary ignored her, seeming to collect her thoughts from the water-stained soundproofing panels on the ceiling. "Adrian Bale was a curator of Egyptian—"

"And Sumerian."

"Excuse me. Egyptian and Sumerian art—"

"Ancient southern Mesopotamia."

Cleary smiled. "In other words," said the detective, "Iraq. I do know that."

Val was beginning to feel they were paying attention to the

wrong things. But it was a day when everything was now precisely all the wrong things. From starting the day at Greta's with chocolate croissants that now seemed unbearably sweet, Val was gliding numb and very nearly insentient in the aftermath of Adrian's murder.

Was it possible her death had anything at all to do with the new exhibit she was curating—what was it called?—that would open in a year? Adrian hadn't mentioned any snags in acquiring the pieces on loan from their permanent homes. But there was the problem of the provenance of those bronze figures from the first century B.C. that the museum—on Adrian's advice—had bought. Since the first Gulf War, the market for fake Sumerian antiquities had flourished. Had Adrian got caught up in it somehow? Did it lead to her murder?

Val didn't believe it. It didn't feel right. If Adrian had been dealing with a jealous colleague or a grudging dealer or exposed forger, she hadn't mentioned it to Val—besides, that purchase had taken months, plenty of time for plotting dire action aimed at Adrian Bale. So...why today? What series of events rolled suddenly and inexorably to this shooting death—today—of her best friend? She had no answers, and looked helplessly at the lieutenant.

Cleary chewed reflectively. "Can you think of any reason this plant would fit into her work at the museum?"

It was a good question, maybe—aside from who pulled the trigger—the only question. "No."

Studying her sandwich, Cleary sat back. "This *Euphorbia*," she said finally. "Is it a houseplant?"

"I suppose," said Val, finding it hard to imagine why Adrian would leave such an excited message over a simple houseplant. "I think they're pretty common."

"Why would the vic—Ms. Bale leave you that message?" Then: "Just for you to come see a houseplant." That was indeed the point, and Val couldn't explain it.

Cleary studied the label on the Diet Coke and then started to pick at it. "But," she said slowly, "you went." Which was when she eyed Val, seeming to imply something that wasn't quite clear.

Val felt herself starting to get wound up. "I figured it was something strange," she explained, a little too loud, "or funny, or really exciting somehow. Like a private joke between Adrian and me." But why would Adrian have called it a *once in a lifetime chance...?*

"Where do you suppose she got this fine example of *Euphorbia*?"

"I don't know. I had the feeling from the way she sounded that—it just showed up. That it was a surprise." It struck her: "Is there a delivery log?"

Cleary pushed away the rest of her lunch. "Not at seven in the morning."

Val was wishing for a three-shot espresso. "Was there anything attached to it?"

"Like what?" Cleary blotted at a wet ring on the desk.

Val's hand flopped in her lap. "Like a card, an invoice, some watering instructions—" How much more lame could she possibly get?

Cleary jerked her chin at her. "How would we know that?"

Was there something she was missing? "You've seen it, haven't you?"

"The *Euphorbia*? As a matter of fact, Ms. Cameron, we have not."

How could that even be? Val felt mystified.

And then she watched Lieutenant Cleary switch directions. Even her voice changed, as if everything they had discussed up to that point had been idle. Place markers for the real substance. "Do you know of any reason someone may have wanted Ms. Bale dead?"

It was ridiculous. "No," Val protested. When a few heads turned toward her, she lowered her voice. "You didn't know Adrian." How could she make this cop understand? "She had no dark history—"

"None you know about."

Val repeated, this time more slowly, "She had no dark history."

They stared hard at each other. "From what we can tell," Cleary went on, "someone followed her inside, destroyed the security camera in that corridor, and shot Adrian Bale—" at that, Val winced, and Cleary's mouth twisted as if to say, *well, it's the truth*, "—from the threshold of her office." She gave a little shrug. "And you say she had no enemies."

All Val could do was shake her head. "None that I know of," she finally admitted, weary. Val tried to picture Adrian's office, the beautiful kilim rug, the horsehair sofa, the bookshelves filled with expensive art books. Like Adrian Bale's apartment, a place of lively beauty and serene intelligence. Of taste and—happiness. Why would anyone want to kill her? Finally, she offered the only explanation that made sense. "She must have surprised somebody in the act of—"

Across from her, with a pinched expression, Cleary was shaking her head. "She was shot in her own office, Ms. Cameron, not out in one of the galleries." It was a key point. "Besides," Cleary went on, "Eva Toscano, the director, assures us no other security zones were breached."

Folding her hands, she waited while Val let it sink in. Then, thumbing through some preliminary paperwork, she added quietly, "Adrian Bale did not surprise anyone in the act of stealing, because," she regarded Val almost apologetically, "nothing has been stolen from the Coleman-Witt Museum."

"All right..." said Val slowly.

"Failing all that, Ms. Cameron, no dark history catching up with her, no wrong place at the wrong time—it's looking good that your friend Adrian Bale was killed for the *Euphorbia milii*."

It seemed fantastic to Val, who suddenly felt argumentative. "Why do you say that?"

Cleary pitched the empty Diet Coke into a trash can across the aisle. "Because it's nowhere at the crime scene," she said. Then the detective in charge of the murder of Adrian Bale stretched her arms overhead. "Oh," she went on breezily, "there's a big gray urn on her desk, something she was working on, apparently." Cleary added,

"She had cut through a whole lot of bubble wrap. But...no crown of thorns plant."

Then she narrowed her eyes, recalling the scene. "No plant of any sort in her office. Anywhere."

Val felt her shoulders slump. She felt tired. Defeated, somehow. "So whatever it was she wanted me to come and see," she murmured, "...is gone."

The detective said softly, "She told you she couldn't hang on to it very long." With that, Lieutenant Cleary pushed herself back from her desk, shooting a wry look at Val. "I guess she was right."

Greta kept her on the phone for a therapeutic half an hour—for both of them—during that afternoon. The last time Val could remember her aunt being quite that appalled was when the first plane hit tower number one. In those days, the Artifact Authentication Agency was housed in an old pre-war building on E. 38th Street, on the sixteenth floor. Greta described the billowing black smoke wafting east from the heights of the first tower, and her assistant was shouting over and over what a terrible accident, but Greta knew right away. Partly because she was older than her assistant. And partly because she had worked for many years by then in her half-forgotten branch of the Department of Commerce that dealt with evil ingenuity, if only—sometimes—when it came to what was being passed off as genuine artifacts from departed civilizations. For this reason, she was more easily able to recognize it in its more murderous guises.

Her staff pressed against the windows facing south, crying, screaming, helpless, all helpless, as it unfolded. One of them threw up her breakfast. Another one fainted. Throughout the colossal burning and disintegrating into obscene acres of dust and rubble thirty city blocks away from their safe little agency, Greta Bistritz was wordless, appalled.

As she was when Val told her in a voice that was finally choked nearly into silence about the murder of Adrian Bale. Greta, of course, knew Adrian, and for great, long minutes she was silent on the line—that one death this morning of the girl she had known and loved and spoken to about the value of using ion beams to detect art forgeries. "Well, then," said Greta finally, responding to Val's very small inventory of facts about the shooting. "Well, then." Her voice was soft.

Val waited patiently while her aunt thought things over. Telling Greta had dried and hardened and cured the terrible crime that Val suspected was altering her own life for all time. She felt as though she was caught hiking alone at dusk on an unfamiliar mountain trail, when what's apparent recedes in those final minutes before the world turns over and everything better suited to the night emerges. You can't see their shape, you can't smell their flesh, you can't hear their footfalls—until it's nearly too late—but they lurk out of reach in the thin and gauzy air. That's how Val felt about Adrian's murder. It was all those nighttime dwellers that were slowly surrounding her. How could she outwit it? How could she...solve it?

By the time Greta's voice came over the line, Val had pretty much forgotten she was even holding her phone. "What are you going to do?" her aunt put it to her.

"I'm going to finish up some line edits, cry into my beer somewhere on the way home, and watch a string of inane movies until I fall asleep."

"That sounds like a worthy plan," said Greta, "and one I pretty much plan to pursue myself, but what I meant was," her voice dropped as she bit off each word, "what are you going to do about Adrian's murder?"

7

Val found herself staring over the lid of her laptop. A box from Bouchon Bakery at Rockefeller Center sat waiting her attention, where Ivy League Ivy had set it sometime after Val told her and a few key other players that she had lost a close friend that morning and would appreciate a quiet afternoon. Within an hour Ivy had knocked, given her a long, goopy look, and set the box on her desk. "Best chocolate chip cookies in the city," was the whispered comment, whereupon the girl had slouched out and shut the door noiselessly behind her.

"Thank you, Ivy," Val called to her. "I really appreciate your kindness." It was entirely possible, thought Val, that she had somehow misjudged the assistant editor, but she would have to add that to her list of inquiries—third behind the murder of Adrian Bale and the possibility of transforming Killian's *Plumb Lines* into something Val could put her name to publicly. For now, though, all Val could do was set her fingers on the cookies, then lay her head across her arms and try to cry.

But nothing came.

Nothing aside from a little *frisson* of what felt like shock.

At the end of the afternoon, Val shut down her computer and slipped into the charcoal mid-length jacket she kept at the office for days that turned out colder than she had thought. This was one of them, and she knew it had nothing to do with the temperature. She pulled the chain on her table lamp, grateful for the familiar rasp as her office lost light, then she walked through the deserted outer office. All she heard was the air forced through the vents. Pretty soon the cleaning crew would turn up for the night shift. The ding of the elevator, the heavy slide of the brass door, and down she went, alone, her hands thrust deep into her pockets. Adrian. Adrian was nowhere at all. And Val was left alone for the rest of her days to try to find themes in books where none truly existed.

She knew she was going to walk all the way home to her apartment on E. 51st Street. Not because the air might do her some good, but because it was the simplest thing to do. The thing that wouldn't require digging around for her MTA card or raising an arm to hail a cab. Somewhere during the walk home, she would duck into a dark, quiet bar and knock back a couple of drinks. The elevator reached the lobby and seemed to rest indecisively for a moment while it decided whether to open. The elevator, that old lusty clanging box, was wiser than Val. The door slid open and out she stepped, craning her neck to catch sight of the weather. Drizzle?

The lobby guard flashed her a quick grin from behind the Art Deco desk, where a tall man stood with his back to the elevator. "Night," Val called, grateful for these small moments of normalcy.

"Ms. Cameron." The guard slung her a quick salute, then eyed the man at the desk.

Now what?

Val slowed as the man in the long gray coat turned toward her. He had very short dark hair streaked with gray, brown eyes that seemed a little too intense, and he needed a shave. He was pale and lean, ready for something. The coat he wore hung open, pushed out of the way by his hands thrust into his pockets. His suit was dark gray, single-breasted, well cut. He looked Val over quickly without so much as moving his head. Then those intense eyes settled back on hers. "I'm Bale," he said.

At that, Val shuddered, and covered her head with her arms.

And began to wail.

They didn't get far. Half an hour later, Val and Antony Bale were sitting across from each other in one of the green flocked booths at the Old Town Bar. She was holding on to the stem of a wine glass, staring woodenly at what was left of the Pinot noir he had ordered. Without a word in the lobby of the Flatiron Building, he had grabbed her upper arm and guided them both to a bar five blocks away. Farther from her apartment on 51st, where at that point in time every step downtown felt like a doomed journey away from everything she wanted from the rest of the worst day of her life. Farther from the happy kingdom of her bed, where she could dig down under the light tent of her comforter.

As they skirted puddles and raced to beat the flashing Don't Walk signs, all Bale murmured was that he'd put her in a cab later. She grunted. The topic of transportation was about all she could handle. When they reached Old Town Bar and he swung open one of the gleaming brass doors, Val stumbled, thinking how happy Adrian would have been that Val had finally broken down and met the beloved Antony.

Nothing could ever make any of it right.

Val had slid into the booth, exhausted, and propped her chin on her hands. Partly to keep from sobbing. Partly to steady her hands. Why couldn't she control herself? The bottle of a Chilean Pinot noir showed up, and the silent waiter poured a sample. Bale breathed, swirled, sipped in a way that Val could tell was a matter of long custom. An imperceptible nod to the waiter, who then poured two glasses, set the bottle down, and left.

Bale folded his arms on the table and gave her a steady look. "It's good to meet you, finally."

She felt terrible. "Please don't remind me."

"If it helps," he said with a small smile, "I wasn't all that keen either."

"Oh?" This possibility had never occurred to her.

"My sister had terrible taste in friends," he said, settling back. "It was part of her charm."

Now she was interested. "Who are you thinking about?"

"Denise from camp. Kathy from camp. Nina from dance squad."

She could tell the list was longer. "I don't know any of them."

"Neither did Adrian, after a while."

"No reason I'd be any different, is that it?"

He sipped. "Maybe we all just got busy."

She took a noisy breath, wanting something kind to be true. "Maybe." Something seemed called for. She raised her glass. "To Adrian," she managed to say before her throat tightened up.

He eyed her. She knew she sounded shaky. Wordlessly, he pushed a clean white hanky across the table to her. As her fingers closed over it, she nodded a thanks. He raised his glass to his sister, and Val could tell he was working to control his expression. They drank in silence for a few minutes. It was a fine Pinot noir, but Val thought she had finally found the one thing an excellent wine couldn't cure.

When Aunt Greta's love, Ben Biderman, had died suddenly several years ago, she told Val that color left the world for a year. As if her vision had lost all the rods and cones and whatever else sets us apart from dogs. Color finally returned. And all it managed to do was underscore the fact that Ben himself would not. The world insisted on being beautiful despite the loss, which made it all the more painful. There's a lot to be said, Greta concluded, for monochrome.

Settling into the corner of the booth, Val was aware that Adrian's brother was composed. Not a restless sort. Not the kind of man who needed to rustle or utter half-sentences just to hear himself exist in the world. That first look at him in the lobby of the Flatiron, it was the same quality she noticed now. She wondered if Bale's nature had been shaped by the monastery. Years of silent devotions—she swiped at her eyes with his handkerchief—whatever those were. But she had no energy to ask, even if she had any business asking. With no reserves of anything at all, she sank against the paneled wall. At the end of that particular day, Val needed something good or nothing at all.

As he slowly poured them each a second glass, she watched the play of light from the sconce on the deep red color filling her glass. It was a whole big firmament of absence inside her. She was in a place other than dead. Maybe an anteroom where not even grief could sit.

She studied his face, at his careful concentration with the bottle. She couldn't imagine what he was feeling. Her face hurt when she whispered, "I'm so sorry." For a moment those dark eyes settled on her, then he bit his lip and nodded. She held up the hanky, giving Antony Bale a shot at it. "I'm okay," he said. Then: "I took the first flight when I heard."

Val held her glass, not drinking.

"I went straight to the precinct house to hear firsthand from the homicide cop just what had happened to Adrian."

"And that's how you heard about me."

He took a sip. "And about the voicemail from Adrian." Bale perked up. "If it's all right with you, Val, I'd like to hear it. Adrian had called me as well." Antony Bale reached into the pocket of his suit jacket and pulled out his phone. Pressing through to his sister's voicemail, which he put on speaker, he set the phone on the table and played her message: *Listen, kiddo, I've got something of yours. Well, the abbey's, at any rate. Did I tell you Prior Berthold gave me a Victorian urn for the museum?* Her voice dropped. *I discovered a stowaway, Antonio. Call me.* Then, after a second: *Love you.*

Val sat staring at Bale's phone as though it contained a miniaturized Adrian.

"The head of our abbey, Prior Berthold, had given Adrian a Victorian Jasperware urn for the Coleman-Witt. The lieutenant said the urn was found at the crime scene and entered into evidence." At that, Antony Bale sighed. "We've had a death at the abbey," he said finally, with a frown. "A young monk named Fintan. Smart kid, very devout. Hard to read. A secretive sort." Then he took a long sip. "He fell to his death yesterday," he said softly. As he rubbed his eyes she could tell how very tired he was. "Maybe the day before. We'll know soon. His mate says the boy was distraught over the disappearance of the urn." He looked Val straight in the eye. "That urn. The very one the Prior had given her." Bale's eyes slid off toward a stylish blond who passed the booth. "And then I got the call about Adrian's murder."

Val held her glass against her cheek, letting the information sink in. "The boy Fintan," she asked Bale. "Was it suicide?"

Pressing his lips together, he held up both hands. "We don't know. Was he that distraught? If so, why? How terrible could the loss of that urn be for a devout boy to commit that particular mortal sin?" Val must have looked unconvinced—and his comment reminded her that Antony Bale was, after all, a monk—because he exhaled and rested his hands on the table. "In the view of the Church, Val. That's what it is. By me, in the pantheon of mortal sins," he said, leaning toward her, "suicide would not make the cut." When she gave him a small smile, he called over the waiter and ordered a cheese plate. "The question is," he spread out his fingers, as though he was measuring the table, "what did the boy Fintan have to do with this urn?"

"Maybe it wasn't the urn," she tried out, thinking about Adrian's message. "She said she discovered a stowaway."

"So what is she talking about?"

Val shook her head. "Here," she said, pulling her phone out of her purse. She cued up the message from Adrian but said softly, "I can't hear her voice again right now, if you don't mind," and without looking at him, added, "Antony." All she could manage was a grim smile as she offered him her phone. As he took it, his hand briefly brushed hers. Suddenly so much contact after seventeen years of sheer avoidance. Maybe anytime now the world would go monochrome for both of them...

Frowning, he listened, his dark eyes darting around, landing only for a second on Val. He suddenly sat very still as he got to the end of Adrian's message. Val felt her heart starting to race. Something had struck him, she could tell, and all she could do was wait while he teased it out. He set down the phone and stared at it. "Listen," she said, her voice dropping, "it's the *Euphorbia milii*, isn't it?" Bale was giving nothing away. "It's the thing Adrian wanted me to see, the thing she couldn't hold on to for very long."

Antony Bale grabbed her arm. "Did you see it?"

She pulled back a little. "No, I never made it inside the building. Why, what's—"

"I've got to make a call," he muttered, scraping his hand over his short, dark hair. "Excuse me—" He opened his hands wide as though he was trying to pat everything comfortably back into place. Suddenly everything—everything beyond the violent death of his sister—had gone completely wrong.

"Wait," she said as he started to slide out of the booth, "wait. It's gone." When Bale looked at her, his eyes were wild. "The plant. The *Euphorbia*. The lieutenant told me it wasn't at the scene of the—crime."

Bale went utterly still. "Are you telling me it was stolen?" His voice was so low she could hardly hear him.

It was important to be clear. What could she say for sure? "The cops didn't find it. The plant is not there." She searched Bale's face, trying to gauge the impact of that information. He was unreadable. As he told her he'd be back, the waiter arrived with the cheese plate, nearly dropping it as Bale pushed by him. Val watched him head quickly for the entrance to Old Town and step outside, settling his phone by her ear. She broke off a corner of a slice of Gorgonzola and discovered she was so profoundly tired she could hardly lift it to her mouth. Even chewing a cracker felt beyond her. She'd been drop-kicked into a world she knew nothing about—cops, monks, secretive dead boys, disappearing plants, fake manuscripts, clogged pipes in Beverly Hills, and an Ivy League Ivy who had it in her to make kind gestures. Not even eight hours' sleep could revive her. And she'd promised Aunt Greta to meet her at the office of the Hunter College professor who had a beef with a holding at the Morgan Library at noon tomorrow.

Val felt small. Smaller. Alice after "Drink Me." Her clothes were looser. Her shoes hung half off her feet. Her silver bangle bracelet could slide right off her wrist. And in her mind neurons were sparking and popping into oblivion like stars. *Get to go cheer for New Jersey.* Leaning her head against the paneled wall, listening to the bar noise like a distant love song, Val closed her eyes and didn't give a damn if she was vulnerable. Before she drifted off, her fingers curled around the phone in her lap.

"Val, I have to go." A hand touched her shoulder, and she jumped. Bale was sitting beside her. Something was different. "I'll call you tomorrow. I'm staying at the Iroquois over on 44th." He slipped a business card under her hand. "Here's my number, if you need it." She squinted at him, caught the sharp smell of rain and citrus, and ran her hand over her eyes, trying to wake up. The wine weighed her down. "I called the abbey," he said, barely audible. "It's the middle of the night over there, but I managed to get one of the more sleepless monks—" He winced a smile at her. "He's checking something out," he went on, distracted, "and will get back to me."

"And you need to be alone." She nodded slowly, not really understanding a thing. Her fingers tried scrabbling at her coat, which Bale managed to slip out from under her.

"Right."

As she pushed herself out of the booth, he held her coat open for her and eased her into it. "Did you find out something about the plant?" she said softly, buttoning up with fingers that felt too small for any serious work.

"It's not a plant." Bale pulled three twenties out of a black billfold and left them on the table. As he straightened to his full height, he slowed, leaning his head close to hers. His breath ruffled her hair. "I'm pretty sure what Adrian found," he said tensely, "is not a plant."

8

She discovered the business card the next morning when she was walking to the subway in the cool, shimmering spring sunlight and rooted around in her purse for her Ray-Bans. Her one extravagance that had nothing to do with having aromatic oils rubbed into her body twice a year, which was all she could afford. On this morning after Adrian's murder, Val tried to trap the fact of it in some inaccessible part of her brain, for the time being, so she could earn her paycheck and get through the editorial day. She slipped on the sunglasses and looked at the card Bale had given her the night before. The logo on the left side was brown, white and gold, featuring a crown, a shield with three stars, and an upraised sword. The motto: *Zelo Zelatus Sum Pro Domino Deo Exercituum.*

> Br. Antony Bale, Cellarer
> Burnham Norton Abbey
> Sidestrand, Norfolk NR27, U.K.
> 1-216-533-6174 (US)
> 01793 744860 (UK)

Cellarer. Did the abbey make wine? Was Bale a vintner? When she realized she was famished—nothing since that corner of Gorgonzola last night, which, she realized, even Adrian's brother hadn't shared. It felt disrespectful to Adrian somehow. The things of the flesh. For her best friend, no longer a joy, no longer a bother. No longer an issue.

Hunger, sex, the first gray hair, the latest UTI, the inescapable root canal. Bills, Facebook, dark thoughts about growing old alone and forgetting things like love. Would that happen to her? Had Adrian simply been spared?

Val turned into a Starbucks across Third Avenue from the subway entrance, snagged a tall dark roast of the day and a butter croissant, which she tucked into her red tote. By the time she slung her tote and her purse onto her mostly clean desk at Words on Fire, the coffee was half gone, but the croissant was still ahead of her. There were a couple of new yellow Post-it notes stuck to her laptop, the red light was flashing on her office phone console, and she realized with horror she hadn't charged her iPhone before falling into bed the night before. Down to seventeen percent charge. Val swore, then tugged open a desk drawer and pushed around the junk until she found a charger.

Four missed calls, all gone to voicemail.

Aunt Greta, reminding her of the noon meeting at Hunter.

Lieutenant Cleary, needing to clarify some points about her interview.

James Killian, wondering if they could get together to discuss a new project. Val frowned. In terms of Killian's present book, whole chapters needed to be rearranged. Content needed shifting. If Killian could lift that swill to the level of social commentary, they might really have something. But she'd have to hear him out about his "new project."

Finally, Antony Bale. "I could use your help," was all he said. "Call me." His message clocked in at 10:32 last evening. She'd already been asleep for two hours.

Killian she could put off until the afternoon, possibly even tomorrow. No need to call Greta. Cleary she'd postpone until after she'd gotten some food in her stomach and some serious work done. For a bad moment she wondered exactly what needed to be cleared up about her interview yesterday. Val had thought it had been a conversation—hell, not an interview. Her arms went cold when she wondered whether Homicide was thinking she could possibly be implicated in Adrian's murder. No, if her imagination slid off in that direction, she was a goner. Good for nothing.

So she made the call she had angled to make all along.

She snapped her fingers against the white vellum card and called back Br. Antony Bale, Cellarer.

They agreed to meet at six p.m.—somehow, Val would have to make it—on the front steps of St. Patrick's Cathedral. There was a five thirty Mass that Bale wanted to attend at the end of his daily two hours spent in contemplation. Soon, a trip to the Coleman-Witt to see the scene of the crime—if he could get in—and talk first to the director and then to the guards who found Adrian. To Val, he sounded rushed. When she tried to prolong the conversation—Bale was the closest living relative to her dead friend—by asking whether he had heard back from the insomniac monk, Bale put her off. "Let's talk at six." A beat. Then: "I can't do this over the phone." After they said goodbye, she wondered why he suddenly seemed to be throwing himself into the investigation. For the homicide team, it was still early days. Had they lost his confidence that quickly? What had Adrian's brother learned that—did what?—upped the ante for him somehow between hearing about her murder and the day's objective to study the crime scene?

The *Euphorbia milii*. The plant Adrian had enticed Val to come see, the plant she said she couldn't hang on to for very long, the plant that wasn't a plant...was at the heart of it somehow. What had Adrian gotten herself into? As Val pulled apart the croissant as though it was a party favor with a cheap little toy inside, she stared at nothing. In her experience, answers never just offered themselves up, neatly displayed and labeled like an exhibit. She powered up her laptop and scanned the *New York Times* homepage.

There it was in the Metro section: *Local Curator Slain*. Adrian Bale, Coleman-Witt, Egyptian and Sumerian Art and Antiquities, found dead in her office. Suspected foul play. A quote from Terrell Hampton, museum guard who discovered her body. Bale often worked early before the museum opened. A quote from Eva

Toscano, director, who praised the murdered curator's expertise and professionalism and mourned her death. Bale was working on several projects at the time of her death. A quote from Lt. Cleary of NYPD Homicide inviting persons with information to call this number.

In short—Val closed the page—Adrian Bale had been reduced to just another violent crime statistic. Maybe, when it came right down to it, that wasn't so bad. Somehow Cleary had squelched any mention of the security camera's being shot out—for that matter, no early theories of the crime were either ruled in or ruled out. No persons of interest. Yet. No brothers of the victim, no best friends. Val could see how the coverage left a lot of freedom of movement— without exciting any anxieties for the person responsible. The killer. It was a new thought for Val, this killer. Had that person overheard Adrian leaving a message for Val? Or not? And was that message totally irrelevant to the murder? Right before she died, Adrian had unwrapped an urn given to her by Antony Bale's prior. She had made an exciting discovery: a "stowaway." She had called Val.

And she had died.

With a funny little *frisson* that made her doubt even the smallest things around her, Val wondered if she herself was at risk. Not possible. Not at all possible. She had no connection to the urn, and no connection to the plant—whether or not it was an actual plant or, for that matter, missing. The sole link to Adrian on the day of the murder was...her phone. Could the killer have overheard Adrian leaving Val the voicemail? Could the killer have assumed Val knew more about whatever was at the heart of the murder than she actually did? Adrian's phone held Val's contact information. *Where was that phone?* Tucked safely by the CSI team into an evidence bag and shelved at the 20th precinct? Or—

In the hands of the killer?

Bumping her hip as she rounded the corner of her desk, Val opened her office door with a clammy hand and stood in the doorway. Trying not to sway, she gripped the frame. Right at that moment she could use some of Antony Bale's quiet poise. With no more information than she had, all Val knew was that she had to stay busy every hour of the livelong workday until she could meet Greta at Hunter College and talk to someone completely unrelated to Adrian's murder...and then on the steps of St. Patrick's soak up whatever news Adrian's brother had discovered since they had split a bottle of something—Malbec?—last night at Old Town.

"Ivy," she said, surprised that her voice sounded as next to normal as it did, "could you please get James Killian on the phone and get him in here as soon as possible?" Whatever the fake plumber to the stars had in mind in the way of a new project suddenly sounded downright fascinating. At that moment, Val believed she would have written him a contract for even a loathsome memoir. Ambitious and good-looking and disturbing— what she needed in the worst way was to be disturbed by someone extremely far away from the death of Adrian Bale.

9

"Tell me again why I'm here," said Val, cupping her aunt's elbow as they stepped out of the elevator on the 8th floor of Hunter College, undecided how to find the office of Saul Bensoussan, Associate Professor of Romance Languages, Chair of Latin and Caribbean Studies.

Greta narrowed her gray eyes at Val and opted for her airy and stuffy routine. "Because the man has discovered what he believes is a fake manuscript. You like manuscripts. I thought you might be interested." She slanted a smile at Val. "Besides, who knows, dear? He might have a book in him."

Val pointed to the left, then bumped her wily aunt. "No, really, why? Not that I don't enjoy your company." She wasn't about to launch into her resolve to fill every conscious minute with material that was either dense, knotty, or completely beyond her probably for the next few months, until the shock of Adrian's death receded by even just a little bit. While she was in the building, she'd see if she could audit a class in quantum physics.

Greta had the decency to look put out. "Oh, all right, if you must know," she hissed, then pushed back a beautiful hank of her Lauren Bacall hair. "We're short-staffed at the moment. Three of my field ops are on assignment, and I thought if I could interest you in Bensoussan—"

Ah. "In Bensoussan," Val repeated carefully, knowing her aunt very well indeed, "or in Bensoussan's case?"

Greta grabbed Val's shoulders. "Oh, why split hairs? Especially now, with Adrian's death. It's good to immerse yourself—"

An incorrigible matchmaker. Val eyed her mother's younger

sister, then sighed. "Somehow I'm not finding murder a turn-on, if you can believe it."

Her aunt stepped back, colliding with an earnest girl pulling a rolling suitcase. Back-saving wheels for serious students. "Then please check out his gripe so I can close the file and archive it." She lifted her elegant shoulders. "How hard can it be? An old manuscript at the Morgan—we're not talking a pattern of international smuggling here." They arrived in front of the closed door to the office of Professor Saul Bensoussan. "Besides," Greta lowered her voice, "it's about fifty-fifty he's got it wrong. He teaches literature. He's not an expert in art forgery." With that, she rapped on the frosted glass of the door.

"Venga!" came a voice from inside.

Val followed her aunt into Bensoussan's office. Her first impression was of heat and light, filtered through a single, old window with an exterior haze of scratches and city grime. The glossy white walls were rimmed with large framed posters of Gabriel García Márquez, Paulo Coelho and Isabel Allende, all exuding warmth and a kind of quiet cheerfulness. Suspended from the ceiling was a jungle of mobiles. One was a beautiful chaos of colored paper birds in flight. Another was tiers of different metals cut into the shapes of children that, when the pale currents hit them, moved to tunes only they heard.

Surrounding two nice Crate and Barrel bookcases stuffed masterfully with books was a gallery of framed book jackets, book reviews, book events—one a signed photo of what appeared to be Coelho shaking the hand of the man standing behind his desk, smiling at Val and Greta. She had expected a young academic hotshot who had made a career decision not to pay too much attention to wardrobe. But that would be someone other than Saul Bensoussan. White polo shirt, pleated khaki pants, a sport coat that looked like it had been altered. And bobby-pinned to his head, a blue and white yarmulke in tiny crochet.

The professor extended a hand first to Greta, who introduced herself and passed him her official DOC badge. He glanced at it, smiling, and then turned to Val with a questioning look. "My niece...and assistant," Greta said smoothly. "Valjean Cameron." With a sweep, Bensoussan indicated the old wooden chairs that had been painted two different shades of glossy red and decorated with bold blue frogs and yellow snakes. Val folded her hands in her lap and wondered if she'd have time to grab a sandwich at One East Ace before going back to her office.

"Well, Professor," Greta smiled, "what have you got for the Artifact Authentication Agency?"

Bensoussan raised both hands as though he had scrubbed them down to a new layer of skin and was letting them air dry. He had a high forehead, Van Dyke facial hair, and hazel eyes. Either he never smoked or drank coffee, or else he had a professional teeth whitening job done recently. All very groomed. Very nice. Val looked around. Everything was just enough, nothing too much. There was a normalcy to this place, but a heightened one. Life of the mind set in a playful nature. His students must love him. Twisting his wrist toward his office walls, Bensoussan explained he was a professor of Latin American literature. But as a Mexican Jew, he leaned toward Val and Greta, he had a special—here he studied the flying bird mobile for the exact word—feeling for the history of the Inquisition. "I have been researching that three-hundred-year period for a few years now. Tracking down documents," he went on in lightly accented English, "searching for any literary work to come out of those times." He fell silent.

Overhead, metal children danced a shy gavotte.

"And—?" prompted Greta.

"Eight years ago I was given tenure based on my monographs on various, oh, cultural aspects of the Mexican Inquisition." His eyes disappeared in his smile. "Un caffé?" he offered. When they nodded, he turned to a small espresso machine at the edge of his desk and set to work, adding water from a glazed blue pitcher and grounds from a small covered urn. "For me," he said slowly, scratching his chin, "the problem is that I was logging many hours of research and finding much in the way of very interesting material. But literature?" The smell of strong, exotic coffee circulated. Val thought she might not need to duck into One East Ace after all...

Pouring carefully, Bensoussan handed them their coffee in cups that looked like they had been painted from Frieda Kahlo's palette. "Gracias," said Greta in the extent of her Spanish—the professor smiled—and Val muttered a thanks. With a demitasse spoon he slipped one tiny cube of sugar into his own cup. Then he stirred reflectively, telling them he had studied all the documents, the last will and testament, the diary, and original liturgical prayers written by the famous Jewish martyr Luis de Carvajal. With the exception of his brothers—one who had become a Franciscan friar, two who had escaped the Inquisition in New Spain—Luis's entire family had been put to the stake. On a trip to Istanbul, Bensoussan told them he had even uncovered an account by one of the escaped brothers who had made it safely to the Ottomon Empire, where religious toleration ran high.

"So," he finished, "I was finding enough prose to analyze for a book, but," here he brushed off some stray coffee grounds from his desk, "what I was really hoping for was a work of prose fiction."

"And then—you found one."

"I did."

"The satire." Greta sipped.

He tipped his head.

Sliding to the edge of her chair, Greta set her demitasse cup on Bensoussan's desk, next to the framed photos of his family. "Tell me," she said finally, "why did you come directly to us?" To Val, it was a very good question. "If you believe you've discovered a fake at the Morgan Library," Greta scratched behind her ear in a gesture Val knew well, "why didn't you go straight to the authorities at the library? Why," said Greta, opening her hands wide, "did you go over their heads?"

Bensoussan heaved a noisy sigh and collapsed against the back of his seat. "Yes, that's the problem, isn't it? Why come straight to you?" For a moment, he rocked softly, looking in turn at Marquez,

Coelho, Allende, as if something was at stake Val could never understand. Finally, he spoke: "Security is tight in the Rare Books and Manuscripts Department," he said quietly, with a tight shake of his head. "With that in mind," he announced, "if there's been a fake inserted into the holdings," he stopped rocking very suddenly, "I'm guessing it might be what we call an inside job."

Val shared a cab with Greta, both of them silent on the way to the Flatiron Building. *An inside job.* What baffled her was not what was faked, but why. As the cab pulled over to the curb, Val started to reach into her purse, and Greta clamped her arm. "I'll take care of it," she said softly, her face suddenly looking all sixty-four of her years. It's wrong to expect too much of Lancôme. Greta asked, "Can you look into the Bensoussan matter?" She shook her head in a weary way. "I can't believe there's much of a mystery here, Val, despite what the attractive professor said. Or that it's an inside job. We're talking about the Morgan Library. Even the custodians have world-class creds."

Val opened the door while the bulky cabbie eyed her in the rearview mirror. "Set up a meeting at the Morgan, Auntie, and I'll join you there."

Greta gave her a long look, said quietly, "All right, we'll start out together. But in the event there's something to what Bensoussan says," she raised her voice, tapping on the driver's seat back in a sign to go tearing down Broadway, "for God's sake, we've got to be discreet." Val slammed the door and stepped away from the cab, wondering how she would suddenly develop overnight the kind of expertise that would enable her to eyeball a sixteenth century document and determine whether it was a fake.

Greta was deputizing her to investigate a possible forgery.

Bale needed her help in the matter of Adrian's death.

Even James Killian, fake plumber to the stars, needed to brainstorm a new project.

As Val swung open the door to the Flatiron Building—too late for a sandwich from One East Ace—she felt seriously overestimated. The only unreasonable request Adrian Bale had ever made of her was to rush the stage together after a Nirvana concert.

James Killian was proving elusive, reported Ivy as she tapped her thin little biceps. Val's assistant editor narrowed her eyes at the plate of cookies Val held out to her. "I'll stay after him," she added in a way that sounded like she wondered which of several mysterious acts the man could be up to. There was an eerie tenacity to Ivy that Val was discovering she liked. What followed was a companionable silence. They shot each other a look that to Val came straight off those old World War II posters about how loose lips sink ships. With a grim smile, Ivy grabbed a second cookie and slipped out of Val's office.

During the afternoon, Val thumbed through a hard copy of a manuscript by a former Al-Shabaab member, submitted to her by one of her favorite literary agents, now edging closer to retirement. Was there commercial appeal to an exposé by a deserter terrorist? Probably, sadly. Was this the one to publish? Not without a whole lot of remedial help Val wasn't keen to supply. When the office phone rang, and it turned out to be Lieutenant Cleary, Val was grateful for the interruption—until she heard what prompted the call. Adrian Bale's phone was missing. Could Ms. Cameron shed any light on that? Ms. Cameron could not. Ms. Cameron was busy trying to reconstitute her liquefied insides into some semblance of organs.

"I didn't think so," Cleary said with some energy.

"Did you check her purse?" As if the thought wouldn't have occurred to Homicide.

"On the floor next to the vic's desk. We've got it."

Val took a big, noisy breath. "I see the problem. Why would she call her brother and then call me...and not have the phone right there with her on her desk?"

"According to the cell phone records, the call to you was the final one, at 7:08 a.m." On the other end of the line, Val could hear Cleary thumbing through papers. "And according to security, camera five was shot out at 7:16. Was the victim getting ready to leave the office? No."

"No," said Val, trying to think like Adrian. "Besides, she had lots to interest her just then. An urn, a *Euphorbia milii*—"

"Possibly a visit from you," added Cleary.

Val nodded slowly. "Adrian wasn't going anywhere," she agreed. Suddenly, she remembered: "Find My Phone," she said, excited. "Adrian had the Find My Phone app on her phone. Will that help?"

Cleary sounded skeptical. "If the killer hasn't disabled it already."

"But maybe not—"

"I guess it depends on the strength of her passcode."

With that, Val shivered. "She didn't use a passcode," she said softly, picturing Adrian waving her away whenever Val pushed her on it. *Oh, my life's an open book*, she'd insist, not caring how trite and even a little brainless it sounded, *I've got nothing to hide*. No dark history. Not that Val knew. Not that Adrian herself knew. But she must have figured in someone else's dark history, because now she was lying on a slab in the morgue.

"No passcode?" The lieutenant was shrill. Then she went on to tell Val that, in that case, everyone on Adrian Bale's contact list was now known to the killer. Val's heart rippled as Cleary went on, "And considering you were the last person she called," she paused for effect, "and the content of the message, someone out there might take a special interest in you, Ms. Cameron."

"My aunt will be so pleased," she said lightly. But Val had already made the connections. Whoever killed Adrian Bale had stolen her phone, stolen the finest specimen of a crown of thorns plant, and knew Adrian was talking to Val Cameron about it. The question for the killer, then, had to be how much more did Val Cameron know beyond what was in her dead friend's message?

By the time she left work that afternoon, she had wrangled her fears into that airtight, impermeable mental box where she tossed the most repellent things, locking them up tight, and pushing them into a shadowy corner of her mind until she was prepared to look at them. Which was usually never. What was left cerebrally was what she liked to think of as the light of reason. Humming and highly transparent. She had gotten over her fear of bats, cancer, and the possibility of her high school diary falling into the wrong hands.

By five forty-five that afternoon, as she saluted the faithful guard and sailed out into windy Broadway, she realized there was no way in hell she was going to disable herself in the matter of Adrian's murder by hysterical worry about the killer. Right now she had too little information to defend herself. Maybe—it struck her with a tiny pop of joy—even too little information to incriminate herself in the eyes of the killer. That alone was an incentive to roll up her sleeves. But she still noticed she kept herself very much to the center of the subway platform, and when the N train pulled in, she warily eyed the other commuters.

She jogged up the subway stairs at 53rd Street and walked the three long blocks over to Fifth Avenue. The front steps of St. Patrick's Cathedral were swarming with people. Catholics who had attended Mass were sidestepping tourists snapping selfies with some part of the cathedral in the background. The wind snapped coat hems and loosened scarves. Val caught sight of Bale as he stepped outside, looking preoccupied. One hand flipped his coat collar up as he looked over the heads of the gawkers. She waved like she was signaling a rescue plane. In some ways, maybe she was.

When Bale beckoned to her, she hurried up the steps. She could tell they weren't going anywhere. Not yet. "How are you doing?" she asked as he shook her hand. "Did you get some sleep?"

He rolled his eyes and shot her a wry smile. "Finally. You?"

"Same." Suddenly cold, she clutched at her coat.

Today he was dressed in charcoal gray pants and a white collarless shirt that managed to look clerical. Maybe it was the black, light wool scarf wrapped once around his neck. Despite what he said about sleep, his eyes looked tired. But something else as well. Bale tipped his dark head toward the cool and cavernous interior of the cathedral. "There's something I want to show you." He steered Val around a middle-aged mother wheeling what could have been a forty-year-old daughter with atrophied legs, propped up in a state-of-the-art wheelchair, their eyes sparkling.

At one of the marble fonts of Holy Water, Bale dipped his fingers and made a quick Sign of the Cross. It seemed so automatic. A child in The House of Bale, as Adrian used to call it. For Val, there wasn't a day of her thirty-five years when she witnessed any sort of religious ritual that didn't make her feel like Margaret Mead on Samoa noting the charming and primitive customs of the natives.

As he genuflected, and Val followed him briskly down the center aisle, the old feeling returned. She had been a child in The House of Bistritz where Greta had raised Val from the age of five, when her parents went down with Pan Am Flight 103 that fell over Lockerbie. All those vague, airy verbs and prepositions, she had come to realize, kept that child safe from any final reckoning about that part of her very young life: *went, down, with, fell, over.* They were soft words, words that held no true images as she grew, words she found in other stories where parents who disappeared didn't even figure. The Israelites went down to Egypt. The quality of mercy fell on the gentle place beneath.

Words were potent magic, that much she knew, and they were all she needed to know of faith. Despite all those years of Friday nights with Greta, who lighted two candles—possibly all that was left of Bistritzes in a shtetl three generations ago. Growing up, Val had thought each candle was one of her own parents, Claire and Tom, who were gone—lost was not such a kind word, neither was dead—in an act that had nothing to do with beauty or magic or love. Those, those things were properly, as her atheistic aunt told her, the role of art in the world.

She picked up on Bale's stride as they headed down the center aisle where she still smelled the pungent effects of the smoldering censer. It always smelled like sage to her, some crazy mix of backyard sprout and exotic off-world experiment. He led her straight to the altar, veering to the left of the nave. There, hanging just feet off the marble floor, was a great wood and alabaster Crucifix. Her eyes slid off toward the altar linens, which seemed safe enough. Beside her, though, Br. Antony Bale, Cellarer, was looking at the top of the Crucifix, his tired eyes narrowed. "Look, Val," he told her. No matter how quietly, there was still a subtle echo in the vast chamber of St. Patrick's.

She followed his gaze, up past the alabaster figure suspended on the wooden cross. Her eyes settled on the Crown of Thorns. This was a sculptor whose interpretation of that object was vivid and oversized. What was she doing here? Bale stepped closer to her, and said, "There's your *Euphorbia milii*, Val. What Adrian called the finest example of one you're ever likely to see."

She lifted her shoulders. "I don't understand."

They looked each other in the eye. She could tell from his expression Bale was about to tell her something he had already decided to confide. But deciding it hadn't made it any easier, for some reason. With that, he leaned in, his head turning until his lips were very close to her ear. "Not that one," he said. "The first one." He waited for her to catch up. "For two thousand years, the Crown of Thorns has been in the hands of the Carmelites. Sometime during this last week, it seems the boy Fintan stole it from its secret place in Burnham Norton Abbey."

10

In a daze, Val sat across from Adrian's brother at Eamonn's Bar & Grill on East 45th Street. The atmosphere was warm and bright, with the right amount of bustle to block out the clamor in Val's brain. Somehow a shepherd's pie turned up in front of her which she wolfed down, unspeaking, with a trembling fork. She was pretty sure she had trailed a dab of mashed potatoes across her chin. She didn't care, and neither did Bale, who was reflectively downing his fish 'n chips. How did they even get to Eamonn's? For that matter, how did she get out of the cathedral?

Bale was slicing into his battered cod as he explained to Val the Crown of Thorns that had been removed from the corpse of Jesus when he was taken down from the Cross had been retrieved by two Essenes who had paid the Roman guards to look the other way while they cleared the area. Busy removing the remains of the two crucified thieves to a donkey cart, and even busier breaking up brawls down the hill from the site, the guards sought only to put this wretched day of high drama and foreign ways behind them...there, in the most godforsaken outpost of the Empire.

The Essenes wrapped the Crown of Thorns, removed the nails from the dead flesh, and wrested the metal spear from the wooden shaft of the centurion's forgotten lance. These holy relics, they figured rightly, were now extremely portable, and together the Crown, the nails, the spear had wondrous power, having pierced the temporary human flesh of what was now eternally divine. In penetrating the flesh, they penetrated the greatest secrets on Earth.

Had these objects merely hastened the death of Jesus?

Or had they hastened the Resurrection?

These were oral histories, he went on, and there are hasty labels and explanatory notes that have come down through the ages with the holy relics. The Essenes made off to Qumran with the three relics they had salvaged from the Crucifixion, where they kept them intact until the colony dispersed. But during those early years they devised a brilliant plan to keep those three holy relics—the Crown, the nails, the spear—safe from thieves and opportunists.

"Can you guess?" Bale smiled at Val.

She sat back. Finally: "I'd start a rumor that nothing had been gathered from the site of the Crucifixion. The nails had been melted down in a forge, the Crown had been incinerated, and the lance had been cleaned and stored in the Roman arsenal." Then she narrowed her eyes at Bale. "If nothing exists, nothing is at risk." Val folded her hands, pleased with herself. "Am I right?"

He smiled at her. "What you say makes sense, but," here he lifted a cautionary hand, "it's not what the Essenes did. In fact," he wiped his mouth reflectively, "rather than state that the objects were lost forever, they did precisely the opposite." At that, Val widened her eyes at him. What was he talking about? Bale leaned toward her across the linen-topped table that separated them at Eamonn's. "They flooded the market. Over many years. They made several duplicates of each of the holy relics and sold them to the powerful and wealthy faithful at the dawn of what became the Catholic Church."

"Sold them!"

"Hey," he said, signaling for the waitress, "a hermit's got to live." These fine examples of Essene craft and craftiness have over the centuries enjoyed all-expenses paid travel across continents. From Jerusalem to Byzantium, the circlets and fragments and detached thorns and fragments of detached thorns have shown up in everything from part of the Czech crown jewels, and everywhere, including a church in Pittsburgh. The proliferation of this one holy relic has over two millennia done precisely the job the Essenes intended: taken either devout or thieving minds off the hunt for the true one.

"Which you have."

"Which," said Bale, pointing a spoonful of crème caramel at Val, "the Carmelites have had, hidden, from their very beginnings on Mt. Carmel. Then in 1538 the troops of King Henry VIII pulled down Burnham Norton, and that's when we lost the rest of the hardware."

"The hardware?"

"The nails and the spear from the lance." He leaned his elbows on the table and gazed at Val over his folded hands. "The abbey was plundered and someone cashed in on what was essentially a black market in religious relics."

"What happened to them?"

He shrugged. "The nails could be holding up the sides of a sheep barn in Kent, for all we know."

"Would that be so bad?"

He smiled, then looked away. "Actually, no. I'd rather hear that new purpose for the nails from the Crucifixion—some good solid use to preserve life—than to imagine them in the hands of...what would have to be a very strange collector."

"But the Crown survived."

"The poor, four old Carmelite monks left at Burnham Norton in 1538 managed to save the reliquary with the Crown and kept it hidden." When a smaller version of the abbey was re-built with the original stones, late in the nineteenth century, the Crown of Thorns came back home.

For the Carmelites of Burnham Norton Abbey, it is a sacred trust to house the principal relic of the Crucifixion. "We bring it out for no holy days," said Bale thoughtfully. "We erect no signs. We direct no pilgrims. We mention it in none of our meetings and none of our worship services. Which is why," he shook his head tightly, "I can't understand how Fintan found out about it."

Val sipped her tea. "Do all the monks know about the relic?"

He pursed his lips. "All of the choir monks know we have it.

Only two of them know where. Among the lay brothers," he gave her a small smile, "I'm the only one."

"You're a lay brother?"

"I am."

"What's the difference?"

"I didn't take the same vows." He reached for his coffee. "And," he added with a grin, "I sleep in a different wing."

Val fell silent, trying to gauge the weight of Bale's secrets. There was no way to know yet whether the tightly held information he shared was one of those weights that would grow lighter with time as she simply went on with her days—or whether it would feel like psychic lead that would nightmarishly feel bigger with each passing year, the thing she couldn't find a way around. She felt pulled into the strange and shadowy world of Antony Bale that even Adrian didn't know. Finally, she put it to him. "Why tell me?"

Bale nodded. "Frankly, it's a preemptive move. You would have figured it out—the truth about the *Euphorbia* Adrian wanted you to see. Telling you up front, Val, is the only way I can think of to impress upon you the importance of secrecy. I need to recover the relic. Somehow there was a security breach at the abbey, and this boy Fintan took advantage of it. But why? *Why?* Why would a devout boy steal the holiest relic of the Crucifixion? This boy robbed us, his brothers in Christ, made off with the reliquary, impulsively hid it in an urn, which he then lost, and ultimately may have killed himself in remorse." With that, Bale pushed himself away from the table.

"Money?" she suggested, unhappy with the notion even as she said it.

"If that's the case, there goes one vow. Strange to say, but I'm likelier to believe our friend Fintan committed a whole raft of sins than to think he broke any of his vows."

Val gathered her coat. "What was he like, this Fintan?"

"Smart and pious." Bale lifted his eyebrows. "A deadly combination."

Val buttoned her jacket. "Isn't that you?"

"I'm smart enough. And pious enough to..." here he scratched his cheek, looking amused, "...well, fit. But this boy was plenty smart, and his mind—" Bale groped for the idea "—was the tool of his piety. If you see what I mean. Love of the Lord was what motivated him. All of his ideas seemed rolled up in how best to express that love."

"Oh," said Val, with sudden understanding. "Then he did it for somebody else. For some higher value. It's the only way he would have been able to explain it to himself."

Bale took a step back. "Ah," he said softly while he thought it over. "A moral dilemma, you're saying."

She gave him a frank look. "Maybe not even such a dilemma."

"Maybe not." Bale stared at the floor. "Interesting." He made a move to grab the check, but Val was faster.

"This one's mine," she said.

He put a hand lightly on her shoulder. "You let me offload a whole bunch of troubling information, and then you buy me dinner."

Val smoothed down her jacket, and said lightly, "Oh, I'll think of it as a cheap history lesson."

When he studied her, she felt a momentary alarm at how grave he looked. "No, you won't," he said quietly. She could never pull off flippant, that much she knew. And that much now Adrian's brother knew too. "Let's go."

Go? "Where?"

"To the crime scene," he answered, and as the two of them made their way through the crowd to the front of Eamonn's, Val clutched at her stomach where, at that moment, the shepherd's pie felt like it was sliding back and forth in a cargo hold.

In the cab heading uptown, Bale explained he had heard from Homicide before Mass that the CSI team had finished the job at the Coleman-Witt, if Bale wanted to come by. The museum was open officially until nine that night—Eva Toscano had told them they absolutely had to finish packing up the last of the artifacts from the Anasazi exhibit that closed earlier that week, otherwise the insurance would run out on them and the Coleman-Witt would be high and dry—and Bale could enter through the front. "I had told Cleary I wanted some time in Adrian's office as her next of kin." He shot her a quick look. "I'll face packing up her things some other time."

"I'll help," Val put in.

"Thanks. But tonight I just want to see it." The ride up Riverside Drive was strangely restful for Val. She leaned back, some small part of her settling down from the disturbance of returning to the museum where Adrian had died a day ago. The driver had on the Yankees game, bottom of the second inning, two on base, one out, low and wide—all good words—the bright happy murmuring crowd in the Bronx on a warm spring night set sweetly apart from violent death.

She opened her window a crack, noticing Bale, leaning back with his eyes closed in something that wasn't sleep. Wasn't even pain. His coat hanging open, his legs wide, his hands loosely folded in his lap. There were fine lines at the top of his cheekbones, and a small, hooked scar along his jaw. On some level it was the kind of face that could turn up just fine in a tangle of sheets the next morning. When she suddenly found herself wondering which vows he hadn't made, Val winced at herself and lowered her window. A light evening breeze brought in the passing smells of fresh tar—or maybe it was brimstone.

11

The wind that snapped coat hems on the steps of St. Patrick's didn't make it to the Upper West Side, for which Val was grateful. It made the late afternoon seem warmer. The sun over the Hudson River was suspended at the point in its descent that you could believe there were still a lot more hours left to daylight. But in ten minutes, tops, the light would shift steadily as the sun seemed to hasten to a horizon that only meant darkness. She was grateful, too, that she and Bale headed for the grand front entrance to the Coleman-Witt—it would be a long time before she could muster either the courage or forgetfulness to use the walkway leading to the employee entrance. The walkway the killer had used in pursuit of Adrian. The walkway the paramedics had used to transport her, bloody, to the morgue.

A doorman dressed in a blue uniform murmured a brief greeting as he easily swung open one half of the great glass doors of the Coleman-Witt Museum. In what Adrian had told her was a costly renovation a decade ago, the entrance to the museum had been made to soar straight up two floors overhead to create a Great Hall, where their few fine pieces of medieval armor were housed. Ahead of them, a grandfatherly docent wearing a green double-breasted blazer was pointing out the defensive features of the breastplate on a suit of armor made five hundred years ago in Germany. Sprawled in front of him was a small group of what looked like ten-year-olds with sketch books, their hands swiping across the pages with charcoal pencils. A plump art teacher wearing a denim smock circulated, whispering suggestions. Too late for a school group, thought Val—must be one of the continuing education classes Adrian had helped start a couple of years ago.

While Bale set off to ask a guard for directions to the director's office, Val wandered closer to the sketchers as the docent opened it up to questions. One eager boy shot up to his knees and asked if they could see the spot where that lady got topped. Val pressed her eyes shut for a second. *That lady. Got topped.* Adrian Bale had been quickly reduced to a sound bite on the evening news. And out here in the community, no one could hang on to her name or her accomplishments or the fact that she had people who loved the hell out of her. All anyone else would recall is that she was executed in an instant of blood and bone. Topped. Was it street language? Euphemism? Spot on? All Val knew was, the word was completely colorless, but even so she felt struck clear down to her spine. She shuddered, covering her eyes as Bale stopped alongside her.

"She's coming out," he told her.

Val nodded, tipping back her head to eye the beautiful gilt arches. *Topped.* Had the boy unknowingly hit on something she and Bale could use? Without looking at Adrian's brother because she wanted to voice the question freely as she turned it over in her own mind, she asked the arches sweeping high over her head, "Is it possible Adrian was killed execution-style?" When Bale said nothing, she went on, "What if we've got this thing wrong? What if we're settling too fast on the urn, Antony, and the...Crown."

"What do you mean?" he finally said, quietly.

Val turned to look at him, his hands hidden in the pockets of his long coat, his look difficult to read. "Was Adrian's murder a hit? Was the Crown stolen—" here she slowed, trying to figure it out "—as a cover?"

After a moment of trying on that possibility, he started to shake his head. "Well," he said finally, running his hands roughly over his scalp, "I hope to God that isn't so, because then the Crown's been tossed into a garbage can somewhere on Broadway by now and I'll never get it back."

"Antony Bale?"

Val and Bale turned at the sound of the voice. Eva Toscano was wearing a dusty rose off-the-rack suit in bouclé that looked like it had been roughed up by cats. Her eyes were glazed, her blue-framed glasses askew on her tight face, but her smile soldiered on. They shook hands, Val reminding the director of the Coleman-Witt that Adrian had introduced them at a fundraising function half a year ago. Toscano's red hair had been sprayed into paralysis on this day after her curator's murder, but it was the only part of the poor woman that didn't seem twitchy with lack of sleep over what had befallen her beloved museum.

"Follow me," she breathed, tottering on her heels, and as Bale and Val fell in beside her, Toscano expressed condolences that didn't show any intention of stopping. Adrian Bale was superb at her job, a true expert in her field, a fine asset to the Coleman-Witt, a team player, a friend to all, kind to insects, awesome at karaoke— It wasn't until they reached the offices corridor in the second building that she seemed to run out of items of the list, and, her trembling mouth slightly open, remembered the objective.

Toscano turned to them in a heady waft of lavender. It was a frozen moment. Finally, with her arms crossed, her fingernails picked at the bouclé of her suit jacket. "The NYPD released the...crime scene," she finished, pressing her lips tight, clearly hating words like *crime scene*. And possibly even *NYPD*. Fine for any place outside the holy walls of this repository of beauty and brilliance. Toscano flung out a hand with great distaste as though it was an invitation to cross the River Styx, and they had unreasonably asked to go there. The place beyond.

The three of them headed down the corridor toward what Val remembered as Adrian's office, maybe fifty feet from the side entrance, straight ahead. Leaving Bale at Adrian's closed office door while the director found the right key, Val slipped alone to the side entrance, where she scrutinized the horizontal metal bar and then turned, spying the security camera mounted high on the left wall near the ceiling. Fixed and operational. She wished with a pang she could say the same about her best friend. Narrowing her eyes, Val tried to imagine what had happened. Adrian arriving at some godawful early hour because of jet lag, toting not only her purse, her thermal lunch tote, probably her laptop, but now also a sizeable Victorian urn clothed in layers of bubble wrap. Letting herself in with her key, a trick to shoulder and knee the door open, sidling through, careful not to jostle the gift from the prior of Burnham Norton Abbey. Slowed down with the crap of the day, slowed down with the responsibility of the urn. She slipped through, the door slowly scraping across her hip as she made it through the entrance, the door to the outside stopping short—murderously short, as it happened—of closing tight.

And with the weight of all the stuff, Adrian simply hadn't noticed the door had failed to click. Maybe from lack of sleep, maybe from what Val knew would have been her sheer happiness to be back from her visit to Antony, ready to dig back into the world of Sumerian treasures.

Val's mind went to the nursery rhyme, *For want of a nail...the kingdom was lost*. For want of a click, Adrian was lost. How easy it had been, when it came right down to it, to breach Eva Toscano's fortress walls. Easy to get into the building, easy to shoot out the security camera, easy to find his victim in the very closest office— alone. Was there nothing that hadn't conspired against Adrian Bale on that misbegotten day to end her life?

Val found Bale standing inside his sister's office, the scene of her violent death, and Toscano backing toward the open door. Bale was simply looking around, studying the place, while the director of the Coleman-Witt babbled. Her eyes were suddenly behaving as though she'd sprayed them with insect repellent. She couldn't look, she couldn't stay, it was all, all too terrible, vile, and disgusting, and she would send Terrell to them right away, and please tell her about the final arrangements, she'd be very grateful. "Stay as long as you—" here she flung up her hands as though people made no sense to her "—like." With that, she turned and rushed back up the corridor.

The office smelled strongly of disinfectant. While Adrian's

brother started slowly around the perimeter of the room, registering everything, Val raised the vinyl blinds and thumbed open the lock on the sash window, pushing it up to let in the fresh air.

She tried to imagine being a new hire at the Coleman-Witt, assigned to this particular office. The top desk was completely devoid of anything—no loose papers, no Jasperware urn, no inbox, stapler, whatever was within her reach from day to day—certainly nothing that contained the finest example of a *Euphorbia milii* they would ever in this lifetime see. Some of the things were now the temporary property of the Homicide Division. Some—just the Crown?—were in the hands of Adrian's killer.

A single business card remained. Val picked it up.

Cleaned of the Crime
Tri-County Area
J.D. Hurley, Prop.
What CSI leaves, we do not
Bonded, Licensed, Confidential
A set of phone numbers.

Tossed on the desk as a routine last act before leaving, having cleaned up blood and bone.

To Val it felt like finding a calling card in a coffin.

She slipped it into her bag, in case she and Bale decided to call them.

Bale was turning over common objects—a Krups coffeemaker, a three-hole punch, a stack of Zagat guides—trying to get a feel for Adrian's work life, Val thought. She stood as tightly up against the single window as she could, stepping left and right, trying to see what a random passerby on the street might possible see.

There was no vision line at all from the window to the threshold of the office door, where someone had fired at Adrian. Out of sight from the museum's security system. Out of sight from the street.

For someone, it had been a clean kill.

But from Adrian's desk, with the office door wide open, there was a clean vision line straight out to the corridor where she spotted the wall-mounted metal coat rack across from Adrian's office. From the wire hangers hung a couple of white lab coats, a gray topcoat, a brown leather jacket, and a purple fleece. On the attached horizontal rack, three inches above the one holding the coats and jackets, was the red and silver thermal lunch bag Adrian had been using for the past couple of years, jammed up against other staff's hats, umbrellas, and lunch bags. "Antony," she said, bounding out to the hall and pulling down Adrian's lunch bag. Clutching it in both hands, she strode back into Adrian's office. "See this?" She held it out toward him.

He winced. "Adrian's lunch?"

Val widened her eyes at him, excited. "No." When he shot her a skeptical look, she went on. "Cleary mentioned they had taken her purse—the one next to her desk—as evidence, but they found nothing of interest in it. A couple of old gift cards with a couple of bucks each left on them, a change purse with a few dollars, a comb, a lipstick, old movie stubs, cheap pair of drugstore sunglasses—" Val blew the hair away from her face. "I forgot, that's all, otherwise I could have—"

"What?" said Bale, interested.

"Remember when Adrian's purse was snatched a couple of years ago when she was coming home late at night, right off Columbus Circle?" When Bale shook his head, Val went on. "She lost everything and had to go through that big rigmarole of replacing all her cards. Afterwards," Val said as she set the thermal lunch bag down on Adrian's scrubbed and empty desk, "she was so annoyed that she put together this fake purse—an old Michael Kors bag—"

"As a kind of...decoy?"

"Right. All worthless stuff inside but with just a few bucks to pull it off, if anyone made a grab for it. And only on workdays, when she was in a crush of people during rush hour, or coming home late and the streets were deserted."

Bale rubbed the back of his neck, glancing around Adrian's

office at the Coleman-Witt. "But where's her driver's license, and her wallet, and—"

With a smile, Val unzipped the lunch bag. First she pulled out a French-styled Coach wallet, opened it, and flashed the driver's license and a line of credit cards at Bale. Fingering through the cash—which topped two hundred dollars—she found receipts, a baggage claim ticket, and a Metro card. "This is her purse," Val said excitedly, "her real purse." While she riffled through the receipts to see if there was anything particularly telling—found a few from the recent trip to Norfolk to visit Antony at the abbey—he pulled out Adrian's iPad mini, clutching it with both hands for a quick second as though it might disappear as completely as Adrian herself. "I'll bet her schedule is on the mini," Val said, then she quickly drew out a hairbrush, compact, bottle of Advil, key ring—and a purple Moleskin notebook with an attached elastic band to keep it closed. Val slipped off the elastic and opened the book. In her bold handwriting, Adrian had scrawled, MY TRIP JOURNAL, Norfolk, U.K., and the dates. For just a quick look, Val opened the journal and thumbed to a random page about halfway through her friend's trip to Norfolk, when her eyes settled on the words, *Today I met a man.*

Well, Adrian went on, *not met exactly, but noticed. He might be a sailor, or at least someone who lives a seafaring kind of life. Listen to me, sounding like Herman Melville. Wrong seacoast, I know, but the Royal Navy isn't all that far away, I'm pretty sure. Something in the set of his shoulders in that classic pea coat and the blue watch cap pulled down over hair that looked shaggy and dirty blond made me think of it. Around here, all the available men appear to be either sailors, monks, brewers, or dead. Ha! Anyway, I was reading in a booth at the pub called Olde Bandylegs here in Sidestrand—only about a mile from the abbey— waiting for Antony to turn up, and this stranger caught my eye. Finished what they call a pint, checked his watch, and swung himself away from the bar. I was appreciating the sleek way he moves like something that could take you unawares in the woods—and I do mean take you—when he noticed me.*

I'm a little past the weak-in-the-knees phase of my life— unless of course you're talking a Sumerian goblet—and this is supposed to be a Trip Journal, not some sweaty diary—but I caught my breath. Those eyes (green? gray?) settled on me just long enough to make him slow down, appraising me. For what? Sex? A drink? A discussion of whether the royal babies look like Kate or Will? All three? I gave him that arch look I've seen Val manage many times, and I actually fingered my pearls. Only I wasn't wearing any. With one final glance at his watch, he brushed a crumb from his thigh, which set my heart pounding, watching me the entire time. I could swear he was stroking my thigh. Then, shooting me a quick, slight smile that I'd like to think held some regret, he walked quickly out of the pub. Dear Trip Journal, it was the best sex I've never had.

12

From the vestry of the Robus Christi chapel in Gramercy Park, the man called Animus watched the members of his High Council assemble. Millard Mackey, the veteran of the first Gulf War who kept house for him, had brushed the black trousers and frock coat the head of the organization wore on these important occasions. Garments hung like hell on him anymore, what with the disease, and in many ways he was little better than a coat hanger, no better than a skimpy wire that just does a job. In helping his employer dress, Millard had the task of working around the two canes Animus insisted on using instead of the walker his oncologist recommended. A walker was not at all the right image for the head of this organization he had carefully built, whereas a cane has true mystique. Two, even more so.

Millard, who had suffered burns over half his body in the battle of 73 Easting in southeastern Iraq, and had undergone two reconstructive surgeries to the left side of his head and torso with indifferent results, had lost much of the use of his voice, half his hearing, and all of his left eye. Although his bleary right eye was still perfectly discerning and could execute a Windsor knot with admirable speed and panache, Millard had to steady himself against the frail man who clung to his canes with the wispy remnants of his strength, otherwise both of them would land on the floor. They may have become bent and lopsided men, but Animus always reassured his indispensable Millard that the prophecy at the core of Robus Christi would include them both. Because it enveloped all of the righteous.

At these words, the dogged Millard, half of whose scalp was so scarred it no longer grew hair, would nod and get an equivocal look on his ravaged face like he was trying to decide between taking the train or the crosstown bus. On some level, Animus understood. Prophecy for the likes of Millard fell more along the lines of shrieks about incoming enemy missiles, followed by a minute of scrambling horror, fulfilled in a deafening explosive truth.

Peeking around the doorway of the vestry, Animus watched as one by one, his High Council greeted each other with warm glances as they found seats in one of twelve rows of walnut pews. He called this special meeting to announce that the fulfillment of prophecy was very near. Millard brushed the shoulder of the frock coat with the arm it was painful for him to raise above his waist, so it was clear what it took. "Go, go," Animus whispered, patting the ruined man with a vague fondness. "I'm ready," he assured him. Millard shot him one of his frequent looks that could mean anything from *that's what you think* to *it's tough doing what you do, and I am honored to press your pants.*

When Millard slunk out through the door that led to the other half of the house, the man turned and opened the bank vault he had—at unfathomable expense—installed at the rear of the vestry when a credit union on the Lower East Side had closed five years ago. Two-foot thick reinforced steel, climate controlled, accessible by a combination lock, this vault had become, for his eyes only, the holy of holies. On an octagonal display case in the very center of the space were the precious items. Now, since Alaric had presented him with the final missing element—the Crown—he set aside his canes and opened the glass halves of the lid.

Iron, and thorn, and an ancient leather fragment—which he kept close to him in his study next door—had brought him his life's work.

All collected in terrible secrecy.

No one else except the indispensable Alaric knew the cost.

Alaric, too, was iron and thorn.

We are what we pursue. Nothing more or less.

Pulling himself up to his full height—three inches shorter than when he began his course to fulfill the prophecy—the head of Robus Christi grabbed his two canes and turned the lock on the door to the vault. With a flash of his old poise, he headed slowly into the chapel, spotting Alaric in his gray leather jacket standing at the back with his arms crossed. As the High Council fell silent, he was struck all over again by how very fine they were, each of them. And why not? He had hand-picked or vetted them all. Inventors, IT virtuosos, philanthropists, NASA scientists, a film director, three United States senators. Everyone world-class. Everyone on board for the highest promise of Robus Christi. A Kingdom of God in the Kingdom of Man, for all.

"Evening, Animus," said Malka, the concert violinist who always sat in the front pew at council meetings.

He inclined his head. "Malka."

Then he glanced around the chapel, which looked inexpressibly warm and beautiful in the early evening light. Millard and Alaric had lighted the candle wall sconces, set into the old wood paneling that lined the walls, the little flames going up and up. Next to the altar was the Gothic wrought-iron standing candelabra, all five branches holding the traditional Robus Christi blue pillar candles, alight. The sight always settled his heart. He let his eyes go soft, gazing into that white-hot shapeless place inside the flames. This was their own Gat Smanim, right here on Gramercy Park West.

He leaned lightly against the altar, just enough to brace himself without drawing too much attention to his weakness, which he had carefully kept from each of them, and turned his head slowly to face the Robus Christi High Council. "I have news," he raised his voice as he gazed at the handpicked assembly. Once the prophecy was fulfilled, these fifty would continue in advisory roles and the true democracy of never-ending life and faith would spread like new oxygen over the troubled world.

"How exciting," cried one of his IT experts.

For the past eight years he and his High Council had to take heart with mundane victories. Variances, trusts, mission statements, neighbor conflicts (particularly getting the ordinance about picking up after your dog enforced—hard-won and extremely contentious). So when Alaric came up with the first of the items specifically mentioned in the fragment—tracked down to a junky secondhand shop called Milady's Miscellany in the East End of London—the High Council wept and rejoiced.

When he came up with the second item, two years ago, finally, in a stable in Brittany, the High Council fell silent. They were within one sacred object of what they needed to fulfill the prophecy that was the very engine of the organization. That night, the prayers and communion were especially hushed and meaningful because the possibility of final success loomed large. They were close. And it was partly...frightening.

"Nothing in the papers, I hope," cried one of them.

"No, nothing like that."

"Wait," said Malka with her unfailing intuition. Beaming in the chapel's candlelight, she swiveled to look for Alaric in the back. "Has Alaric—?"

At that, the fifty members of the Robus Christi High Council fixed their eyes on the visionary head of the organization, and waited, poised with what they somehow already guessed was coming. "He has," said the frail man, holding up a hand. "Our very estimable man in the field has delivered the third and final sacred object." They cheered. It struck him that even the High Council never knew the identity of the objects, these artifacts of the Crucifixion, nor what Alaric had done to take possession of them. Difficult choices had to be made in the service of good works. Nothing that comes cheap can also be priceless.

"And now what?" said the IT expert. "When does the prophecy—?"

Animus spoke over the murmurs. "Get fulfilled?" That was the question now, wasn't it? "Very soon," he said with a smile, his mind already listing the final steps in what he had built very carefully over these last eight years. "Robus Christians, you will know."

Gone forever will be the agonizing and unanswerable

questions about a hereafter that in the new world promised by the prophecy will become completely inconsequential. What greater conversion tool could there possibly be than the promise of life in which suffering and mortality play no part? What the prophecy was about to usher in was what he and Alaric had worked selflessly to achieve, a dissolving of all violent differences and impossible sufferings into what only he himself had gleaned from the secret of the acacia wood box: a messianic age without a messiah. The ultimate spiritual democracy.

And, now that the three holy relics had been collected, it would begin with him.

Animus.

At the hour of his death that would be no death at all.

Cued by his slight nod, the fifty members of High Council reached into the racks where hymnals used to be kept and drew out the laminated cards that held the single prayer he himself had written. Then they intoned, "Haec est Robus Christi." After five minutes of chanted prayer, they stood and filed silently up to the communion table that held the small silver bowls the faithful Millard once grumbled were a bitch to polish. Each bowl contained a host. Returning to their seats, the High Council performed the Robus Christi open-handed benediction over the bowls, reciting the credo, *I believe the world to come lives already in the world of man*. Then they set the hosts on their tongues.

After all this time, the frail man still felt his breath catch at the splendor of it. A self-administered host among Peruvians and Laplanders and Masai and Nebraskans, in a world where the promise of perfect peace would prevail. And death would have no place. No claim on humanity. After all. What he wouldn't mention to any of them—not even Alaric or Millard—was that tomorrow he had an appointment with his oncologist, who expressed the desire to discuss in person the most recent test results, and press once again for hospice care. The head of Robus Christi would have to work very hard to keep from smiling.

13

"I could use a drink."

After finding the Trip Journal, Val and Bale spent another hour in Adrian's office at the Coleman-Witt, hoping to get a feel for the crime—and hoping to stumble across some piece of evidence the NYPD had overlooked. Finally, while Val thumbed through one of Adrian's specimen drawers, filled with potsherds dated twenty-five hundred years ago, she slowly became aware of how still the room was. She glanced up from a particularly sand-roughened shard labeled Tikrit, ca. 2195 BC and noticed Bale standing motionless in the center of the office. He had the look on his face she had seen on TV news broadcasts covering tornado survivors standing in disbelief in the rubble of their homes.

Bale was done for the day, that much Val could tell. "Where do you want to go?"

He ran a hand roughly over his head. "I want to get out of this neighborhood," he muttered. "I never want to come back here." To the place where a beloved sister comes to work because she's actually working her dream job, her with her fake purse and totally innocent find of a holy relic she'd picked up by mistake, when she's possibly humming about some sexy stranger in a Norfolk pub and she looks up to see something unexpected in her doorway. A killer. Adrian, who only ever wanted to grow old acquiring and exhibiting what for her were treasures from an ancient desert civilization. Where was a motive for murder in that?

Val zipped the Trip Journal back into Adrian's thermal lunch bag and cast a final look around her dead friend's office. Bale was right. There was nothing here. Adrian had been gunned down for a perfectly impersonal and antiseptic reason. She had the fatally bad luck to be given a Victorian urn that had been made the makeshift hidey hole for a priceless stolen object. The Crown of Thorns. "I'd say..." she went over to Bale and looked him in the eye, "we're looking for a single killer, don't you think?"

"Let's get out of here," said Bale, touching her arm lightly. As Val tucked Adrian's lunch bag under her arm, it felt precious to her. She'd have to talk to Bale about getting it to Adrian's apartment, and he could call Eva Toscano and have the rest of Adrian's personal effects at the Coleman-Witt boxed and delivered to Adrian's as well. As they headed together toward the main hall, Bale's turned his tired face to Val. "A single killer...?"

"Adrian and the boy monk who stole the Crown."

Bale's eyes narrowed. "Ah, but we don't know that. Last I heard the coroner was still out on the cause of death of Fintan McGregor."

At seven fifteen for the next two mornings, Val played a waiting game. Dressed for work both days in her favorite Ann Taylor gold ankle pants, black asymmetrical top and black Dansko clogs, she put in an hour on what she came to think of as her West 73rd Street stakeout and then dashed to Broadway to catch the train to her office. What she was looking for was a face. Any face. Someone she possibly recognized from three days ago when Adrian was murdered.

She was counting on the ironclad routines of early morning New Yorkers. Those Upper West Siders who would leave for work twenty minutes early to get in the line out the door at the Starbucks on Columbus Avenue. The ones who pounded the same route daily in all weather and pricey running shoes. The retired neighbors who ambled with their identical cockapoos long enough for some steaming product they bag, all in time to get to a zumba class at the 92nd Street Y.

Val had called Cleary to see if there was anything new on the investigation, and whether a couple of detectives from the 20th Precinct had indeed hit the jackpot with someone out on the sidewalk that morning who had been able to give them some kind of lead. "We got the runner with the ponytail, and she thought she had seen a Con Ed truck parked up the block. Only no one else did. Still, we're running it down to be sure."

Not promising. "Anything else?"

"Suspicious looking men ran the gamut," Cleary went on. "Young and black, middle-aged shifty Italian, an old Sikh who was about half a mile out of his neighborhood and no doubt about it, up to no good. In short, every stereotype known to man." And the routine door-to-door yielded squat. Nothing out of the ordinary. "You know the MTA mantra, right?" Cleary suddenly piped up. "Plastered all over the trains and buses, 'if you see something, say something'?"

"Right." Val had no idea where the homicide cop was going.

"People report all the wrong things. Nobody seems to have a clue what's important," she grumbled. Like she was referring to love, voting, and paying your bills.

But Val's first solid lead came toward the end of her shift that first morning as she stood in the drizzle that in the city hardly counted as precipitation. She had accosted the runner with the ponytail, who blinked at her and went on in a strained way, lightly jogging in place, about the possible Con Ed truck. Val must have looked disappointed because the woman jogged sideways and added she saw a mixed race guy who might have gotten out of the truck.

"Might have?"

The runner waved a hand dismissively. "He looked like a blue-collar kind of guy. The kind you see fooling around with power lines."

This information told her something about the witness, but nothing about the crime. Still, Val grasped at anything as her bangs were slowly starting to stick to her forehead. "I don't suppose you remember the time?"

One of these days she'd have to break down and buy an umbrella. Something beautiful from MoMA.

Back and forth, back and forth went the runner, like Rocky Balboa on the steps of Philly City Hall. "Past seven thirty. I always turn the corner onto 73rd Street at seven thirty, otherwise I fall behind my PB."

"PB?"

The woman's eyes narrowed at her. "Personal best."

"But the crime occurred sometime before seven thirty," Val said, studying her Danskos, noting how the raindrops were beading up. By a little after seven thirty, the killer would have been long gone from the Coleman-Witt.

"I don't know what to tell you," said the woman, as though Val was being thick and difficult. A very small old woman with short flyaway hair and two hearing aids that pushed her large ears slightly forward joined Val and the runner. Rainwater streamed down the red frames of her eyeglasses. Folding her arms, she puckered her lips and looked thoughtfully from the runner to Val. "Are you with the police?" the runner asked with the most curiosity she had shown since Val collared her.

"No," said Val, turning up the collar of her black raincoat. "It was my friend who was killed."

The runner slung her a quick, sad look that turned helpless. "Con Ed, mixed race guy, later than seven thirty." Dancing backwards from Val, who nodded at her, the runner made a lithe turn and took off up the block, dodging a twin stroller pushed by a hollow-cheeked dad.

The very small woman fixed Val with an undecided look, like she was considering whether to withhold the most graphic parts of Val's sorry Tarot reading. Val waited. "Petra Housman," the woman decided finally, stepping up to Val as close as she could get and thrusting a hand at her as though she held a knife. Val gave the woman her name, swiftly checking out the block to see if she remembered anyone else passing by on the morning of Adrian's murder.

"No luck?" blared Petra Housman. She had large pores on a little heart-shaped face. The teeth were surprisingly white. Pulling herself up on tiptoes, she pointed a finger at Val's nose. "I live across the street from the Coleman-Witt. I was around that morning, I already told that detective. But I'd got back early from my sunrise yoga class at the Y, so I can't help you with the times."

Val felt deflated. "That's okay, Petra. I'll try again—"

"The one you want, see, is that little *frum* girl lives in the next block." With that, she flung her head violently to the side, casting the rain off herself in a horizontal spray.

"*Frum?*"

"Observant. Ortho. Goes to a day school up near Columbia. She walks this block to get to the train."

Petra Housman stood back an inch from Val and clasped her hands behind her back, like a captain on a quarterdeck. "Saw her out of the corner of my eye, as I headed back into my building." She inhaled deeply. "Didn't mention her to the detective." She gave Val a sidelong look, sniffing. "Just a kid, you know?"

Val nodded. "What was she doing?"

Petra Housman grinned, then rubbed at her nose. "Hiding, looked like. She'll tell you. Try again tomorrow. Name's Tali. Good family. Tell her you know me." The woman started to turn, then threw back at Val, "Although you won't need any warm-up with that girl. Very forthcoming. She may not understand what she saw, but you can be sure she won't hold anything back." With that, Petra Housman brayed and hurried up the street, waving a hand overhead at Val. Then suddenly stopped and turned. "That boy she's hiding from?"

Ah. So it was a boy. "Also *frum?*"

"Of course." Both hands were flung skyward. "She keeps waiting for him to find her."

14

The following morning was dry and breezy. Val figured she still had enough clean underwear for today and tomorrow, at which point she would have to break down and throw in a load of laundry, but for the second day of her West 73rd Street stakeout she was wearing what she considered her default outfit—the one she wore when nothing was clean, if she felt hung over, or if for any number of reasons putting together an outfit felt like a sad misuse of her time on Earth. Even though she was seeing Killian at nine thirty and Bale at six, it was one of those days that called for the default outfit: navy blue pencil skirt, white ruffled blouse, thin navy cardigan. She threw a strand of her best fake pearls into her Peruvian beaded bag, in case the CEO called a surprise meeting, and a funky necklace made of old colorful glass and metal typewriter keys, in case he didn't.

She was lumbered by a folding tripod camp stool Ivy League Ivy had actually brought for Val from home when Val mentioned the stakeout plan. "In case you get tired."

"I'm thirty-five."

"My point."

On some level, Val found she rather liked it that she still had moments of finding her assistant editor annoying. But on the second morning in the dry April breeze, Val had strolled by the Coleman-Witt Museum four times, lugging Ivy's camp stool the girl swore by for the Afropunk Festival, wondering if she herself was beginning to draw some attention. She supposed even innocuous default outfits were no proof against criminal intent. The runner passed her with a wave, likewise the two men in identical spandex t-shirts with cockapoos. No sign of Petra Housman, who had probably long since gotten back from her sunrise yoga class. The hollow-cheeked dad pushing the twin stroller looked her over impassively, then shot her a rueful look like he vaguely remembered the days of trolling for dates. Val answered with a slow sip of her cappuccino.

And then she saw what could only be the girl Petra Housman had described.

She came striding along the north side of the street, her shoulder-length dark curls pushed back with a pink paisley headband that were all the rage in aerobics classes. Flouncing along in the breeze, the girl was wearing the plaid uniform skirt Petra had described, only out of range of her family she had rolled it up at the waist until it came to her knees. If that was a long-sleeved, high-necked white top, it had been slipped off and tied loosely around her neck. The *frum* girl was wearing a pretty, white shell cut in a line that showed off her shoulders, and she was carrying the kind of canvas sling bags that newsboys used to tote. To Val, the girl looked about thirteen. Without slowing, the girl suddenly whipped her head around to check out whether she was being followed. The cockapoos had to dodge her.

When she got close, Val stepped out in front of her and resisted the urge to open the camp stool to settle in for what she hoped was a good long gab. "Tali?" Val tipped her head in a way she hoped would set the girl at ease, what with being accosted by a stranger on the way to school.

No need. The girl stopped, took in Val's default outfit with a quick scan, and smiled with no caution. "That's me," she said, then her blue eyes brightened. "Have you been waiting for me?"

No way around it. "Actually," Val shrugged, "yes. Petra Housman said I might want to talk to you."

"Ah, Petra," said the girl approvingly. "She's our accountant. She does good work."

Val thought Petra might enjoy hearing the good reference from the *frum* young teenager. "I'm Val Cameron. You heard about what happened at the museum—" she pointed over Tali's head, where the breeze was ruffling her curls like a flock getting ready to fly, "— three days ago?"

"The murder." The girl named Tali nodded solemnly. "Yes, of course." Then she thrust out a hand. "Avital Korngold," she said with a tone as though she was announcing the winner of the Pulitzer Prize. "Pleasure."

Val found herself wanting to go to lunch with this girl. "It was my best friend who was killed."

The girl cried out, "*Baruch dayan emet.*" She squeezed Val's arm. "I'm so sorry." And she was.

"What did you just say?"

"Ah." The girl stroked her chin lightly. "Blessed is the True Judge. We bless God upon hearing good and bad news alike."

"Good news I can understand, but—"

"Good and bad," Tali shrugged, "both take faith. God's purpose isn't always clear." It was impossible for Val to feel there was any purpose in Adrian Bale's death. "I really am sorry. How can I help?" She reached into her bag and pulled out a stack of business cards held together with a rubber band. She tugged the top one free and handed it to Val, who had a ridiculous moment when she realized she herself didn't carry her own business card. In fact, since her promotion all those months ago, she couldn't even say for sure whether any new ones had been printed. The girl's was plain white linen card stock with gold embossed lettering: *Avital Korngold*, centered, and just below, *Situations*, and below that what appeared to be her cell phone number. "You can call me Tali, okay?"

"Thank you," said Val, slipping the classy card into the little zippered spot inside her beaded bag. "What are Situations?"

"Advice," here the girl made a slow, rolling gesture with her left hand, "on things happening on the job, at school, in relationships." She sniffed modestly. "I have a knack."

"I might be able to use your help on relationships," said Val half-seriously, then wondered why she thought of Bale. Then: "What are your fees?"

The girl raised both hands and averted her gaze. "Oh, no, no," she said. "This is my own mitzvah project."

Nodding, Val leaned against the wrought-iron railings at the building maybe seven doors down from the Coleman-Witt Museum, where just at that moment Eva Toscano was being dropped off by a hired car, aiming for the side entrance like a direct mortar hit. "Tali," began Val, as the girl shifted her weight, listening. "Petra Housman tells me you may have been on this block early on the morning of the murder."

"Correct." Then the girl waited. No agenda, no defense.

"Petra thought you might have been..."

"Hiding. Yes. Down those steps right over there." She pointed to the dark, narrow steps leading to a basement apartment at the head of the block. A few doors away, and across the street, from the scene of the crime. "Whenever I think that idiot Sruly Levinson is following me, I duck down those steps. Then I wait for him to pass by. When he does, I dash up and follow him. You see, that puts him in a bad spot, because he cannot stop and wait for me. Entirely too much face would get lost." A pause while a different truth occurred to her. "Not that the face of Sruly Levinson couldn't stand some losing," she said softly, then stood up squarely and looked at Val. "But that's neither here nor there. You need to know what I saw on the morning of the murder."

"I think it qualifies as a Situation, yes."

"Agreed. And you have already questioned Petra and the scrawny runner lady and the cockapoo couple and—" She snapped her fingers. "Did you get the twins' dad?"

Val thought about it. "No."

"Then don't. He didn't come down this block that morning."

At that, Avital Korngold, Master of Situations, put her mind to work on the problem, pacing back and forth in front of the wrought-iron railings, pressing her little stack of business cards against the posts, like a playing card smacking the spokes of a bicycle wheel. Then the girl strode up to the side entrance of the museum, cocked her head this way and that, causing her thicket of curls to flop. She wheeled, eyes narrowed, scanning the parked cars jammed bumper to bumper all the way down the south side of the block, across from the museum. Then she came back to Val, looking—if it was possible—both clear and inscrutable at the same time. "There was a truck," she said with certainty.

The runner had been right after all. "The Con Ed truck?"

Tali smiled broadly. "It wasn't a Con Ed truck, although I can see how you might make that mistake. The colors were exactly the same."

Val's breath caught. "Then what was it really, Tali?"

"A kosher bakery truck." The girl did a little time-step.

Tali Korngold, Situations, Tap Dance.

The girl went on to describe a blue and white small truck, out of which a delivery man emerged with a cardboard box of bagels and rugelach. "I'm guessing on that," she cut off Val, who was about to ask. "Maybe this big." She motioned with her hands. A two-by-two white cardboard bakery box with a lid. "The kind they drop off for the men's club Sunday mornings at our *shul*. No biggie."

"What about the delivery guy?"

"He was nobody I noticed, just some guy dressed maybe in gray, gray shirt, gray pants."

"And the truck? Did you catch the name of the bakery?"

"Oh," she nodded vigorously, "it was from Etz Chayyim. Lower East Side." Then she added brightly, "You could check."

Val raised her eyebrows at Tali Korngold. "That I'll do."

Tali whipped out her phone and checked the time. "I'm going to be late, Val, so I'd better get going."

"Do you need me to square it with your school?" Together they started to hurry toward Broadway. "Wait, wait." Val lifted a hand. In the absence of a business card, she scribbled her name and cell number on the back of her Starbucks receipt. "Here, Tali. Call me anytime if you remember anything else." Suddenly it struck Val she should have a conversation with that little stalker Sruly Levinson as well. Tali carefully tucked the receipt into her newsboy bag. "Tell me," said Val, "did you manage to get behind Sruly that day?" It would be interesting to learn what the boy recalled of the bakery truck.

"Actually, no," the girl said with some surprise. "He probably turned down 74th instead. And there I was—" she acted like he had let her down in an extravagant way, "lying in wait down those basement steps." As she started to turn at the corner to head to the subway entrance, she froze. Her features all seemed to collect in the center of her face. "He may have bested me that day, now that I think about it." Then she looked up at Val and smiled. "Oh, well. I'm only thirteen." She shrugged. "I'm not an expert at every situation yet." Then: "Bye, Val!" And then, "Maybe I'll stop by your office sometime. Where is it?" She was halfway up the block, her rolled-up plaid uniform skirt and great floppy bag swaying as she ran.

"Schlesinger Publishing," Val called after her. "Flatiron Building. Anytime."

Tali Korngold stopped suddenly, causing a woman in a tan business suit to plow into her. "Val! Something else!" Val loped up to her. "You know," she said, dropping her voice as her eyes darted around the pedestrians. "There was something about that bakery delivery guy that struck me, now that I think about it."

"Go on."

"While I was hiding and couldn't figure out what was holding up that idiot Sruly, I'd been waiting for like fifteen minutes or something—" here she scrutinized Val for sympathy "—the bakery delivery guy came back out of the side entrance to the Coleman-Witt Museum."

"You saw him come out?"

"Mind you, my mind was occupied with possible Sruly scenarios, right?"

"Of course."

"Even so, I glanced briefly at the guy and it struck me as...odd."

"What did, Tali?" Val touched the girl's arm.

"Well, he went into the museum with your usual box of

pastries and nosh, right? Then why did he come back out of the museum—maybe not even five minutes later—with the very same box? What kind of delivery do you call that?"

And with that, Tali Korngold turned on her heel and ran all the way to the subway entrance, her dark curls airborne like a flag behind her.

By the time she arrived at the Flatiron Building, Val was ready for her second cup of coffee. She'd have to settle for whatever flavored K-Cups Ivy had tumbled into the basket next to the Keurig coffeemaker in the break room. For the call she needed to make to the Homicide detective, Val wanted to mingle on the pedestrian mall outside the Flatiron with the early morning gathering of office workers putting off for five more minutes the final succumbing to another eight-hour stint in a cubicle on an upper floor somewhere. Some sat sprawled with Venti bold roasts, some sat tensely pulled in, single thumbing their phones in hopes of something either startlingly wonderful or mildly interesting suddenly appearing on the screen.

Val shook open Ivy's tripod camp stool and slung it at a table where someone had left a half-eaten cheese Danish and a crumpled napkin. Pulling out her phone, Val looked quickly around. She never quite believed the pedestrian mall was really going to work. Any day now cabs and buses would suddenly agree that this long block set off for humans who wanted to hang out was a spectacularly dumb idea they were no longer willing to honor.

Shay Cleary picked up on the third ring. "This is Cleary."

"Val Cameron, Lieutenant."

"Yeah? I'm in the middle of something here."

"I'm calling about the Bale murder."

"I figured," said Cleary, who suddenly sounded like she was angling closer to the moment of truth on the Bomb Squad. "What have you got?"

"A witness."

"Which one?" She sounded offended, like there could be no witnesses not already known to her.

"Avital Korngold." Situations.

"Okay," said Cleary, humoring her, "who's that?" Then she shouted to someone nearby. "Marcus—over there!" Back to Val. "Sorry. Go on, but make it fast. I don't have all—"

Val glanced at her watch. James Killian was coming in forty-five minutes, and she had to review her notes on *Plumb Lines* and figure out how she could handle whatever new idea he was hot to sell her. Eight forty-five a.m. and already she was tired. She took a deep breath and laid it all out for the homicide detective. "Korngold routinely walks past the Coleman-Witt on her way to the subway. On the morning of the murder she spotted a delivery guy going into the museum by the side entrance. Nondescript, but carrying a large covered box of what Korngold believed were pastries. She—"

"Pastries?" A beat. "What makes her think—" Then she let out a strangled cry. "See it! Marcus, over there. Behind the file cabinet." Then with her mouth pressed against the phone, Cleary said in a low voice, "We have a mouse situation here."

Tali Korngold could handle it. Part of her mitzvah project. Val soldiered on. "She saw the guy get out of a delivery truck from a kosher bakery called Etz Chayyim. She recognized the name. Lower East Side."

"I'll give them a call." Cleary shouted, "Use the shoe box, the shoe box, Marcus. We want to take him alive." Then back to Val. "Any chance this Etz Chayyim had a legitimate delivery there?"

Val played Tali's trump card. "Not when the guy came out not even five minutes later, carrying the same box."

"Ah," breathed Cleary. "Good cover for the Glock." Then she added, "The murder weapon. Ballistics report just came in. I'll give them a call and see what—" As Cleary whooped in the background and the mouse got boxed, Val murmured a soft goodbye.

Good cover for the Glock.

Good cover, too, for getting away with what Adrian Bale had assured her best friend Val was the finest example of *Euphorbia milii* they would ever in this lifetime see. For Adrian, for smart, funny, beautiful Adrian, that had actually been true.

Val pushed herself off Ivy League Ivy's camp stool. Folding it carefully, she walked slowly into the Flatiron Building for just another day at the job.

15

He minded the woman.

It surprised him how much.

Alaric turned the white Escalade he had rented under one of his aliases onto E. 51st Street from Third Avenue just as a light rain started to fall. Two twenty p.m. This was his second shot at being able to double park right in front of the building. The first time, he was thwarted by a Coors delivery truck. As he bullied his way in front of a yellow cab who rightly gave him both the finger and the horn in their short-lived competition around the truck, he continued in fine, Caddy splendor on down the block. It wasn't long before Alaric's mind slipped again to the woman at her desk.

In some other, normal world, wherever that may still be, he would simply have stepped onto the threshold of her office, done his two-second perfect scan of the scene, leveled his weapon and fired. Without a bead of sweat, without a racing heart. He became a master of sloughing off human feeling many years ago. Ever since those double-wide trailer days when his half-sister would crawl into his bed and slip her trembling hands down into his pajamas, and his mother broke his jaw when he finally worked up the nerve to tell her. His jaw healed only okay, but it made him look older and street-wise, there in that shithole of a place where there were hardly any streets to get wise in. As he grew, it gave him a kind of speculative, sizing-up look that women seemed to like. His mother stopped whaling him, but his half-sister only snickered, *you tole on me, ya sweet little shit, ya tole, ain't you a fine one.*

He had found his way to a small brick Catholic Church just

four miles away from the double-wide, where he confessed to all sorts of things, just so they'd let him stay—bad thoughts, bad deeds, bad intentions, bad.

He read the balding priest right, him with the eyeglasses from Sears and the paunch. That parish priest gave him a bed in the rectory basement and three squares a day and once tried getting the kid to open up by saying: *You're a handsome fellow, boy, and there will be those who take advantage of you.* And the boy just polished the communion plate and waited for the priest to be one of them. It never happened.

But the handsome boy with the jaw broken by his worthless mother started to make stealthy searches of the priest's rooms while he was out on sick calls. The boy saw secrets as his insurance against eviction, starvation, or even just nighttime hands thrust deep down inside his pajamas. His fingers learned speed and precision rifling through underwear and toiletries and personal papers, his eyes settling with no expression on the Crucifix hanging over the priest's bed.

And he recalled how he felt something strange and wondered if it might be shame. It was as if the beautiful little dead Christ fashioned out of silver closed his eyes not in the death the whole damn story seemed to be about, but in grief. Grief for the boy standing before him, trespassing in ways for sure different from his half-sister's, but still trespassing. When he stopped to think about it, it was all hands down the pajamas. That was the day he actually had something to confess. And that was the day he determined to become devout—*Lord,* he prayed, *let me be worthy*—and to find a way to make a fine living away from this place where the riverbank breeds boredom and evil.

So he minded killing the woman.

That poor blundering kid monk had told Alaric what happened to the Crown there on the ridge. On the directive from Animus, Alaric had been reassuring to the distraught boy—after all, he recognized in the boy a very old, familiar desire to be worthy. The boy wasn't at all terrified when he turned away and Alaric brought a rock down with two hands on the back of the erring head. And Alaric had picked the body up heavily, weary from something he didn't quite understand, and released it over the edge of the cliff.

He should have minded the boy more.

But for now it was the woman. The recent one, not the sly, chain-smoking ferret in heels who owned the East End secondhand shop in London where he had found the lance after two years of searching. And she had figured out what it was, put up a fuss, set a new and exorbitant price, and the only way he could settle their differences was to leave her strangled on the floor of her shop. No, the one he minded was Adrian Bale, who had unwittingly transported the third and final relic of the prophecy. When Alaric shot out the security camera, he made his way silently down the corridor, and stepped into her doorway.

They stared at each other for two agonizing seconds.

It was her, the woman from Olde Bandylegs Pub.

But how could that be?

He felt so rattled that he shot her in the head as though he could obliterate her barest memories of him. Oh, he was going to have to kill whoever possessed the Crown anyway, but it threw him that he knew her. As he actually found himself wishing it had been someone else, he double-parked in the spot where the Coors truck had been. Then he pressed the hazard lights and quickly scanned the street.

Alaric slipped out of the Escalade, which he locked, and stepped lightly up to the sidewalk and hit the panic button. The screeching wheep that wouldn't stop brought the doorman at a loping run to check out the drama on 51st Street. Alaric slipped inside and strode to the tenant directory. *There she was.* Although he had checked her office, just to be sure. No more surprises, not like he had with the Bale woman.

Her name was fourth down alphabetically.

V. Cameron. 5-B.

*   *   *

Norfolk

By the time Bale set foot on the grounds at Burnham Norton Abbey, the sun was high in the sky and the wind was coming off the North Sea. In this part of the world, he liked both sun and wind, and he liked them together. Sunlight was always reassuring and wind kept him alert to the unpredictable. Abbey life was so needfully routine that Bale had come to relish the unexpected. Not murder, he thought as he let himself in through the kitchen door. There he nodded to Brother Sebastian, the stooped monk with pendulous dark eye bags who headed up the kitchen. Sebastian was rarely seen without his pin I AM IN SILENCE, which Bale cynically suspected was a ploy to head off any complaints about the abbey food.

As he left the kitchen, the distinctive smell of industrial grade dish detergent that somehow never smelled as though it cleaned followed him out. Bale strode along the cloisters, where Brother Martin laid a hand on his arm. "Welcome back," said Bale's pal, the monk with a thatch of dark hair as tangled as the weeds he attacked in the garden beds.

"Thanks. Any new information on the boy?"

Martin sighed, which always deepened the furrows in his face. "Inconclusive. Back of the skull crushed. Rather impossible for the ME to tell whether it occurred before or after the tumble off the ridge. Looks like it's going down as death by misadventure."

Bale rubbed his face. "I'd say murder is a misadventure, wouldn't you?"

"Oh, the greatest. Go get settled. You'll be pleased to hear you missed every single one of the morning prayers." Bale smiled. Then Brother Martin leaned in. "And your sister, Antony? You know I'm sorry as I can be."

Bale nodded once, tightly. Brother Martin was his closest friend at Burnham Norton, but it was a very old habit of Bale to keep information to himself. Trust, he had found, was highly situational. "The investigation is—what do they say?—moving along."

Brother Martin took a step back, scrutinizing Bale. "I know better than to ask whether you've got a theory of your own."

Bale studied the graceful arch at the end of the east cloister. "It's early days yet," he said with a soft smile.

"Early days yet, that's right," hooted the garden monk. "Another way of saying get your snout out of my trough. You'll tell me when you can."

As Cellarer, Antony had been responsible for the hiding of the Crown. It had made a kind of sense, when Prior Berthold had suggested the task to him. After all, in the most basic way imaginable, storage was lay brother Bale's job at the abbey. Nuts and bolts, cases of altar wine, Q-Tips, toilet paper, cans of creamed corn, and the Crown of Thorns. He, Berthold, and Brother Martin were the only monks who actually knew its hiding place. The Prior had suggested Martin as a third—a safeguard in the event something knocked out the other two—based on an implicit trust he had of the man. A trust Bale had only ever felt for his sister Adrian.

"You'll be wanting to check in with the Prior," said Martin, clapping Bale on the shoulder as he headed toward the abbey door that led to the garden shed. "He's in the office, poring over paperwork in what he called 'Brother Antony's tragic absence.'"

Bale made a grab for his friend's robed arm. "The young monk named Eli. I've got some questions for him."

"Ah," said Martin, narrowing his dark eyes. "He's with me today. I'm saving him from Sebastian. The boy hates the whole silence thing. That one, Eli, has a taste for the careless speech of others. Mind you, he's pretty much trash on my patch, but I can manage. Interesting lad, that one, I can tell you." With a billowing wave, Martin turned away. "I think today I'll tell him we're viewing our weeding as a silent devotion, just to play with his head." He grinned. "Bye, Antony."

Bale watched his friend leave, loping along the cloister. Off to his job as garden monk. At times Bale suspected he himself was a bit of a trespasser in the house of the Lord, among all these genuinely good brothers who toiled at the liturgy and the daily workings of the abbey out of what seemed to their Cellarer a rather threadbare hope of better things to come. Bale had always found himself strangely sentimental about people who sacrificed much for an idea that clung on in their hearts despite the evidence of their senses.

He liked men and women who believed there was something ineluctably beautiful about scrubbing stonework for the glory of a God they would never in this—or any other—lifetime get to see, which was why he chose to lend his talents to a religious community. He liked men and women who made good honest efforts despite outcomes, which was why the figure of Christ still interested him.

Bale let himself into the dorter where the lay brothers and male guests stayed. It was a strange, cool place, always dim regardless of the time of day or the season. Nothing seemed to penetrate the thick stonework right at this place, and sounds were only ever muffled. For Bale, it was a perfect place, this spot where he left behind the public and devotional life of the abbey. This was the place where Bale could always find something cached inside himself that could still surprise him. In that moment, he pushed back into the dim stony source place, hoping for a bolt of insight into the connection between the death of the thief Fintan and the murder of Adrian. Because what connected them, it was clear, was the relic. And now its second theft. But in the space at the foot of the steps to the second floor of the dorter, what Bale found himself thinking about was Val Cameron.

Then he took the stone steps three at a time up to his modest cell on the second floor, where he would shower away his fatigue from the red-eye flight and the train from Norwich, and change back into his brown wool robe that identified him as a member of the Carmelite order. Antony Bale, Cellarer. For everything else about him that he kept strenuously out of sight, there was no order, no robes, no promises rather haphazardly kept.

16

Bale sat down in the upholstered chair motioned to him by the Prior of Burnham Norton Abbey. There he waited in silence for the Prior to set a match to the kindling in the fireplace insert. At seventy, the Prior was a sack of skin draped on a skeleton, a man too studious to pay much attention to meals. Berthold kept his head close shaved and went barefoot as much as possible, in the Carmelite spirit. But none of his scrupulous behavior helped him in terms of warming his meager flesh. The Scotch did. The fire did. And Antony's frequent news of the outside world. All three at once would probably make him fan himself with the most recent issue of *Catholicism Today*.

Berthold sat back on his knees and together they watched the satisfying little sparks and crackles start up. "I like what begins," the Prior said in that beautiful and irrelevant way Bale had always appreciated. "Everything is still ahead, you see." Bale himself was undecided. He liked what flourished and had the capacity to make him senseless, but didn't. "Well?" prompted the Prior as he handed him a double shot of Oban in a souvenir glass from Svenska. Then he raised his own. After a soft clink, each of them sipped. Smacking his lips once, the Prior swung around a chair to face Antony. "What did you learn?"

Bale stared into his drink, then lifted his eyes to his host. "The fact my sister was killed within twenty-four hours of the death of Fintan McGregor tells me there's a single killer at work here."

"Frankly, I find that notion terrifying," he said with a lightness Bale could tell he didn't feel.

"I feel nothing."

The Prior shot him a skeptical look, then stretched his legs out stiffly in front of him. "So it's the Crown." He closed his eyes. "A simple snatch for a collector somewhere in Buenos Aires," he mused, waving his shot glass. "What do you think?"

It was a good question. After a moment, Bale pushed himself out of the Prior's chair and stared at the framed print of Giotto's "Crucifixion" on the wall alongside the fireplace. On the poor head of a bleeding Jesus Christ near death was a Crown of Thorns where the tips of each barb disappeared into flesh. As much the centerpiece of the story as the dying man himself. Through the ages, when it came to pictorial representation, the Crown was outsized, drawn disproportionately big to the scene.

Was that still what was at work behind the double theft in the past week of this holy relic kept hidden by the Carmelites since their days in their first abbey on Mt. Carmel?

Bale opened his own empty hands and stared at them. In the mind of someone willing to kill twice, so far, to possess it, was the Crown for some reason disproportionately large? Finally, he turned to the Prior. "This is no maverick art collector at work here, Berthold."

The Prior challenged him. "Why not?"

Bale shook his head. "A collector hires a thief for a simple smash and grab job, no matter how finessed. No," he said, turning what was left of his drink in his palm, "whoever is at work here, Berthold, hired a killer."

"I'd much rather be dealing with a collector, you know," the Prior said peevishly.

Bale sank back into the blue upholstered chair, gazing into the spreading flames, blue and yellow and red. A flame was never just one color. "We're not." Bale rested his elbows on his knees, then finished off his Scotch. "These killings," he said softly, "are desperate, and intense. As if there's some sort of time pressure at work in the operation, something we don't know about yet."

"Ah, you think we're looking at an operation."

"Yes," said Bale slowly, his heart pounding. "I believe we are."

The Prior slung him a sideways look. "Have you heard anything, Antony, anything in your—"

"Networks? No, not a whisper." The Prior of Burnham Norton Abbey was the only one who knew about Bale's occasional intelligence work. He had to. Without his plausible cover stories, it wouldn't take long for the brothers to get suspicious about those times when Antony Bale was absent, in service to the most ectoplasmic of the spook agencies in the U.S. As an American member of a religious order housed in Europe, he had a certain freedom of movement that carried with it very little notice. Consequently, Bale handled discreet little "maintenance" operations.

Known informally throughout the agency as the Network Administrator, he was sent in when terrorist activities—the Charlie Hebdo attack late in 2014 had been his last big assignment—made agents' anxieties run high, threatening to disrupt the network. Not even Adrian knew. His assignments were a rare indulgence—like a bottle of the finest single malt Scotch, or an accomplished woman who seemed to like his company—that came at opportune times, say when he was pacing entirely too much in his cell.

"Listen, Berthold," he said with energy, "I've got to start with the boy's murder. It's the only way to get closer to understanding why his killer needed the Crown of Thorns specifically, and—" he lifted his hands helplessly, trying to figure out motive, "either killed him in a rage when the boy misplaced it..."

"Or," interrupted the Prior, "in fact, he may have been told to kill the boy regardless."

"Ah," murmured Bale, suddenly infinitely sorry for the boy thief, who had no doubt expected something quite different in the way of a reward. How big was this operation, after all? It struck Bale it could be centered literally anywhere in the world. How would he ever figure it out? He needed more resources than either Val Cameron or an aging monk with a taste for fire and Oban could provide.

When Bale realized he had been holding his breath, he ran his tense hands through what was left of his dark hair and started to pace. He knew then he had to keep it small, had to narrow it down to the murder of a young monk up on the ridge. "Help me think it through, Berthold." The other man nodded curtly, and Bale continued. "No sooner does Fintan McGregor steal the Crown than he misplaces it in a stunning bit of bad luck, for both him and Adrian, and then he gets brained and helped over a cliff."

"The Crown goes home with your sister—"

"Whereupon she's tracked down by the one who got the information from the boy—" Bale suddenly stopped. The pressure in his chest was all he could think about, and maybe it was what the Prior would call a blessing. Better some pain that demands attention than the tendency of the mind to draw the image of Adrian at her desk, marveling over what she had inadvertently brought back from her trip to Norfolk, looking up in her innocence to find a figure suddenly appearing in the doorway. "It's otherwise entirely too coincidental that whoever killed her stole the Crown she pulled from the urn."

"As you say," agreed the Prior. "Too coincidental."

If the boy hadn't stolen the Crown of Thorns for his own mysterious purposes. If he hadn't panicked before he could...do what with it...when his mates were about to find him out. If he hadn't hidden it in a piece of pottery given to Adrian from the Prior as a gift to the Coleman-Witt. If only she had discovered it before leaving the abbey and called in Bale, who could have returned it for safekeeping, and if she hadn't flown back to New York with it on her lap, he imagined, the whole way.

"Keep talking," said the Prior.

"Some questions."

"Go on."

"How did Fintan McGregor know where to find the Crown?"

The Prior of Burnham Norton Abbey jabbed at the logs with a wrought-iron poker. "What else?"

"Who was he working for? Was it the killer?"

Berthold made a face. "Interesting distinction."

Bale whirled to look at him. "Where did they meet, those two?"

"Do you mean—" a slow wave of the hand "—who introduced them?"

"No." Bale raised a hand. "Where did they have discussions? Where did the ill-fated, expendable Fintan conspire with the man who was ultimately his killer?" Bale stopped there. "How are those for our early questions?"

Prior Berthold stood up very straight and walked behind his desk, trailing a hand across the walnut wood stained through the decades from wet cups and glasses, and fugitive cigar ash. When he stopped, he stretched his bony robed arms out straight in front of him, the fingers lightly tapping the desk top. "You're forgetting, I think, the central question to this whole business."

Was it possible? Bale stopped pacing. "Tell me."

The Prior turned his palms upward in a gesture of wide open charity. With a smile, he asked Bale softly, "Why Fintan?"

Why Fintan McGregor. Why a nineteen-year-old boy from a working class background who was considered by his teachers generally smart and good-looking and well-liked.

In a Victorian novel, he would be the Best Boy at school. And in that novel, his interesting character flaw would be his tendency to overreach. When you had so very much going for you, there were no limits. No limits and plenty of ways then to rationalize the mistakes. It was Eli, the small, clever monk who mentioned how pious Fintan was.

Bale felt this was an important addition to the picture of the murdered boy. Well-liked, appealing—after all, when his mates were bounding across the grass to him that awful night and he had to stash the stolen Crown, it was his popularity that put him on the spot.

But where did his piety come into play? Bale sensed from the way Eli described it his piety was something Fintan downplayed. If a popular boy downplayed a trait, it was because what he let his friends see was just the tip of the iceberg.

How far beyond the liturgy they all learned did Fintan

McGregor's knowledge—or passion—really go? Too deep, too wide, for the Best Boy to let it show freely? Where had the boy spent his time away from the abbey? Who had met him, taken the measure of him, and recruited him for some dark purpose the young Fintan had no way to judge clearly?

"I'll find out," said Bale, setting the empty shot glass on the Prior's desk. "And I know where to start."

Berthold grunted. "Are you with us for a while?"

"No. Once I've got at least an outline of the killer, I'm heading back to New York."

The Prior of Burnham Norton Abbey regarded the ceiling with narrowed eyes. "I'll say you're at a convocation of cellarers in the East 40s near the United Nations."

Bale shook his head. "Too much information." The Prior had a tendency to take the bones of a perfectly good cover story and add just enough unnecessary embellishment that it only aroused interest.

"All right, Antony," the Prior warded off the criticism. "You went to a convocation of cellarers in Teaneck, New Jersey."

"Perfect." It was death to envy.

Bale was heading quickly toward the door to the abbey office when the Prior called, "See you at Compline, then," in a way that would not tolerate his absence.

"Yes, right. Compline it is, then."

"And I have a special role in mind for you." He flashed his Cellarer a wicked grin.

Bale winced. "At your service," he said with no particular gusto. "Does it involve a vocal solo?"

The Prior wheeled his desk chair closer to the desk and peered at some papers as though he was looking over a tablet of cuneiforms. "Possibly," he answered, riffling through the stack. "I keep trying to work in a *paso doble* for you, but, alas." At that, Antony Bale made a slight bow. Berthold went on: "We are still just a poor religious order with very little wiggle room in the liturgy."

The two men smiled at each other. "If you could find some,

Berthold," said Bale softly, "then I believe I would be happy in this life forever."

The Prior settled himself and from the stack chose what appeared to be a bill from the local hydro company. Never a pretty sight. "Yes, Antony," murmured Berthold. "I know that's what you believe." Then he gave him one of those fond looks Bale imagined a good father cannot keep from his face when he realizes a beloved son wants to become a sculptor, and not a widget-maker, like himself, instead. "But who," said Berthold quietly, setting his reading glasses in place, "would be your partner?"

17

Bale let the boy Eli drive Brother Martin's old Toyota Tundra pickup truck on their errand together. The young monks referred to the brute as Tunnie, and, to Bale's knowledge, not one of them had ever been enlisted as driver. Until that afternoon when Bale had found the boy raking through a cover crop that had been planted for the winter in one of the distant beds. The boy had the doomed look of a galley slave on his face. Bale had to silently agree: this one was terribly underused. In fact, in ten years' time, Bale might nominate him to replace himself in the *ad hoc* intelligence work.

When he invited Eli to come along in Tunnie—Eli could even drive—to help out Brother Martin by picking up some manure near Mundesley, the rake got dropped, then tripped over, and off they went. As the boy shifted into third, his eyes kept darting from side to side as they tooled along. Bale could tell that the boy behind the scratched wheel of the old pickup was hoping something would dash out in front of them—even a rabbit would do—that would let him test his prowess. Back straight, foot straining to reach the gas pedal, slightly discomfited without his robes...it made Bale sad that for a boy of nineteen in a religious order, driving an old farm truck on a pretext of an errand constituted a wild adventure.

No wonder he and the others, Fintan included until the final night, escaped after the Night Office into the woods to smoke and drink and exchange colorful exaggerations about their sexual experiences back in their former lives. Their lives in struggling neighborhoods where the "calling" to the monastic life often signified security and even a kind of stature. Bale looked away from Eli. They were too young, by him, to be recounting stories of long-ago love like old graybeards by a woodstove.

In sudden astonishment, the boy neatly jolted Tunnie out of the way of a pothole where the winter's ice had done its worst on that patch of road. "Good save," commented Bale, mildly. The boy acknowledged the compliment with a quick, tense nod. He was now on the hopeful lookout for other road hazards, although avoiding a misguided rabbit might still make a nice statement about his regard for life.

"Priestley's Farm, then, is it, Antony?" Eli shot him a quick look.

"Down this road another five kilometers." Since Bale had already given Eli this information, he could tell the boy was hankering for some conversation. So was he, only he was undecided how much to tell the young monk. Trust is the thing in life that shatters completely. And irreparably. What was the least the boy Eli needed to know about his friend Fintan McGregor that he would take Bale's questions seriously? That Fintan had stolen and then misplaced the Crown of Thorns from the Crucifixion and was then murdered, possibly for his carelessness?

All Eli now knew—because Prior Berthold had squelched the suspicions about Fintan's death—was that Fintan had peed in an urn, which he then surreptitiously searched for in his mates' lockers, and fallen off the ridge to his death. From Brother Martin, Bale had learned that the lads were jumpy and hangdog, reassessing a world, Martin thought, where in their simple, young minds, a disrespectful pee leads to a tumble over a cliff. Could have happened to any of them. No, if it could happen to Fintan McGregor—smart, handsome, pious old Fintan—it was for shit sure it would happen to the rest of them, only worse. Whatever that was.

Which was the better innocence for this boy to lose in their next moment together, rattling along in Tunnie on a needless errand? That his mate Fintan was a terrible thief of now historic proportions? Or that the salve of death by misadventure had befallen the Best Boy? Something had happened to him. Not a story wherein what the young monks would see as an act of sin—the terrible theft—would make them have to reconsider what they had all thought they had known about the dead boy. He had fooled them all. Excluded them all. Stolen a holy relic either for gain or fame or—worse yet—just to hurl a grand Fuck You to the abbey where Compline was always lovely and the monks were such regular blokes.

Bale made up his mind. "Eli, we're trying to understand what happened to Fintan that night."

The boy's head whirled to face him, then his eyes turned back anxiously to the road. Bale could see the boy's foot pull back slightly from the gas pedal. "So am I," he said with a catch in his voice. "No one tells us anything." It wasn't a complaint as much as a statement. "Death by misadventure," he snorted, giving Bale a very skeptical look. One that confused Bale. Did the boys somehow know Fintan had been murdered and were a source of information just waiting to be discovered?

"What do you think happened to him, then?" Bale said softly.

Although Eli's eyes were on the road, Bale could tell what the boy was looking at had nothing to do with road hazards. "Fintan had been sneaking around so much lately..."

"How lately?"

They rumbled over a cattle grid. "I'd say the last, oh, month, maybe. I caught sight of him one afternoon in town, when Fintan had mentioned he was off to town to mail a package to his auntie in Leicester.

It was the first any of us had heard of this person, you know what I mean? Then, when I was helping Brother Martin turn over that new garden bed and I swelled up from that bee sting, and Prior Berthold drove me into town, that was when I caught sight of Fintan coming out of the Olde Bandylegs Pub with a girl."

"Who was she?" Bale kept his voice casual.

"That American girl who works there. Her name's Melanie. Word has it she's doing a year abroad at Norfolk."

Finally, thought Bale, a lead. He'd find this girl later. "What else?"

"What else did I see that day?" When Bale nodded, Eli went on quickly. "Oh, I stayed out of sight well enough and watched the girl hand Fintan her bar apron in a way that looked plenty playful. Then the two of them got on a motorbike and went out of town."

"Which way?"

"Toward the beach." Eli bit his lip. "The Vespa," he added gravely, as if all the truth about Fintan's fate resided in this one detail, "was pink."

"I see," murmured Bale.

At which the driver of the farm truck heaved a mighty sigh. "We're pretty sure Fintan was, well—" the boy monk seemed uncomfortable with something—the slang, the image, something "—shagging the American girl."

Bale scratched his brow. "Because he rode a motorbike with her?"

Eli snorted. "Because he kept it a secret. That's the way Fintan was. Not like the others, who have to blab about every dirty thought they've ever had, or let out hints about stealing altar wine. Or like me—" The boy made a sweeping, oratorical gesture, then quickly grabbed the wheel again. "I have no life of sin...either to blab or tease or hide with all my might."

"Eli—" said Bale humorously, about to rumble the idea by his driver that perhaps pride in sinlessness was sin.

"No, really, Antony. I'm just not drawn particularly." The sign just ahead on the right was a matter of local granite and gray, weathered poplar. PRIESTLEY'S FARM was burned professionally into the wood. "Actually," said Eli as he turned smoothly off the road and into the driveway, "I think I'll most likely have to confess tailing Fintan that time, maybe just a week ago. Which way, Antony?"

Eli braked Tunnie, which meant his entire leg was fully extended on the pedal. The gravel drive angled off to the right, toward one set of well cared for white buildings. Whatever lay straight ahead disappeared over a hill that obscured anything beyond.

Antony sat forward, leaning his arm on the dash. "Make a right, Eli." With a roar Tunnie picked up speed and Bale lurched. "What do you mean you tailed Fintan?"

For a minute, the boy fell silent. Bale thought he was regretting the slip. They bumped along—Tunnie's shocks, thought Bale, needed to be replaced—and it was the first time since they climbed into the abbey's farm truck that the young and clever monk beside him seemed less than frank. Then the boy blurted, "It's probably worse than I thought at the time, Antony, now that I think about it, but—" He looked quickly at Antony Bale, his voice suddenly high and trembling. "I really couldn't help myself."

Bale gave him a small smile. "Sin's like that, you understand."

"It's what makes it irresistible, I guess," said the boy darkly. "Devil in a blue dress and all that."

"Or on a pink motorbike."

The boy leaned closer to the wheel, and growled. "Oh, it was nothing like that. I didn't catch them...at it." He rolled his eyes. "There are more sins than that, you know." He shot him a look that reminded Antony of the fourth grade teacher who confiscated his stash of X-Men comics.

"If it's even a sin," Bale put out there lightly. "What did you see, Eli?" He touched the boy's shoulder. "Here's the horse barn. You can pull over."

As Eli inched closer to the proud white barn that seemed to speak to them in muffled whinnies, he was shaking his head in disbelief, it seemed, at his own craven behavior. "It was that day I saw Fintan skulking around corners. Like I said, he'd been acting strange and, oh, aloof. At that moment I thought, now this is getting ridiculous, and I was going to tail him and find out what he was up to." The boy jerked Tunnie to a stop.

"What was he up to?" asked Bale.

Eli turned to face Antony and slung a companionable arm over the back of the seat. Even in the midafternoon sun on that April day, shielded from them by the horse barn, Bale could tell the boy's eyes sparkled. With a fond shove at Bale, Eli laughed, "Fintan was following you."

After he delivered Eli and a load of Priestley's manure to Brother Martin, who waggled his long, strong fingers in glee, Bale headed to Sidestrand to the Olde Bandylegs Pub. From the little more Eli had told him, he realized how Fintan McGregor had discovered the secret cache where the monks safeguarded the Crown of Thorns. And Bale himself had unwittingly led the little thief right to it. As Cellarer it was his routine to make the rounds of the abbey's treasures on the first of the month. Truly, it was a bit like his and Adrian's great Aunt Cecilia who overvalued her Depression glass and Hummel figurines, because she believed in her kindly old heart that if she treasured something—Apple Tree Boy was her favorite—it was one of a kind and priceless.

For the most part, the abbey treasures were not particularly either old or valuable. A silver communion plate presented by the Vatican to the first prior back in 1924 when the Burnham Norton Abbey was rebuilt. Mass-produced altar linens from a cotton mill in Leeds back in 1867. Still, on the first of every month, Antony the Cellarer dropped by the storage places for each of the treasures. Kind of a roll call. Just to be sure no mice, for instance, had gotten to what Prior Berthold called the priceless altar linens, or that the communion plate Brother Sebastian particularly loved for its grapevine decoration was tarnishing. Or that the Crown of Thorns was undisturbed in its hidden place.

Antony Bale went down into the crypt whose single occupant was the first head of Burnham Norton since the rebuild. At the far end of the small, dank room where they would really have to take a harder line against mold one of these days was the single coffin on a stone plinth, and there, just two rows up from the floor, was a cache. To check on the Crown, he had to kneel, carefully pulling out the two gray stones that looked no different from any of the others, set them aside, and draw out the soft purple and gold velvet bag that protected the relic. On that day nearly two weeks ago, Bale was pretty sure he had opened the flap and gently pulled the object partially out of the protective bag.

Today the cache was empty.

It must have been that day Fintan followed him to the crypt, listened while Bale jimmied the two stones from their places, holding himself carefully out of sight. In the dim light that somehow only intensified the smell of ages and decay, the boy must have held his breath as he witnessed the drawing out of the holiest relic in Christendom. How could he have kept from exclaiming? And how could he possibly have known that what felt like soaring victory was really the first step in the inevitable direction of his own violent death? And Adrian's?

Misadventure never shows itself until it's too late.

For the first time since his sister's murder for the stolen Crown, Bale felt strangely responsible. He must have gotten too damn complacent in his monthly treasure rounds. It had never struck him he was being followed. Maybe he trusted—that word—the monks, the brothers, the formidable walls of Burnham Norton Abbey so dangerously and completely that he in his carelessness had set in motion the circumstances that had led to Adrian's murder. He shuddered as he pulled up to the pub and rested his head against Tunnie's steering wheel.

18

Bale found Melanie Ruskin stacking beer glasses in the Olde Bandylegs Pub in Sidestrand. A pink Vespa, apparently the wheels of all the truly great sinners, was parked outside, looking docile enough. To the credit of Olde Bandylegs, there wasn't a flat screen TV anywhere in sight. It was a traditional kind of pub, one where a wheezy old setter dreaming in the corner was more welcome than the field exploits of Manchester United. Bale realized it was a brew pub with a couple of homegrown lagers and milds. The Olde Bandylegs label featured an illustration of an old man and older dog, both bowlegged, walking away down a country lane.

It must have been in one of the old wood booths with embossed backs crudely depicting the Norfolk coast that Adrian spied a guy she had written about girlishly in her trip journal. Maybe if something had happened between them she would have delayed her return to New York, and no hidden Crown would have found its way into her hands, and she would still be alive. If, Bale wondered, there was such a thing as destiny, could it really hinge on something as capricious as a fleeting moment in a Norfolk pub? If the guy had stared at her one second longer, if one of them had taken the initiative, would Bale still be taking his sister dancing?

The American girl named Melanie Ruskin wore a yellow pullover and khaki skirt that hit just above her knee. A safe, collegiate look for a girl with dyed black hair in a severe cut with a bright blue hank tucked behind an ear. A line of silver studs mounted her right earlobe, and around her neck was a lanyard with a vapor pen attached. She had large green eyes that tried to look less large under a spray of sandy eyelashes, and a nose that was just a little too pert to work with the stabs she made at an alternative look. At what Bale took for twenty years old, Melanie Ruskin was coping with being cute when she longed to be edgy, retro punk, unsettling.

As he slid onto a bar stool and she gave him a quick look and then a double take, which he could tell annoyed her about herself, he was close enough to catch the brushing of fine powder across her tight, pale cheeks, and the carefully plucked eyebrows. A college girl doing a term or a year abroad pushing all four corners of the envelope of looks, a whole lot safer than nearly anything else. She'd be the girl with the blue bangs and the pink Vespa. The girl who could get it on with—gasp—a monk. She could be that girl. Keep them all guessing. Including herself.

Gliding silently across from Bale, the bartender was a beefy forty-something guy with a surprisingly high voice and a problem with blinking. "Help you?"

Bale eyed the drafts. "Pint of Wee People's Jig, please." On the shelves along the mirrored wall behind the bar, the Jig was a lager, and to the label showing the bandy-legged old man and dog, a leprechaun—also bandy-legged—had joined the walk down the country lane.

"Our signature brew." With five solemn blinks, the bartender drew the draft in ceremonial silence.

Melanie set glasses on a tray and started toward the kitchen. "Crispin, I'm off."

"Right, Mels."

As she started to shoulder her way through the door, Bale heard her humming a piano étude he remembered from his own lessons thirty years before.

"Melanie?" he called after her as Crispin carefully set down the pint of Jig and glided over to serve an old man with a black watch plaid muffler wound up to his chin.

"Yeah?" She turned, her large green eyes settling on him. Bale was wearing jeans, a light sweater and the jacket that was known around town as "abbey wear." Navy blue with the gold insignia of Burnham Norton. He hated it, but it was what he invariably wore when he wanted to hit a particular note with outsiders: a small piece of abbey wear would make him seem trustworthy but not too terribly set apart. Not too intimidating. For a monk, a regular guy. But with Melanie Ruskin he wasn't sure what registered. Besides his age.

"I'm Antony Bale," he told her as she moved closer, setting down the tray, "from the abbey."

She cocked her head, a wary look crossing her face. "Okay..."

Bale took a quick sip of the Wee People's Jig and motioned toward the empty stool beside him. "Can I buy you a drink? I need to talk to you about Fintan McGregor." At that, the girl's shoulders jolted, like a long and weary exhale was finally letting go of her. But she didn't move. To Bale, she looked unbearably young in that moment, before a time of blue bangs and an earlobe stacked with silver studs. "I know he was your friend," Bale added quietly, "and I'm trying to figure out what happened to him. I'm hoping you can help."

Melanie Ruskin chewed her lip, then came to a decision. With a tense nod, she swung a leg over the bar stool next to Bale and took a seat, tucking her scuffed shoes behind a rung. "Crispin," she called to the bartender, "I'll have my lime cordial with a water chaser." To Bale, she slid a quick look. "I'm my own designated driver," she explained, pushing up the sleeves of her yellow sweater. A pink tattoo curved its way across her left wrist. *Chapter Forty-Two*, over a stylized ocean wave and a breaching white whale. Inked in a place Melanie would see throughout her day, rasping along on her pink Vespa or setting down pints in front of customers or tucking into her mac and cheese. Bale felt he had just been handed the secret code.

He pointed in a small way to the tat. "*Moby Dick.*"

A beat. But it had won him a closer look by the girl next to him. "Yes," she breathed, waiting to see what else he would flourish unbidden in front of her startled and staring eyes. Somehow the quality of her disclosures about poor thieving Fintan would depend on what kind of connection he could make. What would a smart, literary girl, twenty years old and yearning for identity, with blue bangs and multiple piercings and a dark side she flogs to offset her pert nose, find meaningful enough to wear inked on her wrist? Chapter Forty-Two was right about the place in the book for Melville's clanging note of existential terror, so Bale took a shot. Turning from her, he made himself gaze thoughtfully into the Wee Folks Jig. Finally, he uttered, "'The Whiteness of the Whale.'"

"Yes," said Melanie. "Of course."

Bale narrowed his eyes at nothing in particular, drawing on smoky college memories. "'A dumb blankness full of meaning.'"

In silence the two of them, their forearms braced against the bar, drank companionably. His thumbs slid through the cold condensation on his glass. It was a good beer, if a little on the hoppy side. Out of the corner of his eye he noticed Melanie tucking her blue bangs behind her ear with trembling fingers. He could tell she was going to try him on something simple first. "So you're a monk?"

He nodded without looking directly at her. "A lay brother."

"What's the difference?"

He smiled at her. "The scope and quality of the vows."

She chugged enough lime cordial to add a good helping of water to the glass. "Plus you talk."

"We're not a silent order."

Melanie Ruskin grunted. "Sounds like a nice gig. Food, shelter, hanging with your friends all the time."

"Well," said Bale, "there's the whole God part of it too."

"Oh, I suppose," she muttered.

"Ah." Bale searched the aged tin ceiling of the pub, bringing out the only other line from Melville that he remembered, maybe because it pinned him, writhing, on the specimen board of his own mind. "'The colorless, all-color of atheism.'"

Melanie turned sharply toward him. "No," she corrected him,

with a pout that suddenly stripped her of the last five years, "not necessarily." Then: "Not at all necessarily." With that, she began to pick at the label on the lime cordial bottle with a ragged fingernail. "At least I'm still trying to figure it out," she blurted. Both Bale and the girl realized at the same moment how it sounded— an abbey full of monks had long since given up the noble effort—and they looked closely at each other. "Sorry," she said, her lips barely moving.

Bale shot her a small smile. "Believe me, doubt slinks around many of us." Then he shrugged. "Maybe it's what sharpens faith."

"Could go either way, Mr. Bale," she observed serenely.

"Could go either way."

Melanie seemed to relax and enjoyed a long, slow sip, her pert little nose high in the air. She seemed to be considering, and Bale let her take her time. It was, he sensed, the only way.

Finally, she burped discreetly and stared at herself in the mirror behind the bar. "Fintan was kind of like that," she told him. "Sharpening his faith on something, but I couldn't tell you what." Turning to face Bale, her sweater tugged across her breast. "It wasn't doubt, that much I know."

"What makes you say that?"

She sat up straighter, restlessly crossing her legs. "Oh, I'd say Fintan McGregor was more about absolute certainty than much of anything else, sad to say, but," here she shook her head, "even so, he wasn't someone who needed to persuade you, if you know what I mean. Whatever he believed, he wasn't the kind who wanted to," she squeezed her hands together imploringly, "share it with you." Bale let out a laugh. "In fact," the girl went on, "I'd say he very much wanted to keep it all to himself, no sharesies. Except for the occasional slip. Do you know," she dropped her voice, shooting a quick look around the empty pub, "it wasn't until the third time we were together before I even knew he was a monk." The word *monk* came out sounding a lot like *psychopath*. "It really kind of freaked me out, to tell you the truth. Then there was just one more time after that, when I had pretty much decided I couldn't take it anymore—"

"Take what?"

"Oh, the sneaking around, the secret meetings, what he called our 'trysts' out in some damn field or the other—"

"Fields?"

"I've got a tent some locals let me pitch when I can't take living with the fine Norfolk family who puts me up. Some space, know what I mean?"

"Right."

"And Fintan was kind of a drama queen, if you really want to know. If he wasn't avoiding our being seen together, he was letting little hints drop that he was destined for great things. Things he was working on in secret. Prophecies, yada yada."

Bale kept a straight face. "Any specifics?"

Melanie wiggled her fingers mid-air. "No, but I could tell if I pressed him he'd spill the beans." She sniffed. "Here's how I saw it. I wanted a fling with a Brit, right, something simple and fun I could share with my friends over Mojitos when we all got back from our study abroad. But Fintan was way more intense than I bargained for. Everything mattered so damn much to him it finally wore me out. Even," she added, as she clinked Bale's glass of Wee People's Jig, "even if I was the least of all the things that mattered."

He said softly, "Did that hurt?"

She gave it her world-weary best. "No, some affairs are like that."

The sagacity of the twenty-year-old.

He was careful to nod quietly when she slung him a look, gauging his reaction. Or maybe just trying out the theory. Then she made a quick study of him and seemed to decide that whatever Bale might have to say on that score, it couldn't possibly be from personal experience. "But that was it for the secret meetings." He wanted to keep her talking.

She looked puzzled. "What do you mean?"

"You mentioned your secret meetings with him."

Her head pulled back, one hand clamping her chest. "Not with me. We were strictly about what he called 'shagging' in my tent in a field, and that was about all the privacy we could find, what with his no money and my tight budget."

"Then..." Bale gave her a sidelong look, trying to follow the conversation.

She leaned closer with a funny little smile. "No, his secret meetings with some guy."

Bale kept it casual. "Fintan ever mention a name?"

"No, but to hear him need to clear out of the tent to get to a rendezvous with this dude, you'd swear it was totally like *Mission: Impossible* stuff." Melanie, thought Bale, was closer than she could ever possibly know to the truth. Stealing a holy relic for what Bale was coming to believe was some dark purpose devised by others—a dark purpose made darker when the boy was hurled over the cliff— had, in the end, turned out to be a final impossible mission for the pious young monk. Melanie went on, imitating the dead Fintan: "'I must go, he's meeting me,' that sort of thing. Really preoccupied."

"I wish you had heard a name."

Her face fell. "It wasn't really misadventure, was it, Mr. Bale?" And then, as if he might not have caught her meaning, "Fintan's death?" She chewed her lip and, past the blue bangs and tattoos and multiple piercings, there was such fragile sadness in the girl's face that Bale felt himself slump.

He wanted suddenly with a kind of raging desperation at the world to pack her off—to pack them all off—to someplace safe where they could contemplate the likes of Melville and God and each other in perfect peace and safety.

"I don't believe so, Melanie."

And as she tried not to break down, all she managed to say was, "I guess it all caught up with him finally, then, didn't it?"

"At nineteen. Just a boy in a monastery. Not such a long life. Not such a far way for...whatever it was...to come." As he watched the girl with the pink Vespa try to shake it off, he asked, "Did Fintan ever tell you anything concretc about the guy from the secret meetings? How he looked, how he sounded, how he dressed—"

She brightened. "No, but I caught sight of him one time."

Bale set down his glass. In that moment, even the hoppy little Jig held no interest. "Tell me," was all he said.

"I was driving us back to the pub one time and suddenly Fintan's clutching me tighter, right? I tell him quit it, he's strangling me, and he gets up close to my ear and practically spits in it telling me, 'That's him. There. Out there, crossing the field.' So I looked and caught sight of the guy crossing the field, but away from us, wearing one of those sleeveless field jackets with lots of pockets and a khaki colored Tilley hat. I know because it's exactly the one I want but it costs a bundle."

"What else do you remember?"

"I asked Fintan where's the guy going, and Fintan said all he knew was that he was living kind of rough, maybe in a tent like us, but not to ask him anymore because he wasn't at liberty to say." Melanie smiled. "That's the way he talked, sort of stilted but in a charming kind of way. 'Not at liberty to say.'"

Where could Bale go with it? "And that was the only time you saw this guy?" A one-time chance sighting wasn't going to get him any farther in the investigation. Even if Melanie had seen more of the mystery man of Fintan McGregor's secret meetings, there was no proof he was involved with the boy's death. Nothing to say a man striding across a perfectly public field wearing a Tilley hat and a sleeveless vest was up to anything at all criminal. Just a tourist spending a beautiful April day in Norfolk doing a walkabout. Frustrated, he gave the bar a kick.

"Actually," Melanie said, "I did see him one more time. At Olde Bandylegs."

Bale turned so quickly he nearly overturned his glass. "When was this?"

She mused, "Oh, week and a half ago, maybe. Fintan wasn't around. The place was crowded, and I overheard these two guys talking just down the way from where you're sitting right now. One was old Mr. Devlin, a retired lawyer of some sort, from Norwich, likes his Jameson's, and the other was...Fintan's guy."

"What were they talking about?"

She lifted her eyebrows. "Birds," she said with a little shrug. "Fintan's guy was a birder, it turned out, from what he was telling old Mr. Devlin, who kept pressing him for more info just to keep the conversation going, I could tell. And Fintan's guy was going on about shrikes and warblers and hawks and whatnot, so I couldn't help but listen. How he was tramping around Norfolk recording the mating behavior of the Red-backed Shrike, right?"

Bale couldn't see where she was going, but suddenly Melanie messed up her blue bangs with both hands in pure enjoyment. "And?" was all Bale could say.

"Ah, Mr. Bale," she laughed, "it's always fun when you know someone's full of shit, isn't it? Like when you really know for sure, like poor Fintan and his faith and his mission impossible. I knew this guy was no birder."

Bale felt dazed. "What makes you say that?" he managed to get out.

With that, Melanie raised both her arms straight overhead in a quick stretch. "I'm a Zo major back home," she explained. "Zoology. Heading toward marine biology, probably cetology," she was speaking so rapidly Bale could hardly keep up, "hence the Melville, right? But I get my share of birds. And about Fintan's guy, no matter how cool the Tilley hat, which between you and me he was using as some kind of costume, I can tell you—" she motioned to a hovering Crispin for another round of lime cordial with a water chaser "—I can tell you for shit sure he couldn't tell a woodcock from," she gave it a quick think, then sang out, "his own."

19

New York

By the end of the day, when Val emerged from the Flatiron Building with a sigh that may have fractured a rib or two, the wind had picked up and what clouds she could see over Broadway were gathering, blotted by the sky into one general overcast. Even though she had switched out of her heels and slipped on a pair of sensible Keens, she teetered as she set off uptown in one of her rare spurts of exercise. Bad day to decide to hoof it home. Bale had left a cryptic voicemail message that he was beginning to think it was all his fault. He had just gotten back to the city—call him—he'll fill her in. There was the wryness in his voice that was coming to sound familiar to her, but there were so many pauses in that simple message that the only thing that could explain it, to her mind, was pain. How could Adrian's murder, and possibly the boy Fintan's, in any way be Bale's fault?

She shouldered her way through the crowd crossing Madison Avenue as she headed east to Lexington. Then there was the meeting with Killian. A book on scandals in the craft beer biz. He held out the promise of murder, intrigue, industrial espionage, and deep deceit. As he sat there across from her in his tight jeans and stone-washed denim shirt, he sipped something mysterious in a Starbucks cup and agreed to her terms: a two-page overview, table of contents, plus two sample chapters. By agreeing, what he gave her was a slow nod. Whether he thought she was being utterly reasonable or a complete piece of editorial shit, she had no way of knowing—but that was typical of her time in Killian's company.

He had the scrappy look of a Hollywood action hero. Harrison Ford with a crooked tooth. Bruce Willis who took maybe one too many fights out the back, for real. He looked so damned artless she suspected what she was looking at was really the highest form of artfulness and that she, Val Cameron, full-time editor and sometime sap, was just another conquest. On the bright side, a conquest very far down the hall from any bed. And then, as she had a flash of an image of his short, shaggy dark blond hair touching all the tenderest parts of her, she wondered if that was indeed the bright side.

The guy unsettled her. So she circled the wagons.

And he knew it. So she stacked the circled wagons row upon row and shot him a look over her own Starbucks cup—what could be less mysterious than an Americano?—that dared him to leap. When he licked some foam off his lips—she liked to think it was from a cappuccino and not something either inherent to Killian or just a product of the fuggy air in her closed office—she neatened up a stack of bookmarks that were already perfectly stacked.

"You interest me, Cameron," he had said softly, his dark gray eyes running their own itinerary across her face and shoulders, looking, it struck her, for soft spots.

With deliberate slowness, she pushed away the bookmarks and looked him right in the eye. "I don't have to interest you, James, to be your editor. On the contrary," she went on, pushing back her chair to signal the end of the meeting, "you have to interest me." On the one hand, she didn't want to release even a dram of ambiguity into the air. Not on that score. As she stood up with as much grace as possible, she saw him shoot her a swift and troubled look, then gone, like sunlight crossing a cobweb. Now you see it, now you don't, a whole world of enterprise and entrapment.

Somehow she kept a straight face as she motioned James Killian, who slung a light-colored jacket over his shoulder, to the door. She had unsettled him. If Ivy had been there at that moment, she would have fist-bumped her. Suddenly Words on Fire's scribbling action hero stepped in front of her, effectively blocking his own exit. In an instant she took in a tattoo peeking out from the open collar of his shirt, inked initials just below his collarbone. She took in his long torso and perfect height for someone just as tall as she was, with or without heels. She took in some rough old business on his face that might make more interesting telling than scandals in the beer trade. And she took in a patchouli smell that took her to a bazaar in Burma or someplace she'd never in this lifetime see. On a single breath, she said, "Something else, James?"

A beat. "A drink?"

"It's ten a.m." Valjean, ever practical.

He smiled. "I meant later."

"I've got a full work day," she said, when that wasn't really the point, "and I don't think it's a good idea." Was there an opportunity to slip around him?

He looked mocking. "We can talk business."

"We can do that here." She sounded breathless.

"Not what I meant," Killian added with a short laugh. Then one arm went to her waist, gently eased her aside, and opened her office door. His fingers lightly brushed her jaw. "Maybe another time."

Beyond track changes, she had no skills for this man. "There's all the time in the world," she said with a false brightness, hardly knowing what she was saying. At that precise moment in time all she wanted was to get to her eleven a.m. meeting with the guy in human resources about hiring an assistant for Ivy.

"That is true," James Killian told her. As he leaned close to Val, she stood perfectly still.

"Don't cross the line," she warned him, her voice low.

"The problem with me is," he whispered, "I never even see the line." Then he kissed her on the cheek in a way that made a slow and disturbing statement and was gone.

Val got ten blocks before she knew she was no good for the next twenty, and walked slowly down the subway steps, hanging tightly to the railing. Nothing more from Cleary on Adrian's murder, no other call from Bale to enlighten or explain the earlier one...and a meeting with James Killian that made her poor office feel more like an antechamber either to Hell or a room at a Motel 6 somewhere off the Jersey Turnpike. If she didn't think Killian's *Plumb Lines* or buzzy beer book was going to land her at the molten top of the publishing heap for even just a little while, she would seriously consider handing him off to her seventy-something gay colleague.

At her stop, she propelled herself out of the crowded rush-hour car and scuffed quickly up the steps to 51st Street. Suddenly she had a hankering—must have been Killian's power of suggestion—for a tall Sapporo beer and a regular sushi dinner at Sushi You. On the chance she was free, she'd give Aunt Greta a call. Making their customary trades of eel for yellowtail sounded to Val like just about all she could handle. "Evening, *carissimo*," she called out to the doorman loud enough to get him to pop an earbud as she passed.

"*Buona notte, Signorina*," he said, clutching his heart lightly with the exaggerated affection they had both grown to enjoy.

Alone in the refurbished elevator—mirrors and brass trim had for some reason seemed to the landlord like a proud upgrade—she sank back against the wall and closed her eyes. Down the fifth floor hall to the left was 5-B, her home for nearly a dozen years. The thick, carpeted corridor sucked away noise like a blotter, which helped with the overly loud Pandora station yowling at her that Jumpin' Jack Flash was a gas, gas, gas, courtesy of her stoned Stones-loving neighbor in 5-A. Two key turns and she stepped inside her very own two-bedroom apartment, sniffing the heady homemade pomodoro sauce seeping like Bolognese ectoplasm from Mrs. Dellarosa in 5-C. As the keys slid from Val's hand into the milk glass swan candy dish that had belonged to the grandmother she had never known, Val stood very still.

Something was off.

In two seconds, she knew it was her.

Not even reveling with Greta at Sushi You, where Japanese was the first language, would revive her. Adrian was dead, but Val still had to go to work and cosset authors who got weirder by the year. Adrian was dead, and Val still had Verizon and Visa and Con Ed bills to pay. Adrian was dead, and no amount of sleuthing could help her deal with her pain, let alone Bale's. There were still Americanos and yellowtail and the reliably heart-clutching doorman in the world, and she thought maybe those things should offset the rest, but at 6:23 on that particular day, they did not.

In the spare bedroom, she kicked off her shoes and headed for her small, burled maple secretary to stick her State Farm homeowner's policy premium in the tortoiseshell tray—also from the unknown grandmother—that she used for bills. "Maybe it's time to call Tali," she muttered. Although damned if she could sort out all the present situations. Val was at that moment in time incapable of triaging anything new in what had become her life over the past several days.

As her hand reached to pull down the front of the secretary, something she did daily, what with her iPad and bills and the printed out manuscript of whatever Ivy had passed on to her from the slush pile, she pulled it back. Hardly breathing, Val leaned closer to inspect the point of the intersection between the part of the desk that folds down and the frame itself.

Something was off, and—her heart started pounding—it wasn't her after all. She kept the fold-down front of her antique secretary always just a little bit ajar. Over the years something in the frame had warped just enough to make the shelf shut tight when closed all the way, nearly impossible to open without shaking the whole piece of furniture.

Val had lived with it for too long, until one day she had gripped the sides and yanked hard enough that she broke off a hinge. An expensive trip to an antique restoration service made her come up with another method of getting into her desk: if she left the fold-down shelf just the slightest ajar, no problem. And it had become her habit. She knew to a centimeter just how close to completely shut she could push it before incurring another trip to the restorers.

And yet here it was, completely shut up tight.

Her first instinct was to jimmy it open, hinges be damned, just to see what else was wrong. But her hands seemed to lose all feeling as they approached the desk. She felt twitchy with the need to see what was inside—or what should have been inside and was now missing—but she needed to be able to show the desk to Bale and Cleary, without having disturbed a thing.

Then her eyes settled on the Murano Millefiori paperweight on the side table under the window that looked out over Second Avenue. It had been her mother's, and Val used it to control the overflow paperwork. She loved the paperweight; it was classic and colorful with its glass-blown bouquet of tiny buds. But in only one position from where she'd glance over from her desk were the slender, glass-blown stems of the buds visible. With the slightest turn in either direction, they disappeared, and all she would see was a profusion of buds.

Val sat down hard in her desk chair, just to be sure, and stared at the jumble of papers on the side table. She was pretty sure the table itself hadn't been moved. Or the papers. But all she could see in the Murano paperweight were the buds. Slowly, Val walked to the table, moving in a semicircle until the stems appeared. The paperweight had been turned a full 180 degrees. The stems were now facing her window five stories up from Second Avenue, catching what was left of the late afternoon light. To be fair, she could tell they looked better that way, but she needed them to face her as she sat working at her desk. For now, she knew better than to touch them. Better than to touch anything in a home that had been violated.

Val spun, wondering what else the intruder had touched. Or handled. Or taken. But she damn well didn't want to spend one minute more in a place that now looked completely unfamiliar to her. Whoever had broken in had to be a pro with a slick set of lock picks. Not so much as a mark on the front door. Right now, without looking for further evidence, she knew that if it hadn't been for the desk and paperweight, she might never have known someone had been there.

In the bathroom, she swept a few items into a cosmetic bag, and quickly pulled an ivory-colored retro dress with a fitted bodice and full skirt from her closet and a clean pair of underwear from her dresser and dropped them into a raffia tote in the shape of a scallop shell with Key West emblazoned on one side and The Conch Republic on the other. For a bad moment, she stared at her things and wondered if his hands had fingered them, deciding, maybe, what to take, what to leave. Fighting a rush of nausea, Val flung her purse into the raffia tote and bolted toward her front door. Outside. Outside she'd figure out what to do. She grabbed her keys from the swan, locked her door behind her, and ran to the elevator.

Call the cops, she thought as she darted out of the elevator on the ground floor. No doorman at his stand. Had he seen anything? Seen anybody? There he was, helping her arthritic neighbor from 4-C into a cab, hanging on to his cane with the silver dragon's head until he was safely inside. Call the cops. No, call Aunt Greta. It was Greta who would tip some rum into a cup of steaming cocoa, tuck her in on the pull-out couch, and tell Val one more time how she and her sister Claire, Val's mother, had borrowed a boyfriend's white Delta 88 and driven all the way to Mobile, Alabama to register black voters. Claire was just eighteen, and Greta sixteen, and their folks had had fits, but let them go.

She could sleep at Greta's.

But she couldn't ignore what had just happened.

And maybe calling Cleary would be the second thing she would do as she pulled out her phone at a fast walk up 51st with no idea where she was headed. She'd have to call the cops, because even though Val felt her body shrink at the thought, she knew in some small part of her the only reason her apartment had been broken into had something to do with Adrian. Adrian and the stolen Crown. Adrian's murder. Adrian's phone, beside the Crown, the only other thing stolen from the crime scene. The phone with no passcodes. The phone with her friend Val Cameron's name in the contacts. Match that up with the last call Adrian had made—to Val—then the killer knew about her.

Knew how to reach her. Somehow, how to find her.

Had Val Cameron become someone's loose end?

She stood on the corner of Third Avenue and stared at her phone. Any minute now she'd begin to cry, but before that time she had a call to make. There was only ever one call to make, she could see that now as she looked around her, wondering if she was being followed. The killer felt a couple of important steps ahead of her and the day had suddenly turned cold. She pressed the number and waited.

"Val?"

"Somebody broke into my apartment," she told Antony Bale before her throat got too tight to talk. "I'm scared."

"Did you call the cops?"

"Not yet."

"Is there a coffee shop nearby? Or a bar?"

Val did a slow half turn. "There's BXL East," she said into her phone, "on 51st, south side of the street."

"I'll meet you there, Val, in twenty minutes." Then: "Maybe sooner, depending on the cabs, okay?"

The light changed and the crowds on the curb hustled across, barely avoiding each other in the crush. "Where are you? Should I meet you somewhere else?" Narrowly nosing her way around a small Ryder truck, which she managed to buff to a shine with her skirt, Val loped to the south side across the street toward the bar.

His voice softened. "I'm at Adrian's."

"I can come over," she offered, passing the bar's sidewalk seating and grabbing the door handle. "I can help." It suddenly seemed terrible beyond words that Bale was working alone in Adrian's apartment, just beginning the long, painful sifting through his sister's belongings. All Val could picture was a peculiar heaviness to everything her beloved Adrian had left behind. The Netsuke honey pot man on her teak bookshelf. The red and gold silk shawl from a bazaar in what the stubbornly classical Adrian enjoyed calling Constantinople. The framed seventy-eight vinyl of the "Dixie Jass Band One-Step" recorded on the Victor label. A wildly colorful signed lithograph by Paul Jenkins. A stack of napkins a ten-year-old Adrian had kept as a final souvenir from the Automat the week before it closed for good. Paper, vinyl, ivory, silk—everything felt ponderously the same without Adrian, strangely both priceless and worthless all at the same time.

"No, stay put, Val. We're going back to your place."

And that was definitely the bad news. "My place?"

"Let's see what else he was doing," was all Bale said before he ended the call in the middle of saying goodbye.

20

It was all scrupulously small talk from the BXL East bar back to Val's place. Bale was wearing the same long dark gray coat he had been wearing the day they met. Tucked under one arm was Adrian's red and silver thermal lunch bag he and Val had removed from the scene of the crime. In the lobby, Val was grateful Bale didn't catch the goofy look the doorman flashed her, along with two thumbs up, as they headed toward the elevator. As the two of them stopped in front of her apartment and she fumbled her keys, Bale laid a hand on her arm and shook his head. Wasn't going in the whole point to this exercise? Val waited for an explanation.

Bale unzipped Adrian's lunch bag, drawing out a periwinkle blue pair of her wool winter gloves that Val recognized. With a wry look, Bale drew them on, flexing his fingers, and then he spoke quietly against her ear. "Slip off your shoes. Once we're inside," he jerked his head toward the door, "no talking." With that, he set a finger against his lips, and deftly pushed his way out of his own shoes. She did the same. Then he smiled tightly at Val and held out a hand for her house keys. Bale noiselessly unlocked her front door, pushed it open, and stepped aside.

Val slipped by him and looked anxiously around the foyer. When she turned around, Bale had already shut the door with just the merest of soft clicks, and stood momentarily getting the lay of the land. He eyed the kitchen, which didn't seem to interest him, and stood scanning the furniture in her living room. Was he looking for other obvious signs of a break-in? Then he pressed his lips together, coming to some sort of decision, and with an utterly silent grace strode down the short hall to the bedrooms. Val followed.

When he headed into her bedroom, Val was grateful she had made her bed, and that the warm gray walls and glossy white woodwork made this room—for her money—the prettiest in the entire apartment. After she and Wade Decker had broken up—or drifted apart—or whatever it was they did that signaled the end, she had redecorated, even going so far as to buy a beautiful, minimalistic oak platform bed. Which, of course, necessitated new bedding. Which, of course, led to a new set of framed Klimt prints that harmonized it all. Now there was Antony Bale, lightly running a gloved hand under the overhanging lip of the nightstand. Then examining the underside of the rather opaque lampshade.

As he moved past her in the doorway, he pointed with a grim smile to the second bedroom where she had told him about the telltale secretary desk and the turned Murano paperweight. He went right up to the desk and set his hands on either side of the front that was now firmly closed up tight. With a quick glance at Val, he moved to the side table and crouched low enough to check out her story about the disturbed paperweight. A small nod.

She could tell he was staring at the Crate and Barrel lamp on the credenza against the long wall. Here, too, he lightly ran gloved fingers along the overhanging undersides of the desk, the side table, the credenza. When he bent slowly to look up under the lampshade, Val saw his eyebrows shoot up. With great care his right hand felt up inside the lampshade, made a short, fast movement, and returned to view. Between two of his fingers, Bale held up what looked like a small piece of metal, maybe one square inch in diameter. When she opened her hands helplessly at him, he tapped his ear, and she suddenly understood.

It was a bug.

Whoever had broken into her apartment had bugged it.

But why?

Val felt a chill.

Bale gave her a long look with sad, narrowed eyes. She had to look away. But she was aware he had apparently unzipped the thermal lunch bag before she had even met up with him, because now all he had to do was noiselessly draw back the soft lid and set the bug inside the insulated space. Clearly he didn't want to risk the rasp of the zipper, so he lowered the lid into place, then carried the bag by the bottom. *Let's go*, he mouthed at Val, letting her lead the way, barefoot, back through her apartment. While she locked up and slipped on her Keens, he drew out his iPhone, tapped to a playlist, and blasted U2 next to the lunch bag. During the racket, he zipped it up, then stuffed Adrian's periwinkle blue winter gloves into his pockets.

The two of them rode in silence down to the first floor.

Bale looked preoccupied, carrying the bug removal thermal bag by the handle. All Val felt was tense and hungry, staring at the initials penned into the finish of the sleek metal finish of the elevator. The seductive aroma of Mrs. Dellarosa's Bolognese sauce receded by the time the door slid open and Bale waited for Val to alight. And she alighted in a way that felt very far from light. At least when she was mucking around up in the Canadian Northwoods looking to sign a writer of space junk thrillers to a publishing contract, running into a black bear was her greatest fear. But once a barge operator told her a bear could pretty much be chased off by banging together a couple of metal pots, she had a plan. And it didn't involve a slew of professional lock picks, some sophisticated ruse to get by the doorman, diabolically imperceptible care in going through her stuff, and state-of-the-art electronic surveillance equipment.

When they emerged onto the street, Bale took a quick look around, grabbed Val by her upper arm and jerked his head in the direction of Second Avenue, beating the light just as a lurching cab came bearing down on them. There at the corner of 51st and Second was a half-full trash can. With no hesitation, Bale dropped Adrian's thermal lunch bag that was really her daily purse into the can, where it sank out of sight. His hand still on her arm, he gave it a squeeze. "I'm hoping by the time the garbage on Second Avenue gets collected, your intruder will have lost interest in what can only seem like a defective piece of equipment to him. One dead bug."

Bale steered them in the direction of Morning After eatery two blocks down. "What's to keep him from coming back and giving it another shot?" asked Val, who realized she truly believed there was nothing she could do to prevent it. In her arsenal, all she had were pots.

Dodging a gray-haired woman in a purple fleece grimly power-walking against the rush hour foot traffic, Bale eased Val into a narrow doorway where all that was left of a millinery store was its sign CHAPEAUX by Posey. "In about half an hour from now, Val, your door's getting an additional lock that will be impregnable. It will only open to a secure ID, and the password will change daily until we get this guy, okay?"

They were standing so close together she felt his breath on her face. "You called a locksmith?"

A tight shake of his head. "Not a locksmith. Are you hungry?"

"Not a locksmith," she went on, "then who? Who does that kind of work, Antony?"

"A friend. Someone I know from...other file folders in my life. Let's eat."

"Why did you throw it away?"

"What?"

"The bug. Why did you throw it away? Shouldn't we have given it to the cops?"

"And what would they have done with it? Trace it? Try to lift prints off it? Not likely. If I wore gloves to prowl around your place now, believe me, he did." Bale shot her a wry look. "And his fit. And we would have tipped our hand, Val. That little bug would have picked up the hand-off to the cops and any conversation they went on to have about the Yankees' chances until they either bagged and tagged it—or destroyed it."

She looked out toward the street, where she guessed everyone else was leading a normal life that probably had very little to do with murder and any desperate attempts to stay one step ahead of a killer. "I see." Then, she smiled at him, although it felt shaky, like she was losing muscle control in her cheeks. "Really."

"All our guy knows now about his slick bit of electronic surveillance is that he's getting nothing for his trouble. It's not picking anything up." He took a big breath, and slung an arm around her, and when he pulled her in for a quick hug, her hand landed against his chest. "Believe it or not, Val, we've actually bought ourselves some time."

She gave him a gentle pat and took a step backwards. "I say we eat." As Bale dropped back to follow her, Val noticed he gave the street a quick scan. It struck her it was a habit. She'd noticed it before, every time they had been in each other's company since the day after Adrian's murder. For a Carmelite lay brother in an order where, for all she knew, prayer was their riskiest business, there was a kind of hyper-alertness to Bale that she was beginning to suspect had nothing to do with either caffeine or general street smarts. Or even, she thought, catching herself up short, with Adrian's violent death. It was simply the way Bale was. Or simply the way...he had been trained. What else was going on at Burnham Norton Abbey that Adrian had forgotten to mention in all her attempts to bring together her brother and her best friend?

They agreed over Greek omelettes and house salads that she would call the cops about the break-in as soon as they were finished. "Call Cleary directly," he advised, "because it'll be in her wheelhouse soon enough anyway." In the middle of his *doppio*, Bale took a call from the friend—whose voice was clearly female—who was going to render Val's apartment door impassable to mere mortals. He listened noncommittally to what she was telling him, barked a quick thanks, and ended the call. Dabbing a napkin to his lips, he explained to Val that apparently something had come up and his friend couldn't get to the building to install the new security until three thirty or thereabouts.

Val's eyes widened. "In the morning?"

"Right. Have you got someplace to stay tonight?"

With a quick nod, she pulled out her phone and called Aunt

Greta while Bale watched her inscrutably. What followed was her usually cool aunt fumbling for the phone and sounding like Val had caught her making her way uptown through the crush of tourists meandering around Times Square. "Hello? Hello?" Another fumble.

"Hey, it's me," said Val.

"I know."

"Where are you?"

"At my place."

Val was surprised. "You sound out of breath."

"Oh, dinner, you know the drill." Greta let out a cry. "Goddamn stuffed mushroom caps. The devil's own appetizer, I swear. What's up, darling?"

Val rolled her eyes at Bale. "Can I stay with you tonight?"

To whatever alarm mushroom caps were creating on E. 65th Street, Greta sprang at the question. "Why? What's happened?"

Val shot Bale a quick look—*can I tell her?*—and he gave her a slow shake of his head. *Not here,* he mouthed at her. "Trouble at home," was what she settled for. "I'll tell you when I see you," she added. Bale opened his hands like that'd do.

"Hell, honey, I can't," cried her aunt. "I've got a friend coming over."

Hence the mushroom caps. Val should have guessed. Followed by her excellent veal marsala and potatoes mashed with shallots and chervil. "I can sleep on the couch." She shot Bale a smile. "Even arrive long after she's left. Who is it? Veronica?" She speared the last little morsel of feta. The last time her aunt's friend Veronica had come over, the three of them had sat up late polishing off a fine Barbaresco until Veronica caught a cab uptown to her apartment in Morningside Heights.

"It's not Veronica, Val." Greta's voice dropped. "It's a different friend." Her voice sounded humorous. "And he won't be going home after we finish off the wine. At least," she went on, with sounds of scraping a baking pan in the background, "not if I have anything to say about it."

Val couldn't tell whether she felt more shocked at her aunt or herself for failing to see the possibility that the aunt who had raised her, years after the longstanding beau Ben Biderman had upped and died on her, actually still had a sex life. Val won. She herself was the more shocked of the two of them. "Ah," was all she could say in what she hoped was a casual way.

"You'll be okay?"

"Of course." The lie came out of her high and easy.

"A burst pipe? Something like that?"

"A malfunction." Whatever that meant. Although at the moment, Val felt like she was referring to herself. "Talk tomorrow?"

The devil's own appetizer was forgotten. "We're going together to the Morgan Library." Greta was suddenly all business. "Tell me you remember."

What with bugs and violations of all sorts and—well, the company of Bale—Val had forgotten the appointment over lunch the next day with Greta and the Hunter College professor who had called in the Artifact Authentication Agency. "I remember, Auntie. Love you. See you tomorrow. Have fun tonight," she added as she hung up, wondering why she included the company of Antony Bale in with everything else she found unsettling.

"Homeless?" Bale leaned back.

She set down her phone. "I'll figure something out." She glanced at the scallop-shell Key West tote she had grabbed on her flight from her home. At least she had gotten James Killian out of the way until the next time he ambled into her office world. One less disturbance in a time of heightened—tension. Bale was leaning on one hip and drawing out his billfold. "No, no." She caught his other hand where it rested on the table. "This one's on me," she said. "I insist. You came to my aid, you arranged for a—" she blinked at him, trying to find the word "—a friend to make my home a fortress." It sounded very commonplace...

The hand she had caught turned very easily in her own, which he held—and stared at—long enough not to mistake it for just a gesture. She sat very still. "My pleasure," was all he said, then released her hand as he opened the billfold. "Thanks for dinner," he

added, drawing out a hard plastic card he set on the table. Two
fingers pushed the card over to Val. "Take it."

"What is it?"

"Key card to my room at the Iroquois."

"But—" she started.

He smiled. "I'll stay at Adrian's tonight," he said easily. "I
could use the time there. Really. It's no problem. There's the
memorial service day after tomorrow at the Coleman-Witt, and I've
been looking through old photos. And, of course," he said with
some energy, "I'm working my way through everything, looking
for...something." He was slipping his billfold back into his pocket
when the waiter placed a check on the table.

Val picked up the check, and then reached for the key card. "I
accept your offer," she said. She even managed to keep the
primness out of her voice. "I'd like a shot at Adrian's too, Antony. If
you don't mind. I might find something—" She didn't quite like
what she was implying.

"That I might overlook?"

She shrugged. "Or not understand."

"You're right. But let's talk about it tomorrow. You should get
some sleep." He squeezed her hand—that one felt more like a
gesture—and she could see in his face that what he wasn't telling
her was how worried he was. Behind the smile, there it was. And it
had something to do with her. Val might be able to interpret some
of Adrian's crazy notes on mementoes from concerts and dance
clubs, but Bale understood some kind of grim mechanics to the
world that made it smart to worry. When it came right down to it,
she thought, strangely without fear as they slid out of the booth to
head into the Manhattan night, he understood this killer in a
familiar way. Not Bale's first intruder. Not his first killer. Only she
didn't know why.

All she knew for sure as he turned to leave was that she was
grateful for his kindness. She resolved to do whatever she could to
lessen the worry. She grabbed his lapel about as awkwardly as she
had ever been with a man. Pushing right past his quizzical look, she

stepped up and kissed his cheek, registering citrus and scruff. "Thank you," she said quietly, her hand flopping by some way of explanation no more articulate than the rest of her.

Very slowly Bale's thumb and forefinger lifted the strand of Val's hair that always, by the end of every workday, jumped the off-center part and hung over her cheek, out of place. He guided the strand back to where it belonged, smoothing it into place with the backs of his fingers. Val stood very still, and panic over the break-in felt very far away. "Let's head back across town. I'll walk you to the hotel. Then I'll catch a cab."

She nodded, then added her own good sense to the night she could swear had gotten warmer. "I'll call Cleary. But first," Val found herself saying, "let's duck into BXL East and I'll buy you a drink."

Bale scratched his face. "When will all this gratitude end?"

"Is it getting in the way?"

"Of what?" Bale challenged her.

Her breath caught. She let the challenge sit there. No smart answer was quite good enough. She had come up against something else that mattered, besides Adrian both alive and dead, and the excellent books she could bring out into the world. That was all, in that moment, as the two of them walked companionably around the corner and headed up 51st Street toward the Iroquois Hotel. Nothing felt like the truth—because she didn't know yet the shape and color of it. "I take it you'll have a drink with me."

"I will."

She linked arms with him, her raffia tote holding a change of clothes and—she was pretty sure—a toothbrush, bumped against their hips. "You can tell me about monastery life."

"That I can do. And what will you tell me about?"

"Oh, so it's got to be an even exchange."

"Nothing less," he said with an ambiguous smile. "Or I'm not interested."

"Let's see," Val breathed, and repeated the problem. "What will I tell you about?" He couldn't possibly know how difficult the question was. Mostly, in her experience, males got the spray off the skates of her life. Light, quick, easy, gone. There were some, not many, who got to a few of the tender places that had nothing to do with sex. Lines from Dylan Thomas. The bleak beauty of Edward Hopper. The memory of her mother, Claire Bistritz Cameron, chasing her playfully around the dining room table when she was all of three, before Valjean even knew the world could break up into fuselage and blasted wings and scattered body parts over a town in Scotland.

But even these things, shared, were carefully managed by Val. They looked more like intimacies than they really were. They simply passed as revelations. Because she had chosen and groomed them for limited distribution. Oh, yes. Even the memory of her mother. Even with Adrian, who never even knew the difference, because the two of them together had created a friendship that still at thirty-five had all the quippy swagger of their college days. And as she stood there in the nightfall that might very well be limited to where they stood outside the BXL East bar, Val studied the brother she had never wanted to meet.

He asked her quietly, "What will you tell me about?"

The answer, when it came, was easier than she had ever believed it could be. "Anything you like."

21

It was late.

Animus was sitting on the window seat in his study on the second floor of the brownstone attached to the Robus Christi chapel. Millard had raised the window because his employer suddenly felt too weak, and the midnight sounds on Gramercy Park West drifted up to him. With what was left of his favorite port, he silently toasted the month of April and his life's work...and his disease. *Lymphoma.* Every consonant and every vowel of that word was beautiful and had spared him from old age. Had he lived to eighty-nine, like his parents, look at how many, many more years it would have taken his beloved Robus Christi to fulfill the prophecy of what he had come to think of as a sacred fragment.

Instead, now, at fifty-one, lymphoma had centered him, the architect of the organization, at precisely the perfect time in the life of man: still sharp enough to plan, still strong enough to act. The cancer had poised him for what he knew would be coming shortly, at just the right possible moment, between the last of life and what had always been experienced as death. He, Animus, truly spirit, was poised to change man's experience of this forever. Of this exquisite moment, none of the others knew anything, not even Alaric or Millard.

It had to be that way.

It was Millard's night off, so Animus had poured his port himself. From where he sat, leaning against the bay window, he closed his eyes and let the distant sirens and hurrying steps and gay laughter seep into his head like well-learned arpeggios. This room across from his bedroom that he kept as his study held the random furnishings he had found especially beautiful, with no thought of design. A nineteenth-century scrivener's table. A Victorian stuffed egret. A Danish modern settee in mustard yellow. A fifties pinball machine from a roadhouse along Route 66. A chandelier by the glass artist Chihuly. A Victrola once owned by the famous tenor Beniamino Gigli. Even a lamp from IKEA. First issues of *National Geographic,* first editions of the work of Willa Cather, first vinyl pressings of the earliest work of Thelonius Monk. And what appeared to be an old wooden Bible box that held the loose pages in Spanish that, when he was still at the Morgan Library, he had the prescience to Xerox against the rules.

Securing the box itself became utterly unnecessary, as he came to see over his years of preparations; still, he had commissioned a woodworker in the Hebrides to fashion him a reasonable replica. Rosewood was the closest this woodworker could get to the original acacia, and that was fine. A box, a satire, a secret shelf for housing the ancient fragment—the re-creation pleased him in terms of his own sense of completeness. He told himself he didn't need the actual box for Robus Christi—it was mere adornment.

For at the heart of Robus Christi was the ancient Hebrew fragment.

As he pursued the fulfillment of the prophecy he discovered accidentally eight years ago at the Morgan Library, he trembled at his sudden role in human history. He had been forty-three and healthy and just another Catholic who attended Mass from the same kind of unquestioning, fond habit as giving a great-aunt a peck on her wrinkled cheek. He was also a librarian at the Morgan—really more of a hobbyist librarian, what with his independent means—where his job was to field questions about the holdings, provide research materials to credentialed scholars, and make sure nothing met with any gum or Diet Coke in the process.

It was a day of stultifying heat late in June when some female grad student came headlong into the Rare Books and Manuscripts room, with an officious way about her, and presented him with three items on the proper Requested Materials form. Back in the No Admittance area, he had found the biography of Hernán Cortés written by a descendant in the early 1700s, the collection of three brittle maps of New Spain...and a charming acacia wood box that contained what was catalogued in the Inquisition materials as a satire.

A quick scan told him that not only was the document untranslated from the Spanish, but that the eighteenth-century orthography was a nightmare. He'd wish stuck-up missy good luck with this one. As he returned too quickly with the three items she'd requested, he stumbled and the biography started to slide out of his hands. To forestall a disaster of rare documents and maps in a heap on the floor, he gripped the stack tightly with his fingers, and then—something rather remarkable happened.

He felt the tiny, high pop of a spring releasing...

A small, shallow drawer slid out from the base of the acacia wood box that contained the satire in Spanish. And in it...ink on leather, very old—no, very, very old—in what at first glance appeared to be Hebrew. Back in his seminary days, before he left because life felt too constricted, he had learned a year's worth of Hebrew. In the very first line, as he tried to read from right to left, the words *Gat Smanim* sprang up at him through the centuries. *Gethsemane.* And in that moment, he knew one single thing for certain: this was his find. He couldn't account for how this fragment had come down through time, or how it became secretly berthed with a satire from the Inquisition, but it was now in his hands. And no one living had any knowledge of it—had anyone found it in its sliding drawer, it would now be translated, copied, published, studied, coveted, and housed in the Vatican.

This was his find.

And in the moment it took him to set the box on a high shelf temporarily, behind a stack of fresh cheesecloth, he knew he would present the student with only two of her three requested items, telling her apologetically that the third item was currently unavailable since it was undergoing restoration by the museum's conservators. He marveled as he passed back into the room that was suddenly seeming especially well lighted, wondering if he himself was the source of the light. At forty-three, he was in his prime, with half a lifetime still ahead of him. Who knew where it would take him, this prize. What heights. It was enough to make him, failed seminarian, hobbyist librarian, convinced that whatever had come down to him through the ages was meant for him alone.

Stealing the fragment from the Morgan Library two days after he discovered it was a matter of nearly giddy ease. But then, over the next several weeks, he felt a deep disquiet. If anyone actually tripped the spring and the little shelf slid open, its emptiness would be a mystery that might lead to an investigation. As a librarian in that section, he could be questioned. And the prospect of questioning became intolerable.

Finally, one day in a tiny explosion from the overthinking that was getting him nowhere, he did the first thing that came to mind to put an end to it: he made a copy of his translation of the Hebrew fragment and slipped it into what was now the empty secret drawer. To the casual finder, it would look either like a partial translation of the satire itself, or a scrap of some other piece of...well, fiction. How could it ever be linked—on Office Max paper and written with a PaperMate ballpoint pen—to an original two-thousand-year-old fragment of divine prophecy? It couldn't. And, as the librarian in the Rare Books and Manuscripts Room, he could steer patrons away from that particular holding.

No cause for concern.

He rarely touched the rosette in the replica that released the spring to the drawer.

For guidance and inspiration, he had his translation, which he smoothed lovingly with the backs of his bony fingers. And tonight, as always, he had his port. There was a soft knock at the door. "Come in, Millard."

A shaft of light from the hall backlit his housekeeper, still in his light plaid jacket from an evening off. "I saw the light," he managed to say with great effort. "Is there anything you need?" His one good eye caught sight of the half-finished glass of wine. "Top off your port?"

Animus suddenly remembered the night shortly after Millard had come to work for him, what must have been nine years ago. Certainly before he made the accidental discovery in the Rare Books and Manuscripts Room of the Morgan Library. He had found Millard through the Wounded Warrior Project and then found it odd that the veteran he hired made it very clear, when Animus had brought it up in his smoothest politically correct voice, how he felt about that term. "I was wounded," he told his new boss with as straight a spine as he could manage. "I'm not now," he added. "And I was a soldier, not a warrior." Finally, Millard Mackey brayed, "It was my job." The effort at coherent speech exhausted him for the rest of the day.

Now, nine years down the road, in the employ of a spiritual empire, Millard still had some of the homelier practices of the military. And it was during that time Animus recalled Millard standing in just the same way in a soft triangle of light in the doorway to the study. Asking then as now if he could top off his employer's port. And that time, moved by this hardworking, honest Hoosier from Terre Haute, Indiana, the head of Robus Christi had whirled expansively, arms outstretched, showing off his eccentric study to the help.

His only help, but one was all he needed. Before his discovery of the inscribed prophecy. Before the onset of disease that forced him to be more ingenious, planning out meticulously even his smallest movements in his quest. Before this near and inevitable moment when he would cheat death forever. He grabbed his port that night and spun, crying expansively, *Millard, this will all be yours someday. Shall I call you my heir?* (Too much port?) He remembered clapping a hand on the veteran's shoulder, pleased to bestow the strange and wonderful contents of his favorite room in the house.

Soon, as it turns out, he would have no need for an heir.

But in recent weeks, he had become consumed with anxiety over one single loose end.

The translation he had set cavalierly into the secret drawer that day, years ago.

It had been nothing short of hubris, really. And he had never figured on getting fired.

He remembered the day last month he had finally managed to switch his copies of the translation at the Morgan Library. He had ordered an EZ Lite Cruiser wheelchair online for $2,400 and had labored over an altered facsimile—key words changed—of his translation of the fragment that had been shut up tight in the original box for these last few years. When the altered translation was ready, he practiced motoring around in his Cruiser. Millard, red in his half-ruined face, declared it "Sensible, sir," believing, it seemed, that the boss was looking ahead to the need as his illness progressed.

With the altered translation folded and tucked into his breast pocket, Animus parted the pedestrians and the traffic as he motored up the east side of Fifth Avenue the thirteen blocks to the Morgan, where he prayed no one would recognize him, that enough time had passed, enough employee turnover had occurred, that he could do what he had come to do. Betting that the security guard would simply wave through the invalid, he pressed the button for the automatic door at the front entrance. He was in. And nearly ecstatic to meet the wan glances of others at the admirable pluck of this disabled scholar. How people in wheelchairs must hate it...

For him, it was the first time he had been back inside the Morgan Library since he had lost his job rather dramatically seven years ago—the day when he raged at a patron who pointed out that the gentleman in charge of the Rare Books and Manuscripts room always seemed to find some excuse for making some of the Inquisition documentary holdings—the blowsy old tugboat of a female actually said those words "documentary holdings"—unavailable every time she requested them. She then smugly went on to tell him she had queried one of the conservators who looked into the matter and discovered half the official *procesos* from the year 1595 plus some ephemera—here again, the self-important sow's word—including a satire and two affidavits were not actually undergoing restoration. She then demanded the items on her Requested Materials form and crossed her arms in the ugly lavender jacket she must have snapped up last season on the clearance rack at Talbot Outlet.

With that, and for the first unfortunate time in his life, the librarian believed he had lost his mind. "Get out! Get out, you officious cretin!" Truly it was as much a matter of punishing her airy vocabulary as the chance she could trip the spring on the secret compartment of the precious acacia wood box. *Ephemera, queried, documentary holdings.* Even the promise of the prophecy from that final night in Gethsemane was too good for the likes of this imbecile.

Too good by half. His agent, Alaric, was off globetrotting on a modest expense account, hunting down the three key relics from the Crucifixion. The search would take years. Years! And here was this imbecile with bad taste and glasses provided by some glass block manufacturing company calling his bluff on a strictly library matter.

It was intolerable.

He found himself breathless from his own invective at her, while she gaped at him, most of which he would never remember, and he was finally swiping away at some frothy spittle when two security guards clamped him on either arm. Whereupon he was escorted to the director's office, fired on the spot, banished from the Rare Books and Manuscripts room, not permitted to retrieve anything from his desk, and shown the front door.

There he had stood gibbering on the street while pedestrians gave him a wide berth. Banished. When he came to his senses he found himself, oddly enough, on a subway train headed for Coney Island. Banished. Riding to Coney Island aside, he would have thought he had wandered into a particularly unsatisfying fairy tale where life was especially cruel and the worst curses all had to do with exile from the Rare Books and Manuscripts room at the Morgan bloody Library.

That was his thinking for the first few years after he had been escorted from the premises while that self-satisfied harridan with no credentials worth a damn was left behind, groveled to by the staff, and practically made a present of the priceless "documentary holdings" on her Requested Materials form. Was she building a spiritual empire on Earth with virtually no help? Was she altering the future of humanity with virtually no help? No, not her. But in those first few years afterwards, he contented himself with how things stood. He had a priceless document in a pretty little rosewood box made to order. Even a Xeroxed copy of the satire that had mysteriously accompanied the fragment down through the ages.

He had all he needed. A grand blueprint for the kingdom of God among living men.

22

From Bale's room at The Iroquois Hotel on W. 44th Street, Val called Cleary and left a message on her voicemail. The drink together at BXL East turned into a bottle of Chilean Malbec Val and Bale shared over an hour and a half at a corner table in the back, next to a framed print of Bosch's "Peasant Wedding." No carefully packaged revelations were exchanged. No generic stories about monastery life were exchanged. In the soft, steady candlelight, it became shop talk, after all—where they stood in their investigation into Adrian's murder. Bale filled her in on his Norfolk leads, a young monk named Eli and an American college student, Melanie. From the boy Bale had figured out how Fintan had expertly tailed him and then stolen the Crown of Thorns.

And from the American girl the most important piece of information was about the phony birder who had been meeting secretly with Fintan McGregor. Spotted in a field, spotted at the brew pub where she worked. From there the trail went cold, but Bale was sure this was the likeliest candidate for the job of killing a pious young monk who had bought some line from the killer about how indispensable he was to...something. Something of staggering importance. Bale had opened his hands helplessly at Val, who could only gnaw at her lip. They fell silent at the dangerous credulity of the very young. And then they fell silent all over again at the dangerous credulity of anybody at all, knowing that at any given moment it could include the two of them as well.

Was she completely out of her league? Val wondered as she turned down the sleek, neat covers of Bale's bed. How could she ever be sure? As she slipped out of her work clothes and set them on the chair, she felt a little *frisson* of fear. In disposing of the bug so deftly, Bale had bought her some time, but there was no way of thinking the break-in was caused by anything other than her final voicemail from Adrian. And the fact that Bale linked the two murders—a botched theft of the holy relic that resulted in the deaths of both Adrian and the thief—pointed to a killer who acted swiftly at even the possibility of failure or exposure. If Adrian herself didn't know a damn thing and was shot to death, what kind of chance did Val stand? With this killer...this phony birder...there was absolutely no wiggle room. Did that signal his utmost confidence in whatever was driving him? Or did it signal an acidic doubt? No wiggle room for a boy hurled off a cliff, no wiggle room for a hapless curator who had gained possession of the Crown.

But it struck Val that when it came to her, when it came to any possible involvement of the one called Val Cameron in the sequence of events, some chances had been taken. Some odd restraint had been shown. Hadn't it? Adrian's voicemail had been a little cryptic, sure, but the killer for one had known the finest example of *Euphorbia milii* they'd ever in this lifetime see really referred to the holy relic. Would he make the leap that Val, the recipient of Adrian's message, would also make the same reference? Or did the killer call it just right: the one called Val Cameron couldn't possibly have known what Adrian Bale was inviting her to see firsthand was anything other than a thorny plant.

It was suddenly a reasonable assumption for someone who had shown no restraint when it came to eliminating anyone who— unknowingly—threatened him, and Val sank onto Bale's bed when she realized it was an assumption that had probably saved her life. So far. Hence the break-in. Hence the bug. She was on trial. Up for inspection. Under consideration. Now that the killer had the Crown of Thorns, he might be feeling more secure. But he had rifled through the contents of her desk, and he had thumbed through the loose papers under her mother's Millefiori paperweight, looking for any indication that Val had come too close to the secret. And he had bugged her apartment in the hopes of recording any conversations that could identify her as a threat. Where was the line, and when would she cross it?

With shaking fingers, Val pulled together the sheer curtains, watching the street three stories below disappear behind the gauze. She wanted it to disappear. Last summer in the Canadian wilderness, when it came to confronting a killer, she had been strangely serene—because she had a slight edge, and the killer did not. As completely out of her element as she had been in that place of deep, vast waters and towering thick trees, and animals always out of sight that she had only ever seen in the Bronx Zoo. Not for a minute in that week had Val expected to feel at home, and she hadn't. She had only ever learned a few skills to get her through, and ones she truly never planned on using again in this lifetime. Running a motorboat, washing moose muck out of her clothes, paddling, paddling, paddling in the bow of a canoe, her only way to her quarry, and finally...cocking a rifle at a ruthless killer. All circumstantial skills in a place she would never visit again.

But in the final gap between the sheer curtains in the beautiful hotel room Bale had lent her for the night, Val narrowed her eyes at the shadowy figures moving on the sidewalks below, narrowed her eyes at cabs that obscured their drivers, stared unseeing at the lights bleeding red and white and yellow into a haze that suggested, for the first time in her thirty-five years, this was a place Val Cameron didn't know. She was no less out of her element here than she had been last summer when the possibility of running into a bear felt like a calamity. It was suddenly a terrible truth that she stood a better chance against the bear than she did against a killer here in her hometown who was contemplating whether Val Cameron posed a risk. He was stealing Manhattan right out from under her, showing her that it was a mistake to believe this place was home. That she knew it. That she had made a life here.

So had Adrian.

Get to go cheer for New Jersey.

Her phone vibrated on Bale's nightstand. Quickly closing the gap in the curtains, Val sprang for the phone. It was Cleary. She tapped the button and listened to the cop handling Adrian's case say, "A break-in, eh? Tell me what you found." Suddenly her two glasses of that lovely Malbec shared with Bale had seeped into the most remote cells in her brain, fuzzing her enough to take the edge off her sadness. All she wanted was to sleep.

It became a fine goal, an expedition she could sign on to—and as she sank back and turned off the light, she told Cleary that she was safe at a friend's for the night. That she'd meet Cleary at her apartment at eight a.m. to show her the evidence of the break-in. Since there was no urgency, Cleary agreed and hung up. Val turned into the pillow, wondering before sleep hit how she'd get into her place without the secure ID that Bale had mentioned, the faint smell of citrus lifting off the pillow and chasing the Malbec to the remote and lovely places of her troubled mind.

In the morning, Val discovered a text from Bale that had come in at 4:32 a.m. *Check with front desk for secure ID.* One problem solved. She pulled out the change of clothes she had flung into her Key West raffia tote and discovered the ivory-colored retro dress with the fitted bodice and full skirt. In her haste to get out of her invaded apartment, she had at least also tossed a black jacket with sequined trim into the bag too. Before leaving the room, she pulled the covers loosely up over the bed and looked around one last time. Unless the Carmelites were an order that managed to circumvent the vow of poverty, she couldn't figure how Bale afforded this fine, tasteful room at the Iroquois. The woodwork gleamed, the white sheets were crisp and new, and the thick, soft blue carpeting gave nothing away in terms of Room 321's history. Either before or during the stay of Antony Bale.

Val's neck was stiff, she thought more from anxiety than anything else, despite the Malbec's best efforts, and only a large cup of coffee would keep a headache from dominating the day. With a date to meet Greta at the Morgan Library at noon to chase down

Saul Bensoussan's conviction that one of the Mexican Inquisition holdings was a fake, she couldn't afford to let the headache develop. With a strange sort of regret, Val softly drew shut the door to Bale's hotel room and headed down three flights of stairs. The clerk at the front desk smiled and slid her a small, sealed manila mailer that Val tucked into her jacket pocket.

Back on the street, the morning was cool and overcast, as if it didn't even have the strength for outright melancholy. At 44th Street, she took a quick look around to get re-oriented to a street that had felt quite unknown to her in her fears last evening. With a quick stop at the Food Court below Rock Center, where she grabbed a cup of dark roast coffee and a cheese Danish, she made it back to her apartment in twenty minutes. If she didn't know better, Val could swear she was in a hurry to be back home. By her phone she was three minutes early for Cleary, so she waited in the shallow alcove, drawing her black jacket tighter around her. In the perfect rows of black plastic sequins, Val found something more cheerful than anything else, like perfect little black planets tucked closely behind each other. There was a fine, tight order to the rows that on that particular morning felt missing everywhere else.

An old woman with dyed red hair wearing brown suede boots ambled, weaving past Val. A young man in a cheap suit with a blue backpack and mirrored sunglasses skated recklessly toward Second Avenue on a rainbow-colored longboard. Deliverymen talked in the gutter, and she watched a near three-cab collision just past the intersection. Angry horns ensued. Still staring at tiny black spangles on her jacket pockets, Val felt herself smiling. Maybe she was wrong. The city was as reliable as cyclones across the prairies. All the shadows were under her skin, after all.

Two car doors slammed shut. "Ms. Cameron?" came the voice. Val looked up at Lieutenant Cleary, dressed that Monday morning in khaki ankle pants, a narrow striped white button-down shirt, the wings of the collar flipped up, and a jean jacket. The detective slid her sunglasses to the top of her laser-parted black hair, still clipped tight at the nape of her neck. They shook hands. "You okay?" Cleary

leaned into Val, quickly scrutinizing her. A uniformed cop stood at
ease, looking up and down the street.

"Never better," Val told her. They both knew it was a lie.

Cleary nodded, grabbed Val's arm, and walked her a few steps
toward Second Avenue. "Listen," she said, with a quick scratch to
her pert nose, "I want to fill you in on that kosher bakery truck."
She went on to describe how the owner had reported the theft of
one of their delivery trucks yesterday. Right off the street. Couldn't
believe his eyes. He and the driver had nearly finished loading up
the back for the morning's deliveries when bing bang boom it was
gone, just like that. Oy, what a mystery, oy, what a mess—what with
the two Men's Club breakfasts they were catering plus three
preschool Shabbats, uptown, downtown, you got the picture. Then,
he went on, nothing less than a miracle, a minor miracle on a busy
day, nothing on the level, say, of the parting of the Red Sea, *baruch
haShem*, but...the bakery van turned up! Who would have believed
it?

"A patrol car discovered it abandoned near Pier 90," finished
Cleary. "The owner inventoried the goods," she said, "and there was
one box of four dozen assorted bagels and one pound of rugelach
missing." Cleary gave Val a small smile. "Since he decided it was
kids joyriding—although we didn't point out that most kids are
looking for something sexier than a bakery delivery van—we
decided not to mention to him that his truck had transported a
stolen plant, a murder weapon, and a cold-blooded killer."

"Why not?"

Cleary shoved her hands into her pants pockets and gave Val a
frank look. "Do we really want Channels 3, 5 and 8 to get hold of
that piece of information? We're thinking not, for as long as we can
keep it under wraps."

Val shook her head. "But it might bring someone out of the
woodwork, right? Someone else who hears the story and realizes he
saw something—"

"And how long do you think it would take our media outlets to
get hold of your little pal Avital Korngold," said Shay Cleary,

leaning toward Val. "And how long—after that—before the killer knows he's been made? And by a thirteen-year-old kid who walks five blocks alone to the train every day to get to school?" Val felt chilled. "Right now the only blowback we've got from the theft of the bakery van is from the poor owner, who's talking about needing to scrub out the back of the van when he thought kids had stolen some bagels. Now," she jerked her chin at Val, "let's go upstairs and see what you've got."

With that, Lieutenant Shay Cleary went ahead of her and told the uniformed cop to talk to the doorman about anything out of the ordinary in or around the building yesterday. Then she held open the door for Val, who walked past her into the building she had called home for about as long as she had worked at Schlesinger Publishing. At the prospect of returning to her apartment, her mouth went dry, and for the life of her, she didn't know if she would ever get over the break-in. She walked toward the elevator on legs that felt spindly, with Cleary close behind her.

At least Tali Korngold was still unknown to the killer.

But Val herself was not. Whoever he was, he had moved around inside her home, fingered her things, bugged her space, and left—if Bale was correct—without a trace.

23

When Val and Greta met outside the Morgan Library, they stepped into the full-body hug they had perfected over thirty years. Val whispered, "How was dinner?"

Greta gave her three quick kisses, one right on top of the other, then pushed her. "Dinner, I'll have you know, was one of my best. Well worth all the trouble."

"Did your guest stay the night?"

Greta lowered her chin, and said primly, "As a matter of fact, he did. With these academic types, you never know." She grabbed Val's arm and headed toward the glass doors of the Morgan Library. "When it comes to the sack," she explained, stepping to the side to let Val pass inside. "So it's always a risk. Half the time you get the idea they'd just as soon be at home reading Proust. And I mean *during*."

Even as Val laughed, and Greta linked arms with her, she hoped she wasn't about to hear anything more in the way of details. But the details, when they came, were culinary. About ten feet into the soaring atrium, Greta turned to her niece. "The fact that my guest keeps kosher added a certain challenge to the meal." She shrugged. "I bought a new pot, a new pan, plastic forks and knives, and paper plates. *Kashrut*," she gave Val a little bow, "was observed."

"Besides himself, what did he bring?"

"Actually," Greta stifled a laugh, "a camp stove."

"You cooked veal marsala on a camp stove?"

Greta raised her elegant shoulders. "It was delicious. Camp stove may become my preferred method."

"What about the fifteen minutes in the oven?"

"There was really no sense in taking the time to kasher the oven. We discussed it all ahead of time, and he seemed satisfied." She gave Val a wide, thin smile that Val could tell was only partly referring to their sincere attempts at making a kosher meal.

Val felt interested. "How long would it have taken to kasher the oven?"

"Really, darling, I have no idea, but you can ask him when he gets here."

"When he gets here? Why is he coming here?" She was genuinely mystified.

"He thought it made more sense, what with trying to make the case that this article in the Library's holdings of Inquisition documents and artifacts—"

Val's jaw dropped. "Wait a minute," she said, grabbing Greta's arm. "Are you saying the Hunter College professor—"

"Saul Bensoussan, yes—"

The man had to be ten or twenty years younger than Greta. "You took him to bed?"

Greta looked amused. "He wasn't a three-year-old with a sour tummy, Val." Then she looked concerned. "Really, darling, sometimes you have such quaint speech."

"How did it happen?" There was no other way to put it. "Last time I saw you, you were pushing me at him."

Her aunt's eyes widened. "And it was clear you weren't interested, so I called him up."

Val had a quick flash of a framed family photo on the professor's desk. "Did his wife answer?" she said pointedly.

Greta's laugh was merry. "Darling, nobody has landlines anymore. Besides, they're divorced. I wish I could have offered you a bed, but—" At that she rattled off something worldly in French. "Where did you end up staying?"

"At Antony Bale's." Greta Bistritz stopped dead and could only stare at Val, wide-eyed. "Don't get excited," warned Val. "Bale wasn't there."

"Pity," murmured Greta, pushing past her niece, who suddenly felt sacked. "Here's our contact." Heading right for them across the expanse of gray marble flooring was Alice Lorton, Community Liaison for the Morgan Library, one of those ageless, trim native New Yorkers with shorn white hair and red-framed Fendi eyeglasses, dressed in a black pantsuit. As she gestured to a vacant table in the atrium, her silver bangle bracelets clacked softly.

Greta, whose morning-after hair had a heightened gleam to it, beamed at Val, and they followed Alice Lorton, who led the way, soldiering mechanically against a morning stiffness that to Val looked pretty severe. Compared to her, Greta Bistritz glided with good health and swept into a white metal chair, where she perched with suppressed energy. Out of thin air she produced her Department of Commerce ID for Lorton's brief inspection. One hand moved gracefully toward Val. "My deputy in this matter," she said by way of introduction. "Valjean Cameron."

"Thank you," said Lorton, with a nod, handing back the ID. "How can I help you?"

Folding her arms casually on the café table, Greta explained the issue that had recently been brought to the attention of the Artifact Authentication Agency by a scholar in the field of Latin American Literature. Lorton listened carefully as Greta went on. "He has raised the question of authenticity of one of the library's Mexican Inquisition holdings."

"Specifically?"

"Item #JPML 17-203," rattled off Greta from her iPhone, "Drawer 36." She looked up. "The holding consists of an anonymous satire in Spanish, titled 'The Entertainment of Spain,' contained in a finely carved wooden box with an attached lid. It was turned into the Inquisition in 1595 in Veracruz by a priest who believed the work to be heretical."

Val was impressed with how well her aunt described the challenged item. But she apparently had a refresher course last night from the scholarly accuser himself. Alice Lorton looked grave. "What's prompted the scholar's suspicion?" She opened her hands wide. "The attribution? The date? The source?"

Greta smiled softly. "The authenticity. Altogether." She waved a hand. "More than that, I'll let him tell you himself." That, Val knew, meant her aunt didn't have any more details than she did on the day they all met in Bensoussan's office. The veal must have been particularly good.

Slowly, Lorton worked her way through what Greta Bistritz of the Artifact Authentication Agency was stating. "Then he doesn't question the priest who delivered it back in 1595—"

"No."

"Or the fact that this is the satire the priest turned in?"

"No."

Alice Lorton drew a deep breath, her trim head tipping from side to side. "Or even that the year is accurate."

"No. The professor allows for the authenticity of the original holding. His suspicion doesn't lie in what happened over four hundred years ago in New Spain."

Lorton raised her shoulders. "Then...what?"

Gently, Val's aunt told the representative of the Morgan Library, "He's been studying the satire for some time now, on and off, for a book on the literature of New Spain. He knows the document. And he knows the engraved wooden box."

There was simply no comfortable way around the implication. "So you're saying—"

"No, Ms. Lorton, he's saying," Greta clarified, as she pursed her beautiful lips and looked squarely at Alice Lorton, "the Morgan Library has been robbed."

After a moment in which all three of them sat in silence, Lorton got with some difficulty to her feet. "Come with me," she said, heading for what turned out to be the Rare Books and Manuscripts room, up a short flight of steps into what Val recalled was part of J.P. Morgan's original townhouse. As they passed through the massive double doors, Val took in the fact that they didn't have the room to themselves. Four researchers were huddled separately over an array of papers and file folders, and antique books stacked carefully nearby.

The soft flutters of excited keyboarding were the only sounds in the beautiful rotunda that constituted the documentary holdings in J.P. Morgan's priceless collection. The smallest ornate mahogany reading table was empty, and Lorton motioned Val and Greta to be seated. She hastily filled out a Requested Materials slip, then met Greta's eyes. "I'll be right back," she told her, handing the slip to a monitor wearing the pin of library employees. The two of them disappeared into the back, and Val leaned toward her aunt.

"We'll take a look." When Greta nodded, Val added, "And then what?"

Greta leaned back into her chair. "Then we'll see. I'm hoping you can handle it from here."

"Me?"

"Have you seen my workload, Val?"

"Have you seen mine?"

"You agreed."

Val felt caught. "I've got a production schedule from Hell that's looking like Bridgegate, Auntie."

Greta said smoothly, "Then this little investigation should be a nice diversion for you."

Val looked at her hands. "My apartment was broken into yesterday." She went on: "Adrian was murdered and whoever killed her took her phone." Here she stalled, undecided how much to confide. Already, it turned out, she had gone too far.

"What aren't you telling me, darling?" said Greta quietly. So quietly none of the researchers at the neighboring tables blinked.

Val turned to face her aunt. "He broke into my home, searched through my desk, and installed a bug."

Greta hissed.

Val continued, "He knows who I am and where I live and probably where I work. He may have followed me here, for all I know." Val gazed at a section of books halfway up the book-lined wall where the spines glistened in old, burnished gold. Not much felt like gold to her that day, so she stared at them until she felt her eyes go soft. "He wants to find out what I know. And from that information—" Her voice trailed off.

"He'll decide what to do about you," finished Greta.

"That's the thinking."

Greta frowned. "Does Bale know? Beyond your needing a place to sleep?"

"Yes." She gave her aunt a frank look. "It helps," was all she said.

"And the cops, of course?"

Val nodded. Then her eyes slid to her aunt. "Not about the bug. Bale destroyed it."

"I think," said Greta finally, after wringing her hands for an unproductive minute, "you've got the best help you possibly can. Let me know if you can add me to the rest, dear heart, all right?"

Alice Lorton reappeared wearing thin latex gloves and holding a very old wooden Bible box. She spread a soft, clean chamois cloth on the table, then took the antique wooden box from the hands of the monitor. As Val watched her set it down with great care, she suddenly came to a decision. "I'd still like to act as your deputy. You might be right about a diversion."

Greta kissed her own fingers and set them against Val's cheek. "Let's see where it goes," and she motioned to the very old Bible box as Lorton slowly raised the attached lid.

The interior had a soft sheen to it, and it was exactly the right size for the manuscript set inside. Val leaned closer, admiring the still legible script hundreds of years old. The gently curling letters, the centuries-old orthography, the Spanish that conveyed something dangerous and heretical. After a moment, Lorton piped up, "Tell me, what happens if you're right?" She was looking directly at Greta. "If what we're looking at is...is a theft?"

Greta was matter-of-fact. "Then it becomes a matter for the police."

"Out of your hands?"

"Of the Agency? Yes. Mostly our work is routine." Greta took a pair of thin gloves from the monitor and drew them quickly over her hands. "For documents or artifacts with terrific provenance, we've got our rubber stamp—" she smiled "—and into this country or across state lines it goes with our imprimatur. When that isn't the case, when questions arise at the point of importation about the authenticity of an artifact, that's when we launch an investigation. In other words, if there had been any question at the time J.P. Morgan acquired Item #JPML 17-203, the Agency wasn't even in existence. With enough chicanery, anything could have come into Morgan's poor unsuspecting hands." As Lorton sputtered, Greta pressed on: "But we'll never know unless some researcher catches it, right, and draws our attention to it." Greta gave a short laugh.

"Are you saying we've got some fakes in the collection?"

"Without a doubt. But the Artifact Authentication Agency can only investigate what's specifically brought to our attention. That's our mandate. Limited funding, limited human resources." Here she gestured in the direction of Val. "Now, in the case of what Professor Bensoussan has brought to our attention, Item #JPML 17-203 in the Rare Books and Manuscripts holdings from the Mexican Inquisition, the situation is a little different."

"How so? A fake is a fake."

"Ah, but what he has stumbled on here is that the holding he's been studying over the last two years is not the same one he first saw. It's a substitute, you see. Much beyond that he hasn't told me, which means we'll have to—"

At the sound of footsteps heading in their direction, Val turned. It was Saul Bensoussan wearing a Yankees jacket over brown lightweight wool pants. He was nicer looking than she remembered, with his lively hazel eyes and Van Dyke beard; he was also older than she remembered, maybe putting him two years closer to Greta Bistritz in age, and he had an average sort of height and build that seemed more attractive given his air of ease. The good professor was one of those men with the kind of understated confidence she always found appealing. Bale had it. Nothing to prove. Nothing even to hypothesize. He smiled and nodded at Val while he set a hand lightly on the back of Greta's neck. "Ah," was the extent of Greta's greeting. To Alice Lorton, she explained, "May I introduce Professor Saul Bensoussan of Hunter College."

Val muttered slyly, "Sometimes you have such quaint speech, darling."

Greta raised an eyebrow at her.

Bensoussan reached between his legs and slid a chair into place. It was a grand, richly dark, book-lined room he apparently knew well, with its glass display cases holding the permanent exhibits—a Mahler score, an early typed letter from J.D. Salinger, among other things—and he glanced affectionately at the shelves. Shifting in her seat to face him, Alice Lorton folded her hands. "Ms. Bistritz has informed me that you believe we've been robbed."

"I'd say so, yes."

She went on: "That this," her gloved fingertips hovered over the open box, "is not the original holding. That someone has stolen the original satire and replaced it with a forgery."

The professor cocked his head. "No, that's not it at all."

"What?" said Greta softly, her eyes fixed on him.

"Oh, Greta, I'm sorry I wasn't clear." He set a hand on her shoulder. "I have no complaint about the satire." With that, he circled his hand lightly over the manuscript pages five hundred years old. "This is authentic." He quickly pulled out a crumpled pair of thin latex gloves and slipped them on, then lifted the first couple of pages of the satire settled in the old Bible box. Eyeing them carefully, he smiled at Alice Lorton. "No, this is the very same manuscript I've been studying for the last two years."

Lorton frowned. "What then? The box?"

"No," he replied. "Not even the box." He patted the sides of the old box like an affectionate uncle. "We know the satire is five hundred years old. I'd say the box that holds it is considerably older."

Val was interested. "How do you know?" she asked quietly.

Bensoussan lifted the box with both gloved hands and rotated it slowly so they could get a good look. "From what I can tell, this old Bible box—or what we're assuming is an old Bible box—is made out of red acacia wood. Not a native species in New Spain." As the point hung in the air, they all fell silent. Then Val watched Greta set her iPhone on the table and tap through to the record button on the Voice Memos app. When she gave him a quick nod, Bensoussan began. "When I first requested Item #JPML 17-203, a sixteen-page loose-leafed manuscript dated 1595 set in an antique acacia wood box of indeterminate age, it struck me as a little odd."

"Why?"

"Red acacia is native to North Africa and one of the very few species indigenous to the wilderness areas described in the Bible. The *aron chodesh*—Ark of the Covenant—and Egyptian coffins, for example—red acacia wood. But here was this beautiful red acacia wood Bible box holding an untranslated Spanish satire that was turned into the Inquisition in Veracruz in 1595. Do you see the problem?"

Greta's eyes narrowed. "A whole half world away..."

He smiled. "I figured the box had made a transatlantic trip with a family seeking adventure or asylum in the New World. The box had been somebody's heirloom. Not, as it turned out, a big mystery. How it came to be in the hands of that priest, we will never know, unless it was the priest's own family heirloom." That wasn't—here Bensoussan shrugged—what interested him.

Still, he photographed it in the event that down the road he could use some shots in the book he was writing, his translation of the satire, "The Entertainment of Spain," plus literary critical analysis of the work, plus cultural context..."It's an academic coup," said Bensoussan, "finding this satire, this untranslated treasure from the early days of the Mexican Inquisition." He took pictures of the holding from every angle and with the lid both opened and closed.

The lid was elaborately carved with stylized date palms and rock outcroppings that—to his eye, at least—resemble any picture he's ever seen of Qumran, site of the Dead Sea Scrolls...and in each of the four corners, *Hibiscus syriacus*. "Otherwise known," he said, "as Rose of Sharon."

Lorton interrupted him, raising her hands helplessly. "I take it you're saying this—this box dates back to Biblical times? Can you really base that opinion on a species of wood and a native flower?" She glanced at Val and Greta. "Much as I'd like to think J.P. Morgan acquired something even more wonderful than he knew, I really don't think—"

The way Saul Bensoussan held up a hand made Val appreciate his patience. "I agree," he said. "Those things alone are not enough for authentication, although—" here he glanced at Greta, "I'm assuming the Artifact Authentication Agency has experts at its disposal."

"Of course," murmured Val's aunt with a thin smile.

"Then let's give them everything we can," whispered the professor, whose thumbs were poised over the corners of the box. With slow deliberation, he pressed the carving of the *Hibiscus syriacus* in the lower right-hand corner. Soundlessly, a slim drawer slid open. The base of the red acacia box had a secret drawer. Val took in a sharp breath, but it was Greta who murmured, "Ah," and smiled with delight at her lover who brought something to the table even better than a bottle of kosher wine. Set inside the secret drawer was a sheet of paper.

The four of them looked at each other, and Lorton got to her feet. "Wait," she said. Then she walked to the center of the Rare Books and Manuscripts room and announced to the half dozen patrons who were leaning over materials at other tables, "Please excuse us for the next half hour, but we need to clear the room. Now." Five minutes later, Lorton had closed the doors, instructed a guard to stand outside the room, and returned to her seat. "Well, Professor Bensoussan," she said with some energy, tipping her close-cropped head to Item #JPML 17-203, "what have we got?"

Bensoussan removed the sheet of paper, unfolded it, smoothed it out, and set it on the table. Half standing, Val peered at it: handwritten, in English, with a ballpoint pen on paper that could have been bought at Office Max. Lorton raised her eyebrows as she eyed each of them. "Copies, anyone?"

"Yes, please."

"I'll take one."

"And you, Saul?" Greta turned to face him. He was the only one of them who hadn't spoken.

From his breast pocket, the Hunter College professor pulled a folded sheet of paper. "I already made my own copy a few weeks ago. Just out of interest. After all, it's the downstairs neighbor to my satire, right?" He laughed. "You can all see—" he said pointing to the sheet he had removed directly from the secret drawer and spread out on the table, "there's nothing of any real interest to it. Cheap printer paper, a ballpoint pen. Go ahead and read it. Lots of cryptic pronouncements, lots of concrete details. Thorns, iron, death, inheritance, life everlasting—so what is it? A translation from some part of the satire I haven't reached yet in my own translation? Or something altogether different? Some tortured piece of creative writing by a college student who should get himself pronto to the counseling center? What?"

Greta had reached the end of the sheet Bensoussan had spread out on the table. Whipping off her reading glasses, she gave a little shrug. "Do we even care?"

Val sat very still. As she finished reading, all she knew was that the word "thorn" had appeared three times in the short piece. The word "crown" once. Greta could tell something was wrong, and shot her a questioning look. Picking up the paper from the center of the table, Lorton sprang up. "I'll make some copies," she muttered, heading toward the door marked No Admittance.

"Here's why we should care," said Bensoussan as he unfolded his own copy of the paper from the secret drawer. "I made this copy several weeks ago, when I accidentally triggered the drawer for the first time. At that point, my mind was wrapped up with the satire from the Mexican Inquisition. I wasn't paying any attention to the box, the drawer, the paper inside. Old box, funky little drawer, overwrought story by a late adolescent. But when I came again to continue slogging through the nightmare of late sixteenth century orthography, I took a break and idly pressed the corner of the box, and out slid the drawer just as before."

"And?" Greta folded her arms.

Saul Bensoussan spread his own copy out on the table. "The copy I made no longer matched the sheet in the secret drawer."

Val felt breathless. "What are you saying?" Thorns, three times. Crown, once.

Bensoussan pushed back his chair, stood, and shoved his hands into his pockets. "The original paper, the paper I had copied for my files, was gone." He gestured at his copy. "This may be all we have of the original, and I for one am glad we have it." He glanced up at Alice Lorton, who was heading toward them with sheets held out in front of her like an offering. "Somebody, sometime in the last few weeks, stole the original translation and replaced it with a copy, altered in a few significant respects."

Lorton passed out copies of the substituted sheet of paper. "What did I miss?"

Greta tugged at her fine, long nose, mulling it over. "But, Saul, what on earth does it matter? My job is to authenticate artifacts, not decide which is the better story, the original or the rewrite that some college kid stuck as a lark in a holding at the Morgan Library." Her voice rose. "That's not a job for the Agency." By then, all four of them were standing around the research table.

Saul Bensoussan slipped an arm around Greta's shoulders and gave her a quick hug. "I know that, Greta. But then there's this—" While they watched, he took a Swiss Army knife out of his pocket and explained that the same day he discovered the switch he teased something out that had become lodged in the slim space, set back a couple of inches, between the box and the drawer. After he had a look at it, he replaced it as carefully as he could, because he deemed it the safest place it could be, and called the Artifact Authentication Agency.

While Val shined the flashlight on her phone at the spot, Bensoussan slid the knife into the narrow space, and he gingerly worked at making contact with whatever lay inside. Gently flicking at an object out of reach, when he snagged it, he bit his lip and slid a look at each of the others hovering nearby. Then with great control, he pulled slowly on the knife, and very slowly the prize came into view.

A scrap of leather.

No, even smaller than a scrap.

Thin, old, dried, irregularly shaped. As though it had fallen away from a larger piece.

Shorter but slightly wider than a shoelace, which is how it first looked to Val.

Bensoussan then pulled out a clean chamois cloth, which he set on the table, and a pair of tweezers. With infinite care, he lifted the old leather scrap with the tweezers, and, as he placed it on the cloth, turned it over at the very last second. As Val, Greta, and the Community Liaison of the Morgan Library closed in over the find, he stepped back. What they were looking at was a single line of text in very faded Hebrew.

Nobody moved. Val felt a shot of heat move murmuring through the vents and out into the room. Somewhere outside the Rare Books and Manuscripts room came the raised voices of ejected patrons. When Greta asked Bensoussan if he could translate the scrap right there on the spot, he gave her a wry smile. "Prayerbook Hebrew, no problem. I've known the service by heart since my Bar Mitzvah. But this?" With an upturned palm he pointed to the scrap. "I wouldn't presume." Val knew if Adrian were here with them, she could translate the text. But she wasn't, and the rest of them were either ignorant or unwilling.

"In case you're wondering," spoke Alice Lorton finally, her voice high and strange, "I won't be making any copies."

24

After some anxious bickering, the four of them agreed to keep the find under wraps for one week. Lorton didn't want to appear to the Board of Directors to be dragging her feet for some unknown purpose after the news got out. One week gave Greta time through the Artifact Authentication Agency to line up some experts in first century A.D. documents. She expected the process of authentication to be lengthy, but Lorton was immovable: a week was plenty of time to take the next step in the mystery of the scrap. Then she calmed herself down by flinging around some platitudes: *one step at a time, one day at a time, all in good time,* and the ever popular *time will tell.*

One week, said Bensoussan, was enough for him to get through another page of his translation of the satire, pick up his dry cleaning, teach his classes, and take Greta Bistritz out to dinner. With a wry smile, he told them all it was back to his own field for him—he had brought the find to their collective attention, and now he was done. Val herself remained silent. No one questioned how she felt about the Morgan Library's official media blackout for one scant week. But they were all in agreement that there were a few questions slammed up against the little they knew at that moment.

Who had replaced the original piece of writing with the new one? Why, and when? Bensoussan's timeline narrowed down the window of larcenous opportunity to sometime between mid-March and the beginning of April. Lorton said she could check the log for patrons who had visited the Rare Books and Manuscripts room during that time frame and requested Item #JPML 17-203. In some ways, though, to Val—who suspected a mere check of a sign-in log wasn't going to be as conclusive as they were hoping—a different question was much more interesting. "Who wrote the original piece about thorns and iron and death, the one Saul copied," she ticked off on her fingers, "how long has it been in the holding, and—"she felt a sudden flash of something like a terrible insight "—and what exactly was it replacing?"

Some excited chatter swirled. "Who's been around here long enough," Greta practically collared Lorton, "to tell us anything about someone who's shown an unusual interest in this red acacia box and the satire?"

Val held up a hand. "Sorry, Saul, but it's not the box, and it's not the satire the thief of the Office Max sheet of paper was interested in, otherwise we wouldn't still be looking at authentic artifacts—namely, this box," she pointed, "and this satire, which are five hundred years old." He nodded, agreeing.

"I'll see what I can find out," said Lorton, "without arousing too much interest. We're underfunded these days, which is why there's no full-time, permanent librarian in the Rare Books room. Mostly pages retrieve Requested Materials and monitor the room, but..." She trailed off as she headed to the entrance to the Rare Books and Manuscripts room, where faces were jockeying for position in the small glass window. "Step back, please," Lorton announced and she pushed her way into the hall, disappearing into the clamoring patrons.

When she was out of sight and the door had closed behind her, Val quickly took half a dozen pictures of the ancient scrap with her iPhone while her aunt and the professor looked on.

"Let me work on the Hebrew," she said when she was finished, giving Greta a fierce look. "Not you, not the Agency. I have a source for the Hebrew. And it's extremely important, Auntie." As her aunt scrutinized her, and Bensoussan peeled off his gloves and headed to the trash can, all Val had time to add was one whispered word: "Adrian."

Then Greta laid her hand on the side of Val's head. "Keep me in the loop."

Wordlessly, Bensoussan set the scrap in the shallow secret drawer, along with the substituted piece of writing. "Saul," said Val quietly, as she picked up her photocopy of the replacement, "I'd like to do a comparison myself—"

With a smile, he handed her his copy of the original piece he had discovered hidden in the ancient box. "My pleasure. In fact, when you're done with it—" His eyes slid to Greta Bistritz. With a nod, Val tucked both sheets into her purse, and wondered how soon she could meet with Avital Korngold, Master of Situations. And, Val was hoping, classical Hebrew. On some level she couldn't understand, Val sensed the little leather scrap of Hebrew text was an oversight.

The thief—and the thought that the thief had stolen more than an earlier translation or tortured story was deeply frightening to her—had overlooked this scrap.

It had decayed right off a much larger document that was now exactly...where? Replaced by what she was increasingly certain could only be a translation of the full Hebrew document, a place marker, really, a queer little mystery, meant to quell any probing questions about what would otherwise be a secret drawer, standing empty.

As the others packed up slowly, Alice Lorton rejoined them, holding a safe deposit box for the holding and a slip of paper. "The last full-time librarian might be able to shed some insight," she said, waving the slip. "It was before my time, so I can't tell you how helpful this lead will be for us, but still...He lives in Gramercy Park." Val took the name and address from Lorton's hand. "His name is Guy Everett."

Although Alice Lorton had mentioned the former librarian in Rare Books and Manuscripts had been fired on the spot, apparently, for wigging out and being spectacularly offensive to a patron, he had always been considered pretty knowledgeable. Whether he was still at the Gramercy Park address nobody knew. After all, it had been several years since anyone had last seen him. But, considering he had been permanently forbidden to enter the Library—the patron he had insulted was on the Board of Directors—that was to be expected. And Everett had never fraternized outside of work. The couple of Morgan employees who remembered him referred to him as eccentric, but they weren't even positive of that, maybe they were just remembering him charitably. Maybe, when all was said and done, Guy Everett was an uptight, old-school librarian who finally, one afternoon, and with the wrong patron, broke.

Val gave Ivy League Ivy a quick call to let her know she was going to be late getting back to the office, and then headed briskly down Madison to 23rd Street, cutting over to Park Avenue South and the Gramercy Park address on Lorton's slip of paper. What looked like two adjoining brownstones presented a flat, inscrutable front to the public.

Over the dark blue double doors on the right flew a blue and gold flag fluttering no harder than a butterfly's wings in the light April breeze. Two elaborate, interlocking initials—R.C.—was all the flag held.

Whatever stone steps the building on the right had once were obviously replaced, not all that long ago, with a concrete handicapped ramp with switchbacks leading up to the entrance. Enclosing both brownstones was a black wrought-iron fence. Val sprang the latch and stepped onto the short walkway to the front steps of 44 Gramercy Park West, which was flanked by lamps resembling Victorian streetlights.

Running lightly up the ten steps to the entrance to Guy Everett's home, she passed traditional-looking urns holding identical spiral topiaries, and rapped the brass knocker against the rather grand, white double doors.

After a minute, she heard a slow rustling inside, followed by an even slower opening of one of the doors. Framed in the doorway stood a slight man in a three-quarter length dark blue tunic leaning slightly on two canes. In a gaunt, pale face two rosy spots clung to his cheeks. He might be as young as fifty, or as old as seventy. Not happy, not well, not—something. His lips barely moved. "Yes?"

"My name is Val Cameron and I'm looking for Guy Everett."

The man in the tunic raised thin gray eyebrows. "What's the nature of your business?"

She tipped her head at him. "I represent the Artifact Authentication Agency."

One hand lifted a cane and waved vaguely to the street. "My manservant isn't home right now."

She was confused. "Is Mr. Everett your manservant?"

"No," he said with great dignity. "I'm Everett, but I don't receive callers unless my manservant is here."

Manservant? Callers? Val suddenly understood the Victorian streetlights. "I see," she said. "This shouldn't take long." A quick glance into the house, where she could tell Guy Everett wasn't about to invite her, showed a gleaming wood floor, rugless and ascetic, white walls and woodwork disappearing down a long corridor. Halfway down on the left was a font of some sort, with a small Crucifix mounted on the wall above it.

Guy Everett lifted his chin. "And what is it in regard to?"

"We've discovered an irregularity in one of the holdings at the Morgan Library."

At that, he blinked. "I'm no longer in their employ."

"I understand that, Mr. Everett," she said with a smile, "but we've been told you're very knowledgeable."

His green eyes narrowed at her, one hand moving restlessly on the brass handle of the cane. "And what precisely are you asking me to be knowledgeable about?"

Coming from another kind of man, Val might have taken it as humor. But not in Everett. "Item #JPML 17-203, a holding from the Mexican Inquisition."

"Offhand," he said smoothly, "it doesn't ring any bells."

She cocked her head at the strange little man with graying hair held impeccably in place with gel. "A satire, written in 1595, contained in a wooden box that is at least that old."

He appeared to have his eyes on something stepping out of the mists of memory. "I may recall something of it. Who did you say you're with?"

She fudged it. "I represent the Artifact Authentication Agency, a branch of the U.S. Department of Commerce." A little fear never hurt. "We're Feds," she added in what she hoped was a disarming way.

"Ah. Federal," he repeated, and Val sensed he was stalling. "And you're trying to authenticate what, exactly? The satire? The acacia wood box?"

"No," said Val reasonably, "neither of those. Right now we're trying to trace patrons' access to that holding at the time you were still the librarian in Rare Books and Manuscripts."

He gave her a look. "Why? Has something happened to it?"

Val had to make a quick decision about how much information she could offer. How much and how accurate. "A—compartment in the box contains a sheet of paper that appears to be a rather recent translation into English of—"

"The satire?" He nodded nervously at her in the way people do when they want you to agree. "It would have to be the satire..."

"Good guess, Mr. Everett," she said in a way she hoped didn't sound too patronizing, "but our expert in Latin American literature says not. No, it appears to be the translation of a scrap from a document of great antiquity—" On some level she knew she needed to keep the flow of information to a trickle.

He went pale. "A scrap from a document?" breathed Everett.

"A fragment of a fragment." Val demonstrated with her thumb and forefinger. "Something that became detached—"

"Where's the document then?" Suddenly he was truculent.

"That's a very good question," said Val.

With great effort, he pulled himself up straight. "If the document is gone, then how can you know what it is, or even whether it is? Such leaps are bad—bad—librarianship."

"I agree. But I'm not a librarian, so I get to make those leaps."

"You show no method," he rocked back on his heels, "no attention to—"

She got a glimpse of the librarian who had raged at a board member seven years ago. Still, she kept her voice even. "We'll have more conclusive information by the end of this week, Mr. Everett." *Because that's all the time we have.*

He brandished a cane at her. "That's no excuse for—"

She overrode him as gently as she could. "Can you recall any patron during the latter days of your work at the Morgan Library who showed an unusual interest in Item #JPML 17-203? Any irregularities in the sign-in log? What we're looking for is—"

Suddenly, Guy Everett stepped back, warding her off with both hands. "I'm sorry, I have no information, I have no recollection," he was jabbering, "and my manservant isn't at home."

She looked at him, baffled. "But I thought you said—"

He cried, "My manservant isn't at home."

Val couldn't remember any time in her life when a door was slammed in her face, but here it was. Not only had Guy Everett, former librarian, done just that, but she stood in amazement as she listened to him on the other side of the door fumbling locks and sliding a deadbolt. She moved very close to the doors and waited to hear him disappear back down that long hall with the gleaming floor. He didn't. It struck her that the brittle, ailing little man who used to work at the Morgan Library was waiting for the alarming Val Cameron of the Artifact Authentication Agency to head back down his front steps and disappear forever. She decided to oblige. Nothing to gain by sticking around. Everett wasn't going to let her in whether the elusive manservant—who calls the help manservants these days?—was at home or not. It felt like a kindness to make a noisy exit off his front steps so the overwrought Everett could stop cowering inside his own home.

As Val walked quickly over to Broadway and headed north to the Flatiron Building, her mind replayed her peculiar doorstep conversation with Guy Everett. He was fine, she thought, hurrying across the street while she still had the light, up to the point she mentioned what she had carefully called a document of great antiquity. For Everett, somehow, that moment was a game changer.

He nearly lost it. Defensive, incoherent, with just one immediate goal: get Val Cameron off his front step. She had touched a raw and dangerous place in the sick little man in his blue tunic with his holy water font in the background. Val picked up her pace.

There was no doubt in her mind that Guy Everett had information about the box, the satire, the recent translation...and the scrap of ancient Hebrew. It might be interesting to compare either the first or second sheets of paper found in the secret drawer with something in the files at the Morgan Library that Guy Everett himself had written. At that moment, Val realized, as she neared her office, she really did wish she was a Fed. What possible authority could she exert over whatever information or suspicions—or stolen documents—Guy Everett possessed?

And then it struck her with force that he had let something slip.

The box. She was certain, in her attempts to keep whatever details she offered him to a minimum, she had only called it a wooden box.

But despite his denials, Everett had later referred to it as exactly what it was: a box made of acacia wood.

No recollection, no information, no manservant.

Maybe Guy Everett's manservant wasn't at home, but about everything else, he had lied.

25

Antony Bale buzzed Val into Adrian's building off Columbus Circle. As she pushed her way into the cool foyer, she felt a twinge—this was the first time in many years that it wasn't Adrian's finger on the buzzer. Nothing felt right. It was entirely possible that nothing would ever feel right. As she started trudging up the stairs to the third floor, Val shifted the paper bag packed high with takeout containers from Whole Foods. She and Bale had agreed to share chicken wings and a platter of crudités. Plus some kind of flavored San Pellegrino; Val would see what they had.

Ahead was a work session. When she had told Bale over the phone about the trove of finds at the Morgan Library, he was excited to see both Saul Bensoussan's original translation from the secret drawer and the second, newer one that had replaced it. Bale was baffled. "And being baffled," he told her, "disturbs me. Puts me right off my wings." In Val's purse were the copies Alice Lorton had given her of both translations.

When she had returned to the office after the Morgan—and her run-in with the peculiar Guy Everett—the afternoon ran away with her. Between the defection of a longtime copyeditor, a cookbook author hysterical over the cover art for her next release, and the weekly departmental meeting that had five new items slapped last minute onto the agenda, Val hadn't had a chance to study the two translations for herself. Added to that was her realization that she had forgotten her raffia tote in Bale's hotel room, and she'd have to get it at some point.

He stood waiting for her in the doorway to Adrian's apartment. "I just got here myself."

Val had always loved Adrian's place, its warm, funky mix of Crate and Barrel contemporary and oddball pieces from estate sales on Riverside Drive or the Lower East Side, which accounted for the three-paneled folding screen, the washstand minus the crockery, and a bishop's chair.

Crowding floor space in front of the tall windows were thriving split-leaf philodendrons and dracaenas. And the only thing Adrian Bale collected were antique ceramic art tiles that depicted birds, which she mounted randomly across the wall closest to all the floor plans. The effect was like living in an aviary. Bale had started to pack up his sister's clothes and books. Coats were piled neatly over the back of the couch.

"Oh!" Val cried. "My white jacket." Scooping it up, she smiled at Bale. "I forgot I'd lent it to Adrian for the trip."

"She wore it all the time. It's yours?"

Val nodded, holding it against her cheek for a moment, thinking of Adrian wearing it in Norfolk. Val could swear it had Adrian's signature scent—the light, classic l'Air du Temps—and found herself wondering how long it would last. As Antony held a long match to the jets in Adrian's gas fireplace to take the April chill off the room, Val set the white belted jacket Adrian had worn in Norfolk with her own red plaid coat she had tossed over the back of a chair.

The two of them spread out the wings and crudités, the San Pellegrino, and the translations from the Morgan Library on the shapely wood and glass coffee table Adrian had bought at a craft fair in Easthampton several years ago.

Val settled herself cross-legged on the rug as Antony stood over her, pouring the water. He may have been wearing charcoal gray pants and a collarless white shirt, but he was barefoot. Val may have been wearing her favorite black Ann Taylor ankle pants, but she had thrown on a lightweight purple jersey hoodie—with the hood pulled up, pushing her crazy hank of hair farther over her eye.

There in Adrian's abandoned apartment, it felt like a very domestic evening.

On his way to the kitchen for more napkins, Bale cued up Pandora on Adrian's laptop, and Gershwin's "Rhapsody in Blue" pierced the air. A beautiful choice for the aviary. If he let her choose keepsakes, Val suddenly knew she wanted the birds of paradise tiles from Adrian's collection. At least it was something. But nothing was going to be adequate to the memory of Adrian Bale.

As Bale settled himself across the coffee table from her, he sighed noisily. "How do you want to do this?" he asked, sliding a small stack of napkins toward her.

Val squinted at the millwork Adrian had repaired at great expense. "We eat, we drink, we compare." When he said nothing, Val raised her hand. "All at the same time. Good?"

He nodded once. "Now I call that a party."

She raised her glass. "But, then, you live in a monastery."

He laughed hard, and the two of them sorted out the sharing of the chicken wings, the offloading of cut-up vegetables and dip, and the equitable division of an odd number of dill pickles that had somehow made their way into the takeout. When they finally dug in and chewed while they silently studied the two translations, Val swallowed three Kalamata olives and asked, "How are the wings?"

"All skin and sauce."

"As they should be."

"Otherwise, what's the point?"

"Agreed." When Bale extended an open bag of chips at her, Val grabbed a handful. "Here," she said, pushing Saul Bensoussan's original translation at him. "Why don't you read this aloud, and I'll compare it to the second one as you go. Good?"

"Good." Bale swiped a paper napkin across his mouth and slid a pen through the wreckage of the takeout food to Val. Then he smoothed out the translation Saul Bensoussan had originally come across in the acacia wood box when he had first triggered the secret drawer, and turned it sideways so Val could take a look at the sheet for a moment. Reading the original together seemed a good way to begin. Glancing at Val, he asked, "Ready?" When she nodded he began to read it slowly.

...the Son of God in this night among the olive trees of Gat Smanim. For he says what binds his feet, what pierces his flesh, what crowns his head are the way to life everlasting among the world of living men. So are body and soul healed, and death must find another, one who sees not. He who hungers for what is hidden in the divine must begin with what binds his feet, what pierces his flesh, and what crowns his head. Iron penetrates like faith, and the thorn draws blood and truth.

For in the moment of greatest extremity among the most faithful, it is through the sting of the thorn that life flows forevermore in the world of man. In these days hereafter, iron and thorn are man's inheritance. Keep them safe from the eyes of the many, for this is a secret inheritance, and taken together they are the bridge for all to the new world among the kingdoms of men, where pain and strife become but chaff cast away in the breath of the Lord. Let it fall to the most righteous among you to let nothing deter and let no one deny. This is the might of Christ in his final affliction and his promise of a kingdom to come in the world of living men.

Glancing at Val, he asked, "Ready?" When she nodded, he began to read it slowly. In the warmth and quiet of Adrian's apartment, his voice sounded beautiful to her, the two-thousand-year-old words floating all around them. As current as the smell of an extremely fine passel of wings or her very last heartbeat.

At that moment Val could believe that everything around her throbbed—the heat from the gas fire, the Gershwin turned down low, the translated words that push and flee across centuries, just out of grasp. And then she was puzzled. "'Among the olive trees of Gat Smanim'?"

He looked over at her. "'Gethsemane.' Same in yours?"

"Yes..." Val put her head in her hands, trying to work it out.

"An important place name, so if the object of a new translation is to—" She stopped, feeling her way along.

"Obscure the true meaning?" offered Bale.

"Or," with a sigh, she met his look, "to mislead."

"Let's hold off deciding that right now."

"I agree."

"Maybe it's all skin and sauce."

She smiled. "Ah, but even skin and sauce is—"

"—still wings."

"Exactly. The fact that our translator did not monkey with an important place name suggests—" She drummed her fork on the glass-topped table.

Bale suddenly said, "Gat Smanim was too recognizable to change. Do you know what I'm saying?"

"Anyone who had seen the original translation in that secret drawer—Saul Bensoussan, for instance—would see right away if a place name as familiar across several cultures as Gat Smanim had been changed or deliberately mistranslated."

"Still, in the end," Bale leaned back on his elbow, "in the end, maybe the setting wasn't the most important thing about this text." He gently waved Bensoussan's paper.

"Ah," said Val, brandishing half a dill pickle, "then what is?"

Bale picked up where he had left off but he didn't get very far when Val caught a change between the original translation and the substitute. "Hold up, Antony, right there. What was that last word, 'what binds his—'"

"Feet. 'What binds his feet.'"

She met his look. "I've got 'faith.' 'What binds his faith.'" She put a check next to the word. Bale continued to read, but Val soon stopped him again. "Nope, hold up. I've got 'what crowns his heart.' Heart, not head." She jotted another check. "And tell me again, what have you got after 'the way to life everlasting?'"

Bale took a quick look. "'Among the world of living men.'"

"The new translation has 'after the world of living men.'"

They sipped their drinks silently for a minute. Then Bale set his down and turned the glass reflectively. "It's very different, isn't it? Changing only one word—"

"—especially if it kind of sounds like the original—"

"—makes a big difference. Here's how the first section reads in the original translation that Bensoussan found in the box." Bale read: "'...*the Son of God in this night among the olive trees of Gat Smanim. For he says what binds his feet, what pierces his flesh, what crowns his head are the way to life everlasting among the world of living men. So are body and soul healed, and death must find another, one who sees not. He who hungers for what is hidden in the divine must begin with what binds his feet, what pierces his flesh, and what crowns his head.*'"

Bale looked at her and smiled. "You're the editor, Val. What do you make of the changes?" He handed her the sheet, and she set them side by side on the table.

After studying both translations for a few minutes, Val sat back. "It's the same translator at work, right? Same handwriting. Most likely Everett himself." She lifted the sheet Saul Bensoussan had given them. "You know, Antony, there's something about the original that reads like—like—a formula for something. It's pretty concrete. What crowns the head, what binds the feet, what pierces the flesh."

Bale was watching her closely. "Like a set of instructions."

"Exactly." Val gave a little laugh. "A recipe. If you do x, then y will happen."

"I see what you mean. But in the substitution, the translator changes just enough to make it...fail."

Val shook out more chips. "What binds his faith? Pretty words, but now it's an abstraction. Same with 'crowns his heart.' There's just enough figurative language that the basic formula..."

"In the event anyone comes across it—"

"...is utterly lost. And look at the small but important changes he made in the time frame."

"Where?" Bale reached for both sheets.

"Wherever the original translation says 'among' the world of living men, or words to that effect, the substitution uses the word 'after.' It becomes 'after the world of living men.'"

Bale whistled softly. "It's nothing less than the difference," he helped himself to some chips, "between the here and the hereafter."

"After the world of living men, I think," she clapped a hand on her chest, "adds color commentary to—what?—a heaven we've already heard about...and can never prove." Then she added, "Or disprove."

"Is it the kind of color commentary someone's willing to kill for?"

In a way, Val realized, that question was at the heart of what she and Bale were trying to figure out. "I don't think so." She reached across the table and found one single word she tapped twice with the tip of her fingernail. "Behold. One final change."

"Let's see." Bale leaned in, his dark head turning from one sheet to the other. "Secret and sacred," he said finally, his eyes drifting to the small and steady fire.

"In the original, the instructions—if we want to call it that—carry a warning, right? This is a 'secret' inheritance. But in the substitute it's become a 'sacred' inheritance. Here again, the true word has been replaced with one that sounds very much like it, but the point is completely different. A 'sacred' inheritance tells us we should treat it with respect."

"What crowns our heart and binds our faith," said Bale wryly.

She nodded slowly. "But a 'secret' inheritance warns us that whatever the formula is promising may not come to pass if—"

Bale pushed away the sheets, suddenly full. "If we don't kill to keep it a secret."

They finished the meal in silence, at one point Bale disappearing into Adrian's kitchen and returning with a bottle of Prosecco. Something was needed, thought Val, who had felt herself disappearing into the disturbing translations from the Morgan Library, and it might as well be some wine. Along with the sexy, soaring notes she always counted on Gershwin for—pulled from those recesses she had always felt she shared with him. *What crowns the heart,* for Val, studying the blot of flames through the glass of sparkling Italian white wine, suddenly seemed like the better choice for translation...even if not the accurate one. It translated Val, that much she knew. No formula, no how-to with a translated fragment that to her editorial ear sounded self-consciously prophetic.

Over a single glass each of the Prosecco—leave it to Adrian to buy the finest—she and Bale spoke a little about the memorial service the next morning. And what in the original translation certainly sounded like the need for the Crown of Thorns. And the goal to get the Hebrew scrap translated as soon as possible. A comfortable little string of afterthoughts, at day's end, the way couples do as they tug off socks and set their alarms in the low light.

The fire was low, the wine was low, the expectation was low. As she slipped on the white jacket for the short cab ride back to her apartment, she wondered what Bale did when the evening ends with an offer to stay the night. If it ever did. When she realized her cheeks were burning, she concentrated suddenly on fussing with the belt that was proving to be a more complicated thing than she remembered. While she fumbled with it, damn twisted thing, Val reminded herself that the man who was watching her inscrutably, with his arms folded, barefoot, in his gray pants and plain white shirt, had a very full life elsewhere. Quite elsewhere, when it came right down to it, in every possible way. He had duties. And devotions. And genuflections. And mortification of the flesh, for all she knew. Whatever those were. He had chosen a life that contained a very different kind of love. Finally, Val made a frustrated noise at the belt and just let it hang there.

His voice low, Adrian's brother was telling her how she could come back to Adrian's anytime over the rest of the month to take whatever she liked. While he spoke, she stuffed her hands in the pockets of the jacket, her left hand closing around a small sharp object she pulled out. She found herself looking down at a silver and vermilion bottle cap—Olde Bandylegs Mild Caper—as he finished by saying he'd be back in a month to dispose of everything else. In the meantime, Val should help herself.

"But what I liked best," she blurted to Bale, "isn't even here."

In that second, as she looked away to keep herself from crying about her murdered friend, she caught a look in his eyes. He was disappointed somehow. In those intelligent brown eyes, she saw something very much like regret.

26

In the Jasper and Eleanora Witt room at the Coleman-Witt Museum, where French doors led out to a flagstone patio and garden with only the daffodils showing, Bale was alone in the receiving line. The memorial service for Adrian had lasted about an hour, and the Witt Ballroom—which was how a keyed-up Eva Toscano had referred to it—had drawn about forty of Adrian's friends and co-workers. Bale, dressed in a charcoal gray suit and white shirt open at the neck, had officiated.

At staggering expense two years ago, Adrian had told Val, the Witts had footed the bill for renovations to the west building that resulted in the ballroom with its wall of long windows, a ceiling that got bumped up two stories, a state-of-the-art sound system, and hardwood flooring with tasteful strips of Macassar ebony. Built-in caches had been added to the room at elegant intervals, where artifacts from the Coleman-Witt's permanent collection were rotated. In honor of Adrian's career, Toscano had filled the caches with the Sumerian pieces Adrian had acquired.

The cool April morning sunlight was slanting low through the windows, and Val heaved a sigh, pushed herself out of the trim brown leather chair, and walked into the brightest patch. The sound system was on an endless loop of a playlist Antony had chosen from Adrian's favorite music. Everything from the Rondo of Beethoven's "Emperor Concerto" to Norah Jones breathily singing "Don't Know Why." Val gave Bale a lot of credit for avoiding any psalms or excerpts from Ecclesiastes, because Adrian had no use for them, and instead he and Eva Toscano and Val offered reminiscences. Then she read aloud what she knew had been Adrian Bale's favorite poem, "Among School Children," by Yeats.

For Adrian, the final lines, which were actually provocative questions, had always seemed to Val like they held the answer to every obscure thing in their lives, if only they could answer them. *O chestnut tree, great rooted blossomer, are you the leaf, the blossom, or the bole? O body swayed to music, O brightening glance, how can we know the dancer from the dance?* Through drunken and disappointing dates, through sober and soaring academic achievements, these were always Adrian's questions. With enough wine in them, sometimes they would make irreverent stabs at answering the questions. With enough wine in them, as long as Val and Adrian were together, sometimes they almost let the questions go forever unanswered. But never quite.

Val had read the poem without a stumble, without a podium, standing there alone in the center of the ballroom in her navy blue jersey dress and matching heels, her toes touching a beautiful strip of ebony. Then she folded and re-folded the paper, and from among the mourners, her eyes found Bale watching her from the French doors, held slightly open with a reproduction doorstop in the likeness of an Etruscan bull. Nobody else's eyes gave anything away, and maybe the Yeats poem seemed like a peculiar choice to the others. Funerals were the time and place for platitudes—maybe the one time and place where easy and familiar reassurances were craved. *She's in a better place. She's with Jesus now. She's out of pain. We'll see her again someday.* In the face of all those utterances that Bale was no doubt fielding—along with handshakes and fleeting kisses—from the others, Val would always choose the Yeats. She smiled at the thought that maybe Bale would too.

The crowd was thinning, some flowing out into the garden to have coffee and chocolate croissants Toscano had ordered, knowing it was Adrian's favorite breakfast. Others moved gravely toward the rack holding the coats by the doors leading back into the lobby. Val understood how even the smallest gesture meant something when they were all, all of them still on the better side of the grave. Coats got stroked, arms got held, steps got measured. Maybe murder didn't make much of a difference when it all looked like death in the end.

To Val, alone again in the sunlit center of this small ballroom, where she could see in the dazzling light beautiful variations in the tones of the ebony strips, the memorial service was adequate. For that one hour, she had been able to set aside the pain and mystery of Adrian's death. But even now she was starting to feel it all creep back, making her poor skin crawl.

Are you the leaf, the blossom, or the bole?

What was she supposed to think about what had happened to her best friend?

In a corner of the room, Toscano was heading for the patio with the remaining two mourners, as the endless loop was coming to the final breathless chords of "The Sounds of Silence." Bale came up to her, his suit jacket over his shoulder. They stood apart, silent, no one knowing any better than the two of them that no funeral for Adrian could ever be more than just adequate. For a second, he sighed and looked away. Her arms hung at her sides, restless. She felt insubstantial in a high-ceilinged room where grief hung like humidity. Suddenly the bold discordant sounds of "España Cañi" pierced the air—Adrian's choice for the *paso doble*, her favorite ballroom dance that she had taught Val over two sessions at Swing 46—and Bale strode to the closest chair, where he slung his jacket.

No sooner had he rolled up his sleeves than he grabbed Val around her waist and she gasped a small laugh, and together they danced the four fast, turning two-steps of the *paso doble*. After the rapid hip-swinging chassé in each other's arms, she spun away from him, then waited for him to spin up to her and pull her back into his arms. Then Bale passed Val behind him, a matador and his cape, and lifted her over his extended leg. Her hands clutching her skirt high over her hips, she made a feint, he struck a pose.

When the music slowed, so did they, and she arched her back against his hand as Bale danced her backwards in an elegant turning two-step across the ballroom floor, casting all thoughts of murder away from them. Val felt as though she was living inside the music, her feet lighter than she remembered, and that she was something other than terrestrial—she was pulse and air and a flutter of beautiful brass notes.

Val paused briefly, her back up close to Bale, her right leg overstepping his own, and they danced the chassé just far enough apart they could still add the flourish of a drag, and grab hold of each other's hands. He spun her past him, and at the final notes, she came to a stop and arched her back, her arms bent at the shoulders. Very slowly, he extended a hand to her, as if he were making one last remark in what had been the conversation of *paso doble*. Without a word, Val knew they had danced it for Adrian.

How can we know the dancer from the dance?

27

Avital Korngold, of Avital Korngold Situations, was torn between eating her pizza, addressing the Hebrew set out in front of her, and describing the poor personal hygiene of her social studies teacher. When Val called to suggest dinner, the girl chose Noi Due Kosher Café on W. 69th Street, east of Broadway. "Nice little Italian place," she had added in the offhand manner cultivated by thirteen-year-old girls. "I think you'll like it. But let's get there early," she added, with exuberant weariness, "Noi Due is small and the only casual eatery that is also kosher on," here Val heard the girl on the phone suck in a breath then blurt, "the entire Upper West Side," as though the size and sweep of that neighborhood rivaled the planet Jupiter. They agreed on five p.m., and Val called Bale and gave him the address.

Probably the last thing Adrian's brother wanted to hear that day was a dinner plan that took him half a dozen blocks from the scene of her murder. But he was uncomplaining and agreed to meet that renowned Master of Situations, Avital Korngold, anywhere her heart desired. Besides, Italian was—by him—the best comfort food in the world. He said he'd come straight from the two-hour daily contemplative time observed by the Carmelites, and Val was reminded of how very different his life was from hers. When he added, "I manage to pack all my contemplation into about forty-five minutes," she laughed and found she felt better.

That afternoon, after clocking some serious time at work with back-to-back meetings, Val got an email from James Killian, who had attached his proposal for a new book, tentatively titled, *Babes in Brewland: Sex, Intrigue, and the Almighty Buck Among the World's Craft Beer Makers.* Offhand, thought Val, clicking quickly through the fifteen page proposal—how does Killian manage to generate something that quickly?—it caught her interest. At any rate, more than *Plumb Lines*, his tell-all about the Excretory Lifestyles of the Rich and Famous. What famous movie star had a toilet seat covered in leopard fur? What famous rap star had toilet paper made in the image of the Confederate flag?

Only Val's disturbed former boss, who pulled Killian's work out of the slush pile, would find any redeeming social value in such trash. For Val, who was then stuck with it, it took trashy to know trashy, and although Killian himself seemed all right, aside from his cockiness, *Plumb Lines* was finally no better than the crap it described in rollicking prose. Small print run, small format, an impulse buy near supermarket checkouts, swift remaindering, and she'd be done with it.

Still, she thought, eyeing the new proposal, Val had to give Killian credit—he could be on to something marketable with this craft beer industry exposé. In a rare moment of expansiveness that she thought later might have something to do with the heightened emotions of Adrian's memorial service that morning, she shot Killian a quick email. *Interesting proposal. Meet for a drink tomorrow to discuss?* Then she forwarded the file to Ivy League Ivy, with the quick tag, *If I acquire it, will you handle it? Better yet, given authorship, can you handle it?* From her office two doors down from Val's, Ivy shot back right away, *Are you kidding? Killian? I'd consider it a job perk!*

With that, Val laughed hard as she slipped out of her moccasins, and then reached into her lowest drawer for her emergency stash of Chanel No. 5. After quick dabs on her wrists and behind her ears, she grabbed her handbag and turned off her desk lamp. The little click that, for Val, set apart daylight from nighttime. On weekends, she actually missed it. As Val rode the elevator down with two employees whose names she didn't know, only that they were recent hires in the IT department, her phone chirped. Sliding it out of her bag, she saw a text from James Killian.

How's today for that drink?

Val thumbed, *Can't. Tomorrow is soonest.*

When and where?

Where are you staying? she texted back. They could at least meet somewhere convenient.

But he dodged it. *I can meet you anywhere.*

Val gave him the address of Old Town Bar on 18th Street, where she had landed with Bale that first night, and added four thirty p.m. It felt important to meet him during the work day. When nothing came back from James Killian, she assumed they were on, and Val picked up the pace to the subway. At Times Square, she shouldered her way onto the 1 train, which she rode to 72nd Street. Swept along in the human current she emerged back onto the street, then hurried the two blocks to Noi Due, Tali's choice.

When she caught sight of Antony Bale leaning on the metal railing leading down to the entrance to the kosher café, her heart lifted before he even turned to see her and raise a hand in greeting. Wordlessly, they stepped into a hug just as Tali herself showed up wearing a long black skirt, red boots, and a quirky hooded leather coat of many colors.

Gravely, she shook hands. "Follow me, lucky people," she then said, bounding down the stairs and holding open the front door to the café. After she pushed together two of the small, bare-bones tables and plopped herself down across from Bale and Val, she pushed back her hood with a flourish. A star-crossed heroine from a Victorian novel, thought Val, hiding a smile. Stuck in her mass of dark hair were little fake jeweled hairpins. Referring to the server as Chaim, she annotated the menu for Val and Antony Bale, who suggested she order for all three of them. Pleased, Tali raised a hand to summon a server, and Chaim, who was clearly enjoying the girl's presence, ambled over.

Tali folded her hands and glanced ruminatively at the ceiling. Then she declared, "A bottle of Chianti for my friends—the

Bartenura, naturally, if you still have it?" Jotting, Chaim inclined his head. "And an iced tea for me." Tali went on, "We'll begin with the caprese, please, Chaim, followed by two large Brancato pizzas."

"The Brancato is off the menu," Chaim murmured.

When Tali fixed him with a look of deep disapproval, he said, "I'll see what I can do." Widening his eyes at nothing in particular, the server departed.

"The Brancato," Tali leaned across the table, spreading her hands as though no explanation was necessary, "has the roasted red peppers and eggplant, so—"

Bale and Val nodded solemnly.

At that moment a teenage boy in black pants, white shirt, apron and crocheted yarmulke with the Mets logo, slid to the table two over from them where diners had just departed, and started to clear the place of the dirty plates. Tali sucked in a breath, pressed her lips together and kicked at Val underneath the table. The busboy glanced over. "Oh, hi, Tali," he said, and went back to work.

Tali managed to grunt something by way of response in the boy's direction, then added, "Oh, hi," with studied indifference, turning away with a bored little hair fling. Then, to Val, she mouthed, "Sruly Levinson," with a desperation that would have fit nicely with the news the Pharaoh's army was half a league behind them.

Val gave Sruly Levinson the eye, and was struck by the fact that the boy had height, broad shoulders, features more comely than most teenage boys', and a small acne issue that looked like it would clear up with no trace. When she turned back to Tali and shot her a discreet thumbs up, the girl uttered a *tsk* of great disdain, and said, "Parents," leaving Val to wonder when she had crossed the line into parenthood. Next to her, Antony Bale was biting his lip and smoothing out a print-out of the best shot Val had taken with her iPhone of the slim scrap of Hebrew.

Tali gave it a quick glance as the iced tea and Chianti arrived. Giving her drink a vigorous stir with her straw, Avital Korngold Situations raised her glass and toasted, "L'chayyim," which Bale and Val echoed, and the girl pulled the print-out closer to her as she sipped.

"Very nice," said Bale of the wine.

"Of course."

"How do you know it?" he went on, keeping his expression neutral.

She nodded. "You mean because I'm thirteen? It's the one my mom likes," explained Tali. "And she has excellent taste." As the café got busy, when Chaim set the caprese down on the table with three small plates, then left, she whispered that Chaim's father was her social studies teacher, a pious fellow who could describe all the amendments to the U.S. Constitution but couldn't seem to identify a good body soap. She suddenly sat back in her chair and looked at Bale and Val. "Is that *loshon hora*, do you think? The evil tongue?"

Bale looked at Val, his eyes settling on her lips. "What do you think, Valjean?"

Val inhaled, turning to their thirteen-year-old Hebrew translator. "Did you say it to be hurtful?"

Tali considered. "No," she answered slowly, "but that doesn't mean it wasn't, I suppose." She pushed her fork at the share of caprese she had lifted onto her own small white plate. "In my defense," she added with some spirit, "I only meant it to be informative."

Val smiled at her. "Isn't that the rationale of all gossips?"

When Tali gasped and shot her a look that suggested she was judged and found wanting, Bale scrutinized his forkful of mozzarella topped with basil, and said, "I think the measure here is whether the information was necessary." Popping his bite of caprese into his mouth, he added, while Tali studied him, "If it isn't necessary, then—" He pointed his fork at the girl.

"—then it's idle. And it's *loshon hora*. Yes," she said in a grownup way. "I see your point, Antony." The arrival of the Brancato pizza cheered her up immediately. "Yay, Chaim, *todah rabah*! Thanks a lot." The caprese forgotten, the handsome busboy crush forgotten, the girl helped herself to a fragrant wedge. "I'll have to take on more cases to make up for it." Val was impressed as Tali helped herself to two sizeable bites before she wiped off her hands with great zeal and pulled the Hebrew sheet closer to her.

"It's pretty faded," she commented, then pointed with one finger, "and you can see where it's been damaged, right?"

"Will you need more time?" asked Val quietly. Alice Lorton's one-week grace period was never very far away from her thoughts. How long could she wait before—

"Not at all," said the girl. "I translated it right away." Then she dabbed at her lips with a clean napkin.

Val and Bale exchanged a quick look. "And?" prompted Val.

"Understand it's a—a—" she snapped her fingers trying to snatch the elusive idea, "sentence fragment, so what you've got here is cut off in the middle of the sentence." She narrowed her eyes at them. "Is this all you have? It would really help if—" She left it unspoken.

Bale swirled his wine. "We have translations of what we believe comes from the rest of the fragment, but we don't know yet which is correct."

"Oh, well, that's at least something, then. Excellent!" She beamed. "And you should know it isn't Hebrew. Well—" she temporized, her eyes shooting to the ceiling—"the alphabet is Hebrew, actually, but the language is Aramaic." When Val looked at her quizzically, Tali went on, "The language spoken by the people." Tali's eyes sparkled. "It's extremely old, I'd say. Quite a find."

Val leaned closer to the girl. "Tali, we need to rely on your discretion for a while." Then she went on. "Do you understand?"

"This isn't your social studies teacher," Bale said quietly.

Val added, "It's really important." They regarded each other in silence. "Once we have this scrap translated, it should help us piece together the rest of what we've got."

Avital Korngold seemed to deflate a little. "I understand," she whispered. Very slowly, she pushed aside her dinner plate, with her Brancato slices still uneaten, and Val watched her read the scrap in complete silence from right to left. Then, pursing her lips, she nodded slightly. One hand settled on the edge of the sheet, and the other trailed along under the words. "It says, *and let what is brought forth from this place for all time be not agony and death but the words of Yohanan the beloved of—*" Tali pulled her hands into her lap and looked silently at Val and Bale. When Bale spread his hands, waiting for the rest, Tali explained, "Oh, that's where it breaks." A little shrug. "That's all you've got."

Bale asked her to repeat it.

Val pulled out the translation Saul Bensoussan had given her and took down Tali's translation of the Hebrew scrap—the opening line that had become separated from the rest of the ancient document, then slipped into a space between the shallow secret shelf and the false bottom of the red acacia box. As Tali gathered her things, talking about an Adele concert she was hoping to talk her mother into letting her attend, plus the clarinet lesson she was going to miss if she didn't hit the road that very minute, Val and Bale exchanged a look.

With a kiss to Val and a handshake with Bale, Tali thanked them several times, then—with one final check for the whereabouts of Sruly Levinson—she took off. Val sighed noisily and turned to Bale. "The Hebrew scrap changes everything." As she started to talk it through, he sat back and listened, nodding at Chaim when he dropped off a check. "Everett had to discover the main part of that document several years ago, before he was canned. When he went to translate what he had found, he had no idea it was incomplete," she said, reading from Saul Bensoussan's sheet. "Everett believed the document begins with '...*the Son of God in this night among the olive trees of Gat Smanim. For he says what binds his feet, what pierces his flesh, what crowns his head—*'"

"It sounds like a direct transcript of Christ's words."

Val got excited. "But it wasn't, was it? The scribe was taking down the words of Yohanan, the beloved—"

"From there it flows directly into the rest. '—the words of Yohanan the beloved of the Son of God.'"

"John?" she tried.

Bale tipped his head. "Almost certainly," he told her, reaching for his billfold.

Crossing her arms, Val stared at the sheet. "From there it gets murky, Antony. Who then is making the prophecy?" she asked tensely, leaning closer to him. "The 'he' is really unclear. Who exactly is providing the formula for life everlasting among the kingdoms of men, or whatever you want to believe? Jesus or John? Or John paraphrasing Jesus? It begins to feel like hearsay." She glanced at Bale, who set a credit card over the check. "Bottom line? Guy Everett made dangerous plans based on a damaged document."

Very slowly, Antony Bale, Cellarer, Burnham Norton Abbey, Sidestrand, Norfolk, U.K., turned the sheet to face him. Val watched something ripple in his expression. Finally, he tapped a phrase near the end of the translated document. "I didn't catch this before," he said quietly.

"What?"

"This phrase, Val," he went on, "'this is the might of Christ.'" Bale looked up at her. "The might of Christ." He shook his fine, dark head, laughing softly. "I've had my share of Latin."

"I can imagine."

"'The might of Christ'?" he told her with a smile. "In Latin it would be Robus Christi."

Remembering the blue and gold flag rippling outside the entrance to 46 Gramercy Park West, she felt a chill on the backs of her legs. "R.C.?"

"R.C." While Val's mind flew across every fact, impression, statement and half-truth she had come across since the morning Adrian Bale left her a voicemail before she was murdered, she watched Antony, who sat very still, grow quiet. At that moment, all he looked was troubled. "Robus Christi," he said so quietly she could barely hear him. "Val, I think Guy Everett built himself a whole infernal organization."

28

The next day, Millard was under strict orders.

Mr. Everett was committing himself to a silent, solitary retreat in the Robus Christi Chapel for an uncertain length of time and was not to be disturbed. Not for meals, baths, bedtimes, Alaric, household affairs, members of the High Council, or random disturbing women from any government agencies. When Millard widened his mismatched eyes at the last item on the list, Everett wondered if he had gone too far, but then let it go. It was, he squared his frail shoulders, the very least of what he was letting go.

Tightening the sash on the new white silk robe he had saved for the occasion was like signing an executive order. Where they stood together on the threshold of the connecting door between Everett's home and the chapel, Millard gave his employer's bare feet an inscrutable glance, murmured something that sounded like "Have a good time," and disappeared in the direction of the kitchen.

Turning away with difficulty, Everett entered the Robus Christ Chapel on two canes. Sweat seemed to thicken on his skin but dribbled nowhere, and the pain, bad as it was, felt like it was tearing at the undersides of his flesh, scrabbling with claws, trying to free itself. Even the pain knew it was sinking along with this pathetic body. If Everett didn't know for sure what lay ahead, he believed he would be howling in fear at the prospect of death. But the preparations kept him focused. With very little trembling, his fingers locked the connecting door and then Everett headed slowly to the place in front of the altar, where over the last two hours it had taken what was left of his strength to assemble the necessary objects. From the vault he had taken the lance, the nails, and the very precious Crown of Thorns, and arranged them on the dais. He had even lighted the beautiful blue and gold column candles, grateful for the butane lighter, because his eyes teared when it occurred to him he no longer had the strength to strike a match.

Who was there to watch over him in these final moments of this life?

He found himself wishing Alaric would come, out of the blue, unbidden.

He found himself for one single moment wishing Millard would break down the door.

And do what, exactly? Heal this body? Frustrate this prophecy?

As Guy Everett set aside his canes and settled himself on the dais in front of the altar, he decided to forgive himself for his loneliness. Despite the fact that even Jesus Christ, in his own extremity that final night in the Garden of Gethsemane, not far from sleeping disciples and one busy scribe, had companions. What Guy Everett had, instead, was a semicircle of sacred objects, and in a moment of very faint memory, he felt like a child again, surrounded by playthings. His Etch-a-Sketch, his trolls, his Rock 'Em Sock 'Em Robots. He started to reach for them, they were so very clear.

He fingered his well-worn translation of the prophecy that lay safely stored in the hidden drawer of the rosewood box on the table in his study next door. Safe. Across the millennia, across sands and rock and terrifying wide, deep oceans, this prophecy from the lips of Jesus Christ had come to rest in Gramercy Park. Every so often over these past few years, Everett would trigger the spring of the silent, sliding drawer and stare at the ancient leather, whispering his own Robus Christi prayers over the find that had lifted him these seven years ago straight out of the dreary throngs of men without purpose.

Had the Hebrew letters faded even farther into the ancient

brittle animal skin? The Cameron woman who had badgered him on his own doorstep—he was beyond even her now, her and her insinuations that somehow part of the priceless ancient document had become detached from the rest. He hadn't even checked. Within an hour, none of it would matter, ever again. Not the expenses over the past several years, not the necessary deaths in pursuit of the holy objects.

The time was quite close, he felt it in what was left of his body, and his eyes searched a dark corner near the ceiling. It shamed him that despite his remarkable destiny, he, Guy Everett, was still a little bit afraid of death. Maybe resurrection should come tagged with fear as well. Maybe even immortality. Could it grow tiresome? Would it prove to be a horror he never could have anticipated? Everett shuddered and did what he always did when troubled by his own weak thoughts. He studied the translation of the prophecy that a companion hand-chosen by Jesus Christ had inscribed carefully as the master uttered it, hours before his arrest and crucifixion.

With a small smile, Guy Everett closed his eyes. *Binds his feet, pierces his flesh, crowns his head.* Even as the Son of God foresaw the instruments of his own torture, he laid out a path to immortality through precisely those instruments. The nails, the lance, the Crown of Thorns. Right there, there, all around him, within reach of his dying fingertips. He had accomplished—with the help of Alaric, no denying, who was his warrior—the rarest and most priceless treasure hunt in the history of mankind.

He knew what remained: the Crown.

Guy Everett untied the robe, which, with a little shrug—all he could manage—slipped from his shoulders. Fell away. As surely as pain and doubt and fear. Fell clean away. His fingers stroked his naked ribs that jutted like a dozen lances of their own, aspiring to be stilettos penetrating through dying flesh to find the beautiful thick and golden air of Robus Christi. He touched the scar on his right side where he had lanced himself—privately—when Alaric had presented the holy object that the Roman had used at the Crucifixion; that's how ecstatic he had been. The infection had finally cleared up. And he touched the white loincloth that was all that covered him. His feet, with his insteps tattooed with the bold images of nails, seemed very far away from him. As he leaned toward them, where he sat, it was as if his backbone was popping into brilliant nothingness, one bone at a time, like bulbs shot out by bored boys. His breath was very shallow now, and he realized with a strange, remote lance of fear, that he couldn't see.

It was now.

With a cry, Guy Everett clutched the Crown of Thorns, and as he sank back, drove the barbs into his skull in a rush of what he could only call bliss.

29

This time, she arrived first for their drink together, about twenty minutes early. On some level, it was like finding high ground before a battle is enjoined. Not that Val expected a battle. But whenever she thought about this sizzling hot new Words on Fire author—based strictly on his prose, naturally—she found herself muddling around in military imagery. Find the high ground, keep your gunpowder dry, don't go straight up the center. These, she knew, had nothing to do with metaphor, not really. And they had everything to do with survival, based on hard experience.

Val found a booth near the back, and when the bartender raised his eyebrows at her, she ordered her favorite, a Sam Adams Boston Lager, in honor of meeting James Killian and discussing a beer book. By him, it was an exposé of sex, intrigue, and general bad behavior in the craft beer industry. By her, it was a beer book. When the Sam came, along with a paper coaster, she felt herself settle down from the difficult day, her eyes straying back to the entrance. Outside, afternoon sunlight backlit the hurrying crowd, and there was nobody who was demanding a damn thing of her. Happy hour was officially early that day.

Sipping through the delicious head, Val turned the pages of Killian's new book proposal to the table of contents. There was a regional order to the material she wasn't sure she liked, because it might push readers into thinking there were more cultural explanations for whatever particular bad behavior Killian was describing than perhaps there really were. She'd have to think about it. Just then her eye caught the title of one chapter in the section on craft brewing in the U.K.—"Getting Mild in the Midlands." She read the teaser: "The Stakes Get Raised at a Norfolk Brew Pub." For a second, Val felt queasy. Then she thumbed through the pages of the proposal's Overview until she found more information on the Norfolk Brew Pub.

Olde Bandylegs Brew Pub, Sidestrand, Norfolk, U.K.

And the beer was called the Olde Bandylegs Mild Caper. A "mild," Killian described briefly, was a beer dark in color and light in alcohol, one in which malt is dominant and hops take a backseat.

And it struck her forcefully that the bottle cap Adrian had slipped absentmindedly into Val's jacket pocket was from the Olde Bandylegs Pub. Val felt like a seven-year-old kid again the time Aunt Greta had taken her to Miami Beach and had held a mighty conch shell up to her little ear. Not the sound of the ocean so much as a great, deafening rush of air. With stiff fingers, Val drew the bottle cap out of her pocket and held it in her lap. Then she glanced down at it quickly. The graphic showed a bowlegged sprite capering lightly with a tabby cat. The proposal stated that Killian himself had visited each brew pub in the book and had sampled plentiful amounts of the signature brews.

What explained it? Val couldn't take her eyes from the silver and vermilion bottle cap. There was only one place Adrian could have had that beer—at the Olde Bandylegs Brew Pub in Sidestrand, Norfolk, while she was wearing Val's white jacket. And there was only one place Killian could have had that beer. But what if it had been months ago, or a year ago? Something she could put down to a weird coincidence, not this dread that was settling around her heart. Val grabbed her phone and Googled the Olde Bandylegs Mild Caper. What came up was the pub's homepage, where the headlining image was the bowlegged sprite, capering with a cat. *New Member of the Bandylegs Family! Meet the Mild!* And the text stated that the beer had been brought to market three weeks ago.

Three weeks ago.

She forced herself to construct a timeline, to see if an overlap between two people and a new beer was possible. Killian was, in a sense, easy. Val herself knew Killian was in New York for the past week, since Adrian had died. Where he was before this past week, she couldn't say, except for the new fact that he had sampled the Olde Bandylegs Mild Caper, which put him firmly in Norfolk between two and three weeks ago. Adrian's trip to England to visit her brother was a week long, and it would have been over the second week of the Mild Caper's appearance. It meant that Killian and Adrian overlapped for a single week in Sidestrand, Norfolk of all places. At the end of that week's overlap, the Crown of Thorns was stolen from Burnham Norton Abbey, Bale's boy monk Fintan McGregor went over a cliff, and Adrian had written in her Trip Journal about a sexy shaggy-haired stranger in the Olde Bandylegs Pub. And, without knowing, she had made off with the Crown of Thorns on her trip back to the States.

Val pulled herself up straight, shutting her eyes, thinking it through again. It was only a disturbing coincidence, that's all. Both Killian and Adrian may very well have been in Sidestrand over the same time, never met, never even seen each other, and gone their separate ways, story over. Just two New Yorkers who happened, over the course of a week, to be traveling in Norfolk and turning up in the same pub to sample the new beer on entirely different days. Although the general overlap was possible, there was absolutely nothing that put them in the very same location on any given day. Killian was researching his new book; Adrian was visiting her brother the monk.

Just two New Yorkers.

But even as she put it all down to a crazy coincidence, it struck Val that she didn't really know how much of a New Yorker Killian really was. Didn't he tell her he had grown up in the Midwest somewhere? And hadn't he worked out in L.A. as plumber to the stars? When it came right down to it, where did he call home? Then or now? She had a sense from a few vague answers he had given her that he bounced around, a rolling stone, that sort of thing, and she had never pressed him enough for more information. She didn't even know where he was staying over the last number of days while they met to talk about edits on *Plumb Lines*.

Did Killian have a family? A wife and kids? A partner and kids? What did he do when he wasn't tracking scandals in the beer world or bringing to light the strange bathroom habits of the clogged and famous? His jacket bio was, when she thought about it, colorful and unspecific—bouncer, ski bum, short-order cook—the sort of transient jobs no one would question because we all think we know exactly what they mean. One day Killian had appeared, and because he was handsome and charming, that was really everyone's lucky, lucky day. The world is just that welcoming when you're handsome and charming. Just that unquestioning. Just that fatally incurious...

Quickly, Val thumbed through author photos she had on her iPhone, looking for a shot of Killian. And then she remembered. *No, no,* he had waved away the very idea of an author photo—*no jacket photo for me, let my words do the talking*—besides, he had laughed in a way that had charmed Ivy and two editorial assistants, *I'm actually pretty shy.* With that he had scratched the side of his nose in what Val had privately scorned as a Gary Cooper kind of way. So she had no photos of her author James Killian, the humble and shy. This—this, she thought as she paged back to Killian's table of contents, slipping the bottle cap back into her pocket—this was an inexcusable oversight on her part. Her eyes shut in sheer disgust at herself.

"What's the matter?"

She opened her eyes to see James Killian standing, smiling, at the table, slipping off a leather bomber jacket and flinging it lightly into his side of their booth.

She wasn't sure. But until that changed, Val wanted the time together to be utterly seamless. While she pushed back against the little wormhole of some terrible truth in the part of her mind that never tired of jumping out at her in those few dark and endless corridors, her eyes found a close alternative answer to the question *what's the matter?* "This chapter," she tapped the exact place on the page, "'The Brewmeister of Bavaria's Dark History, and We're Not Talking Stout.'"

He flashed her a crooked smile as he slid easily in across from her. "What about it?"

Let the games begin.

Val lifted her chin, then folded her hands in a way she thought he'd believe. After all, she was Val Cameron the Unassailable. "Your research needs to be unimpeachable." She shot him a frank look. "Otherwise it's libel. So, is it?"

Killian sat back, sizing her up. Val kept her expression neutral. "You don't think a lawsuit is good PR, is that it?"

"Yes," she said in that starchy way she was pretty sure amused the man sitting across from her, "that's it." It took all she had in her at that moment to wrinkle her nose at him in what she hoped was a way he'd think was flirtatious. Wasn't that what he was after all along? "Convince me Schlesinger Publishing can trust your research on Herr—" she waved a hand dismissively, "Zussen of Zossen—"

Killian barked a laugh and seemed to loosen up. "Herr Heidrich of Augsburg," he corrected her. She waited in silence. Then he added, "You can trust it."

"What else can I trust?" She said, looking away, then back at him, with a slow smile.

After a moment of measured surprise, Killian leaned closer. "I'd say what you're feeling."

Val let her gaze drop in what she thought was a shy way, then she ran a finger slowly down her frosty glass. "Thank you for teaching me some German," she said softly. He was watching her closely. Then: "Is that all you've got?" The sexiest challenge she could muster.

"I thought you'd never ask." With that, his lips barely moved. When his eyes slid to her breasts, Val was grateful for the table between herself and James Killian.

"How do you know I'm asking?" She raised an eyebrow.

"Asking or telling," he said. "I'm good either way."

Val blinked at him slowly. "I'm counting on it."

Killian gave her a long look that, for a moment, worried her. "What about that line you warned me about?" he said wryly.

She let her eyes rove his face. His green eyes, his crooked jaw line, evidence of old scraps left untreated. In the pocket of the long white jacket Adrian had borrowed for her trip to England, Val's hand tightened down around the bottle cap until the metal grooves dug into her palm. In a crazy way it gave her the strength to ease out of the booth, his eyes still on her, and slide in next to him. Val set her lips very close to his ear. "I think it got lost in a sandstorm."

"There are a lot of those around."

The way he said it—his mind shifting to something outside the moment—made Val think she could lose him. "Not named James Killian there aren't." She reached across him to run her fingers along his neck, underneath his collar. And when his eyes closed for an instant at the touch, she glanced at the tattoo inked on the pressure point above his collarbone. *R.C.* When those eyes opened with a start, as though he never indulged a moment of inattention, she very slowly planted a kiss on his clean-shaven cheek, looking for all the world as though her glance had never shifted anywhere else.

"There's something I want to give you," she told him.

"Besides that?" he whispered, setting one hand on her inner thigh.

Val pulled a business card from her purse, and scribbled her address on the back. With a very frank look at him, she slid the card under his hand that was lingering on her thigh. "My place," she said with a confident smile. As his fingers closed around the card and his eyes never left her lips, she knew with perfect conviction that the man knew damn well where she lived. "I've got some work to finish...first...so, let's make it eight." She needed time. "I like punctuality," she said earnestly, her lips brushing his cheek. "It's very important." James Killian murmured something about aiming to please. Val's left hand slipped out of her jacket pocket, and she covered his hand with the imprint on her palm of a bottle cap from a Norfolk pub that was going to determine his fate. It had already determined Adrian's. She gave his hand a squeeze he might even interpret as fond. "I'll be right back."

On the way to the ladies room, she turned and snapped three quick pictures of him with her phone. He was smiling lazily at his beer, unaware, even with his eyes open. In a post-coital haze before anything had happened. She almost felt sorry for the bastard, slick and clever and ruthless until there was a shot at sex. *R.C.* The same logo as the flag on the brownstone in Gramercy Park. What the hell did it mean? What did her plumber to the stars have to do with the strange little former librarian who lived there? Val made it inside the ladies room, where she leaned heavily against the cool tiled wall, and thought of Adrian describing the stranger. Sleek moves, dirty blond hair, weathered face, his eyes on her thigh. *Best sex I never had.* Now it was Killian's turn. She emailed the photos to Bale with the note: *New developments, send ASAP to Melanie for ID, need answer within hour.*

As Val was holding a wet paper towel against her face, and trying not to sway, Bale shot back: *Who is he?*

One of my authors. Worse, my date. Then she turned on the hand dryer and swiveled the nozzle to her face. How long could she take while Killian sat out there without suspecting a thing? How long could she put him off before he showed up at her building? How long could she put him off after he showed up?

Bale came back: *Stall.*

Won't be the first time, she thumbed quickly.

On it. Stay tuned.

And Bale was gone.

At least when she was seven, and two years an orphan, lost in the rush of deafening air from the conch Aunt Greta had to help her hold up to her ear, at least then she had a pink and white shell. The shell explained it all. Like a small friendly monster breathing on her face in the dark with the sheets pulled up to her chin. A mystery, Greta explained, somehow knowing, of calcium and labyrinths and whorls, and little Val liked those words so much she didn't even want to know what they meant. She had closed her eyes tight and listened. Labyrinths and whorls and calcium invited her into a place that held only rushing air and smelled slightly like the sea, and for those few minutes she couldn't even hear her own terrible loneliness.

Now Bale was gone.

And Killian wasn't.

She wondered if the deafening rush of air would turn out to be her own fatal ignorance.

Val stepped out of the ladies room.

30

You will know, Animus had told him many times. *You will know, Alaric, when the time is near.* Usually these assurances were followed with default phrases the visionary head of the organization would mutter, *when man will shed his veil forever and become the new divine.* That was the most recent one. With the certainty that Animus knew what he was talking about, Alaric had followed orders like the fine, holy lieutenant he was. He never questioned Animus about the prophecy that was meant—according to Animus—for no one's eyes but his own.

But when it came right down to it, Alaric hadn't known. Not a thing. Not a goddamn thing. There where he stood up the street from Leo House, the Christian Guesthouse where he had been staying, on legs stiff with an anxiety he had never known. Not even—to be quite fair—when he recognized the woman he had to eliminate as she sat there in her museum office, steeped in whatever self-satisfaction she was feeling at the moment of her death at his hands. Not even when he had brained the indiscreet boy monk. In work, for Alaric, there was never any dread. But he felt it now as he stood with his phone loose in his hand. Had the rapture—or whatever it was—come and gone and he'd missed it? *You will know, Alaric.*

"Mr. Alaric," came Millard's voice in his ear.

The veteran who kept house for Animus had always been clear about not making contact with the elusive Alaric, so the agent of Robus Christi went on alert. "What is it, Millard?"

"It's Mr. Everett, sir. He locked himself in the chapel almost a day ago, for a retreat, he said. I'm not supposed to interrupt him, but he's not coming out and I'm—"

"Have you knocked?"

"I told you," Millard brayed. "I was instructed not to interrupt—"

"I'm coming." Alaric may not have sensed the time had come, but he could still get there in time to witness the fulfillment of the prophecy. He had sacrificed more than he could afford to review at this moment. A home, truthfulness in all things, the lives of others, and anything better than a nameless hour or two with women who never even needed to know his name. *Good works*, Animus had told him once over his nightly glass of port, *are not always good for everyone, Alaric.*

True, but the agent of Robus Christi wanted to witness the moment of fulfillment more than he desired what was offered to him, elsewhere, for this evening. Like the final eruption he felt with sex, his hands entwined in the red or blond or black hair of the nameless woman of the moment. A woman was never more elusive than when he was in effect pinning her to the sheets. It was wrong, no doubt, to compare those baffling times to what he could anticipate as the unspeakable joy of the fulfillment of prophecy, which would lift him for all times from inexplicable sheets and from the fine trajectory of his Glock.

Alaric set off at a run, crossing 8th Avenue as the light was changing, picking up speed as he headed east on 24th Street and people stepped aside. How much time did he have? *Alaric*, Animus had dubbed him, *Alaric for wings*. Above the gross earthly fray. Only where were his wings now, possibly in the final moments of the lurching cabs and jackhammers and panhandlers populating a Chelsea forever transformed in a world burnished new? He ran harder, his open jacket flapping behind him, dodging a red double-decker tour bus. "Come see!" he yelled, dashing by the stares, his laughter freed from years inside him. "Come see!" Alaric whirled, halfway across Sixth Avenue, rocketing so hard around the corner toward 23ʳᵈ Street that he nearly fell, saved by his hands pushing off against the grimy sidewalk.

And there it was, the blue and gold flag softly twitching in the April breeze over the chapel of Robus Christi. He was gasping as he tripped up the steps to the front entrance, shaking uncontrollably as he pulled out the key Animus had presented to him as a tremendous honor. *The only spare, Alaric.* It was a sign of complete trust. And he had thought fleetingly of the parish priest back on the Ohio River who had taken him in, trusting the boy to be honest, trusting the boy who had fled the double-wide not to pry or steal. "Father, forgive me," Alaric heard the sob catch in his own voice and he let himself into the sacred chapel, "for I have come. Let me share in the moment." And he wanted to add that he had suffered so much, but he wiped his eyes as he strode down the short aisle, taking in the tall steady pillar candles. It was all his eyes could see as they accustomed to the dim light.

And then he saw it.

And he couldn't from any cell of his brain make sense of it.

He stopped in his tracks, staring.

The lance, the nails, arranged in a strange tableau.

"Animus?" he choked.

On the dais, in front of the altar, lay the figure of the emaciated Guy Everett. Clothed in a loincloth. Alaric stepped closer. "Animus?" Louder this time. As leaned over, he took in the Crown of Thorns on the visionary's still head, the Crown that Alaric had stolen. The barbs were rammed into the skin, leaving little pinpoints of blood. Because there was no more blood to flow. Alaric narrowed his eyes. He was looking at a corpse.

What could any of it be except plain and pathetic?

Pietà for one? Was that it?

Wiping a trembling hand across his mouth, he needed to think. Stepped away from the strange, absurd scene. But he couldn't. He was confronted with the heavy blue velvet drapes of Robus Christi that ran along the back of the dais. Was this, then, what he had spent the last seven years preparing for? This...colossal error? Where was the resurrection? The test case for the life everlasting Animus had divulged from the prophecy he let no one else actually see? Alaric paced. Where was the altered world where lion shall lie down with lamb? Where mankind emerges divine in a world free of suffering and death?

Alaric stopped in front of the corpse as he stood there with helpless fists and anger erupted louder and more eternal than sex. With all his might, he kicked Everett's corpse in the puny ribs, hollering his rage to the rafters of this useless place, more profane than a double-wide on a backwoods riverbank. And when he kicked him again, the Crown shifted and half-covered an unblinking gelatinous eye. There was no help for Alaric, who shrieked, whirling away toward the drapes he could only hope would smother him. Instead, he barreled into the standing pillar candles, burning low, waiting, like him, for endless flame, and Alaric made it happen.

His arms flung the candles against the drapes, there and there—and there—screaming until he was hoarse, the drapes going up in flames with a whoosh that reminded him of his soul all those years ago, first burning, and then burning out. He couldn't watch it twice. Not twice. Stumbling away from the smoke and flames of the walls of the Robus Christi Chapel, Alaric nearly fell off the dais, then turned. Then fled.

31

Several things happened after Val left Killian outside Old Town Bar, but not before his thumb lightly traced the outer curve of her right breast. She headed uptown, barely mindful of traffic, and when she came to her senses her palms and forehead were pressed against the cool glass of a Macy's window. How long had she been standing there? She checked the time: just past six thirty. And Killian was coming at eight. Val climbed into a cab, where she clicked off the TV and sank back into the seat that smelled vaguely like leather cleaner. The cab was the closest she could get to a sensory deprivation chamber. She gave the driver her address as his watchful dark eyes studied her in the rearview mirror. When she pulled out her phone to call Cleary, it rang. Aunt Greta. She took the call.

"I'm watching a church go up in smoke," her aunt told her.

"What?"

"46 Gramercy Park West. Wasn't that where you went after we met at the Morgan?"

Guy Everett's home was number 44. "No," said Val slowly. "I was next door. What's happening?"

Rapidly Greta filled her in. "FDNY's still trying to get it under control. Lots of old wood, and it's gone up like a tinderbox."

Val could picture the flag, in blue and gold, rippling right out front. *R.C.* "I think Everett owns it, Aunt Greta. I think both buildings belong to him."

"Well," drawled her aunt, "let's hope he's not the one they pulled out of there."

"Dead?"

"Unrecognizable." Then for a moment Greta sounded distracted. "If it's Everett, I'd say the trail's gone cold, in terms of Saul's fragment, but it's a bad choice of words." Then she added: "We'll know more later. Some people are descending on the site, distraught."

Val made the quick decision that she'd leave her aunt out of whatever the evening ahead—hell, the hour ahead—held. She had something else in mind for the head of the Artifact Authentication Agency. "Auntie, I'm sending you some photos."

Her aunt's voice dropped. "Yes?"

"Show them around the crowd at the fire, okay? Let me know if anybody recognizes the guy."

"Why? What are you on to?"

"Adrian's killer." As the cab pulled over to the curb, Val slid cash into the tray, waved off a receipt, and added to her aunt, "Ask those few distraught people at the scene. I've got to go." With that, Val thanked the driver, ended the call, and slid out of the cab. Barely eyeing her building, she loped around the corner to Second Avenue and headed two blocks down to Le Pain Quotidien, as the rain started heavily. Inside the doors to the rustic bakery café, she called Lieutenant Cleary, who picked up before it went to voicemail. To her credit, Cleary listened without interruption while Val laid out what she had in terms of James Killian, the tattoo, the disturbing overlap with Adrian Bale in a village in Norfolk, the beer book, the beer.

"Where's this guy now?" said Cleary.

"That's just it. He's never told me where he's staying, but," she scratched her cheek with sudden inspiration, "we've texted—can you get his location off that somehow?"

Cleary grunted. "What's your number, Cameron?"

Val gave it to her. "Look," she said, getting to the immediate dirty heart of it, "he's coming over to my place—"

"He what? What the hell..."

"It was the only way I could guarantee he'd show up. Otherwise, if he gets the wind up, Cleary, he'll bolt, and I don't think you'll ever find him, do you hear me?" Her heart was pounding as she stepped inside the café and moved to the bakery shelves. Val pressed her quietly, "Can you get over here, Cleary?"

"You don't even know this is the guy."

"I'm working on it. I'll call you as soon as I know, all right?"

"I can detain him on reasonable suspicion, Cameron," Cleary told her, her voice going high and wide, "but I hate reasonable suspicion."

"Killian's going to show up here with or without a positive ID in—"

Cleary wasn't done. "Reasonable suspicion is for assholes."

"—sixty-five minutes." The truth of it liquefied half of Val's muscles.

A beat. "Call me, you hear me, Cameron? In the meantime, here's what I'll do." And while Val mimed a cup of coffee to the counter clerk, Cleary said it had the earmarks of a classic sting operation. "I can put Horowitz, good man, bit of a cowboy, outside the building as a homeless vet."

"Okay."

"And I can replace the doorman with Chavez, loves undercover, fearless, you'll know him by the nose prosthesis. Me, well," the lieutenant spun the idea, "pumps, pearls, fake-hailing a cab. Sound like a plan?"

"Yes, yes, it's good."

"Best I can do on short notice. Don't make me look like a moron here," she warned. "With pearls, I'm already halfway there, you know what I'm saying? Meanwhile I'll run your number and see if we can get his location."

Meanwhile? There was hardly any meanwhile at all. Meanwhile meant ambling up Fifth Avenue with a soft pretzel, meanwhile meant browsing perfumes at Bloomingdale's, meanwhile meant the guy you date before the really good one comes along. When Val said, "Just get here, Cleary," her voice sounded very small. Not even good coffee could help. It took her a second to realize Cleary had hung up. She sipped, because she didn't know quite what else to do, heading to the back section of the café, past the customers at the long communal table in the center of the place. Past people done with their workday who were after a good, quick bite to eat. When her phone rang and she realized it was Bale, she spilled some coffee as she fumbled to answer.

"Antony?"

His voice was tight. "Where are you, Val?"

"Le Pain Quotidien on Second Avenue." She stood very still. "Tell me."

"Melanie Ruskin made a positive ID."

That's Fintan's guy, said Melanie, who had fortunately been sound asleep in her bed at the home of the fine Norfolk family she'd been assigned. Not out in a tent in a field somewhere. It was the middle of the night when Bale had roused Brother Martin and given him the job of finding the American girl with the pink Vespa. *That's Fintan's guy all right,* she had repeated. And Fintan's guy had killed him. The boy had been recruited somehow to steal the Crown of Thorns from Burnham Norton Abbey, and when he bungled it all so spectacularly, his panic made him a loose-lipped liability and he had been killed. Then Killian had followed the trail of the Crown to New York, where he had killed Adrian Bale to secure it.

"I'm on my way." Then: "Val?"

"I hear you. No, don't come. He'll see you and take off."

"Val, he doesn't know me."

"Right. That's right."

"Tell me where I can find you." The agreed to meet across the street from her building, and just around the corner on Second Avenue, then ended the call. Val waited out the rain in Le Pain Quotidien, pacing, clutching her phone as though it contained all the secrets of the universe plus a few useful weapons. By 7:41, she had edged to the corner building, out of the rain under their awning. Peering around the corner, she spotted a woman with jet black hair that hung to her shoulders, a wide-brimmed green rain hat, pumps and pearls stepping off the curb outside Val's building to hail a yellow cab. One, a Toyota Highlander, slowly rolled down

Second and eased its way onto 51st, its roof light off. Occupied. Cleary stepped back. Sitting up against the building itself was the promised cowboy Horowitz, dressed in shabby gray fatigues and fingerless gloves, holding a ragged cardboard sign Val couldn't read from her angle. Fake doorman Chavez must be inside the building. How long had they been in place?

As eight o'clock got closer, Val's heart started to pound. She had been standing unmoving against the corner building for seven minutes when she noticed the Toyota Highlander yellow cab come rolling slowly down Second again. As it eased its way onto 51st— again—Val stepped out just far enough to see it pass Cleary in her pumps and pearls, her arm raised with no cab in sight. The light on the Highlander was still off.

An odd dread settled in that Val couldn't explain. Suddenly her phone rang.

James Killian showed up on her screen in the dusky light.

Something had gone wrong.

She answered the call, marveling at how normal she sounded. "Hey."

"What's going on?"

Val glanced across Second Avenue at absolutely nothing at all. Why would he ask *what's going on?* The question terrified her. Somehow he had made the set-up with Cleary and the other undercover cops. They were screwed. "Where are you, James? Is eight still good?"

"I'm close." He told her. "What's going on?"

Where was he? All in that moment Val knew for sure was that if she bungled this call they would lose him forever. Everything was suddenly just that clear. She stepped away from the building and tried to look as relaxed and inviting as she possibly could. "Where are you?" she repeated, making an obvious show of looking up and down the street, delighted by his game. "James," she laughed ruefully, "have you found me out?"

His words came fast and slurred. "I got here early, rang your buzzer but nothing. You were out and I didn't know what to do.

Maybe you forgot, so I got in a cab. Kept circling the block, waiting for you to show up. Waiting to—"

"Listen, if tonight's not good for you..." She gave him a dose of disappointment. Where was Bale? How could she get Cleary's attention? And then Val knew: she couldn't. If it was Killian in the Highlander cab, Val was the only one who knew, and now the only hope the plan could still work was for her to go solo.

He blurted, "And then I saw you. What are you doing hiding around the corner? What's going on?" His voice rose, and he sounded very young.

"Oh, shit, James—" she saw the Highlander heading toward her down Second, but then glanced away quickly "—you did find me out." With that, she let her shoulders slump as she did a slow 360, half-expecting to catch sight of him walking toward her with his sexy swagger. Her smile was wide. "I've just been waiting to get the drop on you when you show up at eight. Why do you think I was so specific about the time?"

"What are you talking about?"

"Oh, I had some idea about coming right up behind you, so close I'd stop you right in your tracks." Silence on the other end. "Silly, I know. But, look, it sounds like you've had a rough day." She made a show of scuffing her shoe at nothing on the sidewalk. "You can take a rain check."

"No!" he cried. "I'm almost there. I'll be there." When he added, mumbling, "Thanks for planning a surprise for me," her stomach twisted.

At that moment Val realized that she couldn't meet Killian out on the street. He knew exactly where she was standing, but she had to stick to Cleary's plan and get him to head into her apartment building. "I'm getting soaked," she managed a little laugh. "I'll wait for you inside, James." Before he could respond, she ended the call, running lightly across 51st toward the entrance to her building. For the few seconds she was safely out of sight of the Toyota Highlander, before it rounded the corner, she jogged right past Cleary, telling her in a tight voice, "He's here. He's in the

Highlander cab." Cleary shot her a grim look and gave Horowitz a hand signal.

Val flung herself into the dry safety of her lobby, and turned to face the street. On her phone, 7:53.

When a different yellow cab pulled over for Cleary, she waved him on with what looked like some angry words, and when the driver pulled away, she raised her arm to hail another. It turned out to be the cruising Toyota Highlander as it pulled slowly past Val's building, stopping in front of the French restaurant across the street. Cleary turned her hailing attentions in that direction. Slowly, the door opened and the passenger in the backseat paid the driver, then stepped out. As he stood up and scrutinized the street, Val took a step back.

Killian.

As he turned to face the building, patting the cab to take off, Val thought he looked like hell. Dirty, sooty, shaken. His mouth was hanging open as though he was struggling for air, and as he took a step to cross the street to Val's place, he stumbled and had to catch himself from falling by twisting toward a double parked BMW. The swagger was gone, the cockiness was gone, and to Val it looked like it was all the guy could do to stand up straight. Yet, here he was. Whatever had happened to him, whatever he had done, James Killian had come to Val's. In that instant she felt a profound pity.

As James Killian made it across a Manhattan side street in a rain that might as well be a flash flood in a New Mexico canyon, Cleary and Horowitz set upon him. Out of Val's lobby barreled Chavez, sidearm drawn, and Val, suddenly completely unafraid, followed him. Cleary and Horowitz were shouting over each other, and when Killian began to yell, pulling out of their grip despite the flashing badges, they spun him around, which was when he saw Val.

On his face was a look of sudden understanding. What followed were a string of inhuman sounds as Val drew within ten feet of him, then stopped. Horowitz was yelling "fuck" over and over and Cleary, whose pearls broke when Killian had torn at them, was slapping handcuffs on him with grim determination. "Goddamn grandmother's goddamn pearls you motherfucker," she cried, almost like it was a reason for the arrest. Killian's face was wild, his neck muscles straining as he tried to pull away and tried to make his life something different from what it was, and for a second, he stilled, and looked directly at Val, and in that instant she knew she would never be able to explain for as long as she lived, she felt she was looking at the stricken eyes of an eleven-year-old boy.

32

When the squad cars pulled away and the rain started to let up, Val
turned to see Bale jumping out of a cab on the other side of Second
Avenue and run easily across the street. Shaking the rain from his
head, he gave Val a quick nod and pulled her back under the
awning. As she filled him in on the arrest, and she realized she was
shivering and it wasn't even that cold. After a few wordless
minutes, Val and Bale ambled up the block without a direction. Val
could tell she was weaving, at first, but then it passed, and her legs
felt stronger. It happened right around the time she had let go of
the pity. Twice she turned to look at Bale, who seemed off in his
own thoughts, and finally she came to a stop under the red awning
at BXL East bar, where she told Bale she wanted to stand quietly
and listen to the spatter of the raindrops.

Finally, he spoke. "I'm leaving tomorrow."

"In that case," she said, feeling strangely sacked. Not knowing
how to finish the sentence. "In that case, I'd better get the bag I left
at the Iroquois. The raffia tote," she reminded him, as though it
could possibly matter, "you remember, with Key West on one side,
and..." she trailed off, "the Conch Republic on the other."

Bale looked down. "Right." His smile was grim. "We'd better
go get it."

"And then I guess it's goodbye," she managed with some
bravado. No better fortification on the face of this Earth, she
thought, with disappointment.

Bale lifted his shoulders. "I'll be back at the end of the month," he reminded her. When he asked, "Can I call you, Val?" she heard how tentative he sounded.

"Of course," she said, more pained at the alternative than she could possibly say. His eyes were on something else, reflecting the red, yellow, white of Manhattan streets after a good rain. Bale was looking west, so Val looked east, and added in a strange monotone, "I can help you close up Adrian's place." A shared task...and then what? Boxes get shipped or given away. Keys get returned. Followed by goodbyes more final than either of them can ever pretend otherwise. The easy, easy reasons for getting together finally gone.

Without a word, the two of them started walking west, dodging trash bags glistening curbside from the rain. A pedicab flew by, unaffected by yellow cabs and delivery vans, kicking up a playful spray in its wake. At Lexington Avenue, as the light started to change, Bale grabbed her arm lightly. They darted around a nightfall crowd heading east for some curry, and Bale said, "Val, at some point, you know—" They hit the curb and slowed down, and he released her arm. Suddenly Bale stopped dead and turned to her, his long coat held open by the hands in his pockets. "At some point it has to stop being about Adrian."

She was struck by how completely true it felt. What had brought them together was gone. No, it was only because it was gone that these two stubborn people had been brought together in the first place. *My sister had lousy taste in friends,* he had said. And she had brought all her own prejudices to the table, putting off her beloved Adrian, whose brother was a monk or something that passed for a monk—Val couldn't possibly have cared less—just how interesting could that be to anyone not a blood relative? She nodded tightly a few times at Bale, who seemed to be studying her, and Val pulled her jacket around her as snugly as she could without cutting off her circulation, holding it in place with her crossed arms. In silence, the two of them walked briskly to Fifth Avenue and headed downtown.

At 44th Street, they turned the corner, nearly colliding with two leashed German Shepherds and a dozen middle-aged alumni wearing Harvard ties and trying to remember the words and the tune to the Alma Mater. Mid-block, Val and Bale entered the Hotel Iroquois, brushing a few straggling raindrops out of their hair and heading for the elevator. On the third floor, he held the door open for Val, and when she moved ahead of him into the dark, Bale pressed the light switch.

Val saw her raffia tote first thing on the desk chair. For some reason she felt like an old soldier when she declared, "I will miss you."

Bale hung up his coat, then turned with a smile. "I will more than miss you."

"I was going to say the same thing," Val admitted, glancing around the same room that two nights ago had felt lovely, but empty of Bale himself. "But then," she shook her head slowly, "I edited it."

He set his hands on his hips. "A skill that splashes over to your personal life."

"Sometimes I think it's all my personal life, Antony."

After a long look, he took in a noisy breath. "You're thinking you should go."

"No."

Neither of them moved.

He smiled, rubbing the back of his neck. "Ice keeps having to get broken, doesn't it?" She watched him roll up his sleeves because he didn't know what else to do.

"Maybe that's not a bad thing." For a woman who was there to collect a tote with a change of clothes, she noticed with detachment that she was taking off her jacket. The light was old and golden, and someone had turned down the bed. She gave him a frank look she knew he couldn't possibly appreciate was rare. "You said at some point it has to stop being about Adrian." Bale said nothing, but bit his lip in a way, she thought fondly, he must have been doing since he was a kid. "You should know," she said slowly, listening to herself speak the truth, "it already has." As she stepped up to him, she handed him her jacket, which he folded with care and set across the back of a chair.

Then with no hesitation at all, he pulled her into his arms and they held each other close in a declaration that had nothing at all to do with words. Val pulled back only far enough to turn his face toward her, and she kissed him hard as his hands tightened down around her back and slid to her hips. "No editing," he whispered.

"No praying," she whispered back. "Unless it helps."

"Christ, I hope not," he muttered, leaning his forehead against hers. As she started to unbutton his shirt, she nearly hummed, thinking what a very fine thing it was to do with a set of human hands.

33

It was a woman named Malka Prager, a concert violinist, who had made some important connections for Lieutenant Cleary. A benighted member of the Robus Christi High Council, she had turned up on Gramercy Park West while the FDNY fought the blaze. Greta pegged her right away as someone with more than normal human interest in the fire and approached her. When Greta scrolled through the photos of Killian that Val had sent her, Malka, who by then was tugging at her hair, cried, "That—that's our Alaric!" Alaric, for all the High Council knew, did special assignments for the head of the organization.

With that, the link had been made between Guy Everett and the theft of the ancient fragment, and Alaric—James Killian—who had killed at least two people to get their hands on the Crown of Thorns. But as she watched the firefighters at work, Malka Prager cried for the collapse of the organization—Everett's visionary edifice—founded on the promises of a prophecy pipelined straight to them from Jesus Christ himself. Swords into ploughshares, lion and lamb, a messianic age that proves—here Greta thought the violinist's eyes were especially bright—we are each of us our own messiah. And yes, Malka Prager could provide a list of the names of the entire High Council.

In the few days since Antony Bale had left New York, Val had taken Ivy Breshears, Ivy League Ivy, out to dinner—a work dinner with a bottle of long overdue champagne toasting Ivy's promotion—during which they scrambled to plug the hole in the Fall list caused by axing *Plumb Lines* by James Killian. Val discovered Ivy was only four years younger than she was and had served as president of the International Socialists Club at Brown. And Cleary had doffed the pearls and called Val with the news that the cell phone records had narrowed down the neighborhood where Killian was staying. Inquiries finally led them to Leo House, a Christian Guesthouse on 23rd Street, west of Eighth Avenue, where they recovered the murder weapon, a Glock P18 pistol.

Cleary was exuberant. The pistol upgraded their detention of Killian from reasonable suspicion to probable cause. Now that she was out of the realm of asshole, she could breathe. And she added that right after the fire at number 46, a fellow named Millard Mackey, from 44, identified the charred remains as those of Guy Everett, his employer. According to the ME, this Everett was dead at the time of the blaze. Mackey, who was not considered a suspect in the fire, had since disappeared. When Greta inquired about a wooden Bible box, she was told nothing had turned up—old wood, was it? More tinder.

Val had cleaned her mother's Millefiori paperweight and set it back just right. She had called a furniture repairman to fix the folding lid on her secretary desk. She made a batch of cannoli for her doorman and accepted a pint of Mrs. Dellarosa's homemade pomodoro sauce. She framed a photo of her and Adrian at twenty-three on the beach at Siphnos in the Adriatic, beautiful in their bikinis, their teeth white and ready for life, whatever it held there in the Adriatic sunshine, their eyes glistening with youth, their arms around each other in what they had felt sure would be a lifetime. The framed photo would never be enough, but when it came to Adrian, nothing would ever change that loss for Val. It was beyond the skills of a furniture repairman to fix.

She was even sleeping well at night, which she knew had more to do with Antony, in the home that felt like its old self before violation. Whenever Val felt her mind drifting to the violations of James Killian, she remembered the feel of Bale lying pressed up against her, and she wondered how she'd get through the next two weeks until he returned. She was beginning to think that her heart was a simple thing after all. She still hadn't brought it up with Greta, who was busy kashering this and that in her own kitchen. "Oh, in the interest of saving time," she had said by way of some wacky explanation for her hopes about the Hunter College professor.

The first day after Antony Bale left the city, the night together at the Iroquois was still so fresh that she could forgive herself her tingling skin and forgive herself for watching every video she could find on YouTube of the *paso doble*. But as the days stretched on, the longing was becoming acute. Even Ivy, who sensed something was up and returned after her lunch hour with another offering from Bouchon Bakery, couldn't help. It explained why Val was on the 1 train uptown, first having made a trip to the Lower East Side for a small package in a white paper bag. The white paper bag felt perfect to her.

She emerged from the subway station and walked to the address she had been given on West End Avenue. The late afternoon was a lambent thing, slightly still, slightly warm, the city clamor oddly distant for those few minutes. Buzzed in, Val took the elevator up to the third floor and knocked on the door. Voices rose, feet bounded, and the front door was flung open so hard it hit the wall. "Val," cried Tali Korngold, catching Val in a breathless hug. Over the girl's shoulder Val saw a tall, smiling woman in a colorful headscarf heading toward them. "I'm glad you're here!" Tali took the package of kosher cream cheese pastries.

"Tali," said Val, content she was right where she should be, touched her friend's head with affection. "I have a Situation I'd like to discuss."

34

Norfolk

Since he returned from New York, Bale had fallen asleep twice
during Mass. Not from any real fatigue, but because it all felt
terribly remote. When the brothers spoke to him, it was as if he was
listening through a wall to some other conversation that didn't
concern him at all. The choir monks, through every gallant section
of the Daily Office, sounded as though they were transmitting
across a wasteland. And Bale only ate his meals because it would
excite too much comment if he didn't. By the fifth day, he was
wondering whether he was coming down with some degenerative
disease, something where the five senses disappear practically all at
the same time.

Restless, he barreled out of the abbey near midnight, and was
struck by how beautiful the moon still was, even heading toward its
crescent. Startling and white and pure. He found himself wishing
Val was there with him, warm and substantial, there to see what
was still fine in this old firmament. As they had clung to each other
in bed that night, that single night, he saw for the very first time
that human beings were part of that firmament, too, and it had
nothing to do with eternity, and everything to do with what was just
as mysterious, certainly more perishable, and inexpressibly dear.

It was then Bale heard voices, raised in a tumble of distant
laughter. As he headed in that direction, it felt delightfully strange
that he smelled the campfire before he saw any light from it. Where
the woods started to open up, and Bale was still safely hidden by

the abiding trees and scant moon, he caught sight of a pink Vespa parked by the ridge trail. Around the campfire sat Melanie Ruskin and the three boy monks, their robes hanging open like casual undergrads after graduation.

Bale felt his heart lift when he realized the boys were teaching the Compline service to the American girl. Maybe the half-blue hair and small, literary tattoo was Melanie's equivalent of the boys' loose robes. "Compline?" she snorted in a charming way. "Sounds like farm equipment," at which the boys fell back laughing. One mooed. Another baaed. It was Eli, the clever Eli, who didn't know any better than to provide the Latin root for the word. When she pushed him over, they all laughed again, then a flask got passed, flashing in the thin moonlight. A smoke got passed in the other direction, and Melanie started to tell them about her friendship with Fintan McGregor. She didn't call it an affair this time, Bale noticed, and she didn't call it a relationship. A literary girl, despite the watery path to cetology, she had found just the right word. The others fell silent and listened, their eyes big in the moonlight that caught the scuddering waves below.

Bale turned without a sound and found his way back to the abbey, where he headed for the kitchen. In the weak moonlight slanting through the windows, he made his way down the narrow hallway to the storeroom. There he turned on the single overhead light, then headed to the very back of the room, where they kept whatever they needed less frequent access to—bins of brown rice, canisters of salt, ten-pound cans of tomato paste. And this—he stopped at the thirty-pound tub of semolina flour. *You're crazy!* Brother Sebastian had blustered. *We'll never eat that much pizza. Why in the name of the Holy Mother did you order this much?*

Bale removed the lid from the tub, smiling slightly at the unchanging vat of flour. No better place, as it turned out. Thrusting his hands deep into the fine semolina, Bale carefully drew out the object he had hidden there maybe four years ago—and for this one, not even Martin or Berthold knew the whereabouts. They had agreed it was the safest way. Dusting off the plastic airtight shell, he opened it and gazed at the finest example of *Euphorbia milii* he would ever in this lifetime see. It was as if he was holding an epochal event two thousand years old in his careful hands, marveling that in touching the Crown he was somehow connecting to the flesh of the Crucified Christ.

He had felt a pang when he learned that everything in the Robus Christi Chapel had burned up in the fire—that one had certainly been a nice later example of the Crown of Thorns, which had come to the Carmelites back in 825 A.D. As a splendid early fake, one of the many floating around across the centuries, it had been worth a place in its cache in the crypt where the first Prior of the rebuilt Burnham Norton Abbey was installed. Truly, Bale thought, how could that poor boy Fintan have known that the object he stole was not the true holy relic? Or that Robus Christi's murderous pursuit of prophecy depended on a fake? In the end, it didn't matter whether the Crown the boy stole was the genuine article or not. Either way, it would lead to the identity of the killer.

And it had.

Inside the cheap plastic shell was what was left of this two-thousand-year-old relic, and it was, in its own way, beautiful. Barbs had fallen off and been lost, but some still clung to the brittle, intertwining vine of a coronet. As a younger man, all Antony Bale had seen were the thorns. But when it had come into his care, his feelings had changed. And so had he. Now, really, all he saw was the intertwining vine that through two thousand years had never lost its shape and held onto what thorns it could. It was the vine that struck Bale with awe. That struck him to his heart with what went beyond words and murderous plans and simple yearning. As he closed the airtight shell and lowered it carefully into the waiting flour, that what he was really looking for in his life was a way to become the vine.

Epilogue

Terre Haute, Indiana, one month later

On a hot day in May, the dealer who owned *Foxie's Den of Collectibles* was sitting half-asleep on the milking stool with the sign she had taped to it many years ago. NFS—Not For Sale. Altogether too nice a collectible to sell, and as she aged, it strangely fit her contours well. As she sat drowsily, surrounded by her life's work, she fanned herself with one of the colorful paper fans from her collection of World's Fair fans dating back to the very first fair in Paris in 1874.

She had chamber pots and fox stoles and a gen-u-ine antique Pepsi machine—even an old Philco nine-inch TV that still worked. She had glass and pewter and silver and a little bit of gold. She had papers of all sorts, stacked with beautiful crumbling edges, and christening gowns with lace dissolving into dust. Smells of decay more advanced than her own, always good to remember. Tastes she wouldn't even dare to try—like the licorice drops she had found unwrapped from some seller's great-grandmother's silver dresser jar.

Every day something new joined her in the Den, and it was what kept her there, open, seven days a week, and turning herself out of bed each morning at the age of eighty-nine. Why, just that very morning, there was that poor disfigured fellow who came in to sell her a few little things, things he brought with him when he moved back home to Terre Haute from New York. Not much passed between them, but she saw him fingering a WWII sergeant's uniform as she counted out his cash. As he left, the dealer felt suddenly quite tired and found her way over to her milking stool, grabbing her fan.

Later, she thought, she would have to find a better place for what this poor fellow had sold her. Sometime soon. But for now, with a laugh, she opened the creaking door of an icebox from 1911 and shoved inside a stuffed egret, an IKEA lamp, and a pretty little rosewood Bible box.

Photo by Portrait Innovations

SHELLEY COSTA

An Edgar nominee for Best Short Story, Shelley Costa is the author of *You Cannoli Die Once* (Agatha Award nominee for Best First Novel) and *Basil Instinct*. *A Killer's Guide to Good Works*, the second book in the Val Cameron mystery series, follows *Practical Sins for Cold Climates* (January 2016). Shelley's mystery stories have appeared in *Alfred Hitchcock Mystery Magazine*, *Blood on Their Hands*, *The World's Finest Mystery and Crime Stories*, and *Crimewave* (UK). She teaches fiction writing at the Cleveland Institute of Art. Visit her at www.shelleycosta.com.

Henery Press Mystery Books

And finally, before you go...
Here are a few other mysteries
you might enjoy:

THE DEEP END

Julie Mulhern

The Country Club Murders (#1)

Swimming into the lifeless body of her husband's mistress tends to ruin a woman's day, but becoming a murder suspect can ruin her whole life.

It's 1974 and Ellison Russell's life revolves around her daughter and her art. She's long since stopped caring about her cheating husband, Henry, and the women with whom he entertains himself. That is, until she becomes a suspect in Madeline Harper's death. The murder forces Ellison to confront her husband's proclivities and his crimes—kinky sex, petty cruelties and blackmail.

As the body count approaches par on the seventh hole, Ellison knows she has to catch a killer. But with an interfering mother, an adoring father, a teenage daughter, and a cadre of well-meaning friends demanding her attention, can Ellison find the killer before he finds her?

Available at booksellers nationwide and online

Visit www.henerypress.com for details

THE SEMESTER OF OUR DISCONTENT

Cynthia Kuhn

A Lila Maclean Mystery (#1)

English professor Lila Maclean is thrilled about her new job at prestigious Stonedale University, until she finds one of her colleagues dead. She soon learns that everyone, from the chancellor to the detective working the case, believes Lila—or someone she is protecting—may be responsible for the horrific event, so she assigns herself the task of identifying the killer.

More attacks on professors follow, the only connection a curious symbol at each of the crime scenes. Putting her scholarly skills to the test, Lila gathers evidence, but her search is complicated by an unexpected nemesis, a suspicious investigator, and an ominous secret society. Rather than earning an "A" for effort, she receives a threat featuring the mysterious emblem and must act quickly to avoid failing her assignment...and becoming the next victim.

Available at booksellers nationwide and online

Visit www.henerypress.com for details

ARTIFACT

Gigi Pandian

A Jaya Jones Treasure Hunt Mystery (#1)

Historian Jaya Jones discovers the secrets of a lost Indian treasure may be hidden in a Scottish legend from the days of the British Raj. But she's not the only one on the trail...

From San Francisco to London to the Highlands of Scotland, Jaya must evade a shadowy stalker as she follows hints from the hastily scrawled note of her dead lover to a remote archaeological dig. Helping her decipher the cryptic clues are her magician best friend, a devastatingly handsome art historian with something to hide, and a charming archaeologist running for his life.

Available at booksellers nationwide and online

Visit www.henerypress.com for details

CPSIA information can be obtained
at www.ICGtesting.com
Printed in the USA
LVOW10s1457170417
531099LV00011B/806/P